FOOTPRINTS AND SHADOWY FIGURES

A WWI NOVEL

K. K. SULLIVAN

FlimFlam
Enterprises
Springfield, Nebraska

FlimFlam
Enterprises

www.FlimFlamEnterprises.com
Paperback ISBN: 978-1-7360739-7-1
Kindle ISBN: 978-1-7360739-8-8
Library of Congress Cataloging data on file with the publisher.

Designed and produced by Concierge Marketing Book Publishing Services.

Printed in the United States of America.

10 9 8 7 6 5 4 3 2 1

To all those who have fought for our country
believing that all men are created equal under God,
with liberty and justice for all.

1. DAMN

As buses left the terminal, the dank smell of exhaust permeated the area. On the terminal benches, vagrants tried to find a comfortable place to sleep for the night.

"Damn," said a female voice in the half-lit street just outside of the station.

"What's the problem?" said a male voice, out of the dark.

"My lighter ran out of fluid!" said the female voice.

"Here, let me give you a light, so I can see your voice and put a face to that angel," he said as he struck his lighter and held it up so the glow radiated against her skin. "Aren't you as cute as a bug in a rug. The name is Sullivan," as he swayed back and forth. "Leonard Francis Joseph Sullivan, Capt. U.S. Army. I'm the best man in the catalog. Friends call me Curly. And you are?"

"Kendall, Fredora Frances Kendall, Doctor. U.S. civilian. My friends call me Doc."

"I thought you were a cab driver in that hat and uniform, spouting bullshit about being the best in the catalog." She took a long draw and asked, "Is that in Sears and Roebuck, Gimbel Brothers, Marshall Fields, or Saks Fifth Avenue? I'd like to see that with my own peepers just to see what kind of catalog you're in, Captain Catalog."

A charming smile lit up her face. "So Admiral, I don't know you shit from Shinola." Their eyes met and she asked, "I'm famished. Where would a girl get a bite to eat around here?"

"I know just the spot, Nurse Betty. Place called Old Ebbitt Grill. There's some of the finest dining in all of D.C.. It's not too far from here," slurred Curly. "I would whistle for a taxi, but my lips are on strike and they won't allow it. They are extremely dry, which means I need a drink, care to join me, Roc? I have a flask of the finest Bush Mills right here in my overcoat, compliments of my father, General Sullivan," he said as he patted his pockets and pulled out the little flask with the Sullivan crest engraved into the silver. He unscrewed the cap, took a drink, and handed the flask to Doc.

"You're a gallant knight and chivalrous gentleman. I take it they serve alcohol where we're going?" said Doc, taking long snort.

"Certainly, or I would not be taking you there, Sweetheart," he said as he took a small snort and put the flask in an inner pocket.

Doc let out a piercing whistle and motioned a cab to stop.

"Where to, ma'am?" said the cabbie through the window.

"Old Ebbitt Grill," said Capt. Sullivan as he fumbled his way into the cab, shutting the door beside him.

Doc let out another ear-piercing whistle, "STOP!" She opened the door and moved Curly to the other side of the cab.

"Yes ma'am," said the cabbie, as he looked into the rear-view mirror.

"Like he said, Old Ebbitt Grill. Please hurry, I'm starving!"

"I see you mastered the art of chivalry. Thanks for making sure the taxi was safe just for me."

They glanced at each other and dropped a smile. The cab made its way to its destination.

"Here we are folks. That'll be a buck twenty five," said the cabbie.

Capt. Sullivan patted his pockets.

"Here's two. Keep the change," said Doc.

"Thank you, ma'am," said the cabbie.

"I thought Army Captains paid," said Doc.

"It's called emancipation. Normally I would've, but you had a dollar out there, old Dolly," said Capt. Sullivan.

"Your last name should be Skate, Capt. Cheap Skate," said Doc.

The pair opened the door to the restaurant, and stepped to the desk. "How many," asked the Maitre D'.

"There'll be two, please," said Doc as she and Capt. Sullivan followed the tuxedoed Maitre D' to their table.

"What can I get you kids tonight?" asked the cocktail waitress, dressed head to toe in a black cocktail dress; as a piano played a rendition of *Blue Skies* in the background.

"I'll start off with a double shot of Bush Mills!" said Sullivan.

"And I'll have what he's having, with a beer chaser. Don'tcha want a beer chaser? Don'tcha, Wimpy?" egged Doc as she looked right at Sullivan across the table.

"By all means," nodded Capt. Sullivan.

"So, tell me about yourself?" inquired Sullivan. "Wait a minute, I guess my first question to you is, are you married, or do you have a boyfriend that you were gonna meet at Union Station? Because I wanted to get into a brouhaha kicking his ass, gorgeous," slurred Sullivan.

"Here we are; two double shots and two beer chasers. $1.50 please. Should I have them put that on your dinner bill?" asked the waitress, setting the drinks down.

"No. Here's two bucks," said Doc.

"Why thank you very much, ma'am," said the waitress.

"I'm not married, nor do I have a boyfriend," said Doc as she slammed her double shot down and then gulped half of her beer.

"I came down from Boston on the Patriot, stayed with my folks for two days. When everything opens up on Monday morning, I have urgent business to attend to here in D.C.. Then up to New York City for a week and then back up to Boston," said Doc.

She opened her cigarette case and put a long white coffin nail between her lips. Curly lifted his lighter and flicked it to life. Doc took a deep drag, and blew out three smoke rings.

"About yourself. What have you been doing?" asked Doc, as she held up four fingers to the waitress.

"Left the country in 1937 to do military attaché work, then back and forth between assignments from one military post to another. Just came back. I think I can be at rest now," said Capt. Sullivan, as he loosened his tie.

"Two double shots, two chasers $1.50 again, please. Thank-you," said the waitress, picking up the empties and setting down the fresh drinks.

"You know, men still carry a billfold in America in 1941. And aren't men supposed to pay, or did that go out with the emancipation, too? Maybe you should tighten that tie backup, it would keep more neurons in," said Doc, pausing. "Say Curly, can you give a girl another light?" she said as she rested her chin on her hand, ready to listen intently.

"Does anything else light up other than your cigarette?" replied Sullivan as he sparked his lighter. He lit one for himself, too.

"Pretty sure of yourself, aren't you Capt. Sullivan," said Doc as she slammed her double shot down again, and again, threw up four fingers to the waitress.

"Just like I said Dr. Kendall, best in the Catalog," said Sullivan. "So, where did you go to school?"

"Johns Hopkins," replied Doc, as she blew a long stream of smoke out, adding, "You're about two drinks behind."

"Well, makes sense now. Mommy and Daddy got a little money," said Sullivan sarcastically.

"That'll be $1.50 ma'am," said the waitress.

Sullivan grabbed his billfold and handed her two dollars.

"Why thank you, Sir."

"Well isn't that some shit, Capt. Second-Rate Date. You know that's one dollar and 50 cents, 6 quarters, 15 dimes, 30 Nickels, or 150 pennies that you just paid, plus a 50 cent tip." She leaned back and took a long draw, blowing a large smoke ring that hit Sullivan in the nose. "By the way what's wrong with money?"

"Nothing, as long as you earn it yourself," said Sullivan as he returned a smoke ring back to her.

"My parents have their money and I have my own money," said Doc, as she let out a small belch.

"Outstanding, we're playing an old Sullivan game called Belches and Farts. What a world-class choice, right here in Old Ebbitt's Grill," slurred Curly as he repaid the courtesy with a shot of contemptuous wind.

"Your turn, Doc," said Curly.

"I'm camouflaging my ass-ettes at this time, but I'll let you have the wind this time," said Doc with a shit-eating grin on her face. She tapped her cigarette out in the crystal ashtray.

"Is there going to be a next time?" inquired Curly.

"That depends on you Capt. Rockefeller, United States Army. I suppose you don't make much money, do you?" asked Doc.

"$240 a month and I'm worth every penny of it. I am U.S. Army prime grade," touted Sullivan. "You're an angel, with an angel face," said Sullivan as he looked right at Doc with a long gaze.

"For an Army cheapskate, you're not bad lookin'," said Doc, as she reached up and pinched his nose. "Honk, Honk," she continued…

"Why sir, I trust I may have leave to speak.

And speak I will. I am no child, no babe;

Your betters have endured me to say my mind.

And if you cannot, best you stop your ears.

My tongue will tell the anger of my heart.

Or else my heart concealing it will break.

And rather than it shall, I will be free.

Even to the uttermost, as I please, in the words," asserted Doc, satisfied.

"Ah, *Taming of the Shrew*. That's a funny one, isn't it Katerina. Mom made all of us read old Bill Shakespeare," said Curly. "So, is that what you ponder, my beautiful Katerina?"

"Why yes sir, I sure do," replied Doc.

"Let's make like a tree and go," said Curly. Curly stood and tossed a couple singles on the table. He held out his hand and helped her up.

"Where're we going?" asked Doc as they stumbled toward the door.

"Miami. An old classmate of mine, lives down there. Are you game?" said Curly as he raised his hand to hail a taxi.

"As they say, the game is afoot," said Doc releasing a piercing whistle. A yellow cab abruptly stopped.

Curly opened the door and let Doc in. He slid in beside her and nudged her over. "In 20 minutes, a train leaves for Jacksonville, Florida. You'll wake up to a Florida sunrise, and from Jacksonville we'll catch a train to Miami," said Curly.

2. CAPT. ROMANCE

"Capt. Sullivan," said a female voice.

"Please come in, Private," said Capt. Sullivan.

"Here are those things you asked for. Your cup of hot Joe. And I brought your cigarettes from your valise... and some hair of the dog," said the Private.

"Thank you very much. Please sit over here, and take notes and dictation," said Capt. Sullivan.

"Yes Sir, Capt. Sullivan," said the Private.

"Before we get started, would you care for a cup of hot Joe yourself?" said Capt. Sullivan.

"Why yes, and I'll also take some hair of the dog," said the Private. "I will reciprocate by lighting your cigarette for you."

"You know drinking that hot Joe will put more hairs on your arse... and since you've got seven hairs on your cute little arse already, that's one for every day we've been married sweetheart," said Capt. Sullivan adding, "Especially if the coffee has some hair of the dog in it."

"Oh, Darling those are the seven cutest hairs on my ass. I love when we play General and Private and I get to take dictation. Next time I'll be the officer and you can be Private," Doc whispered as she lifts her left hand into the light. "I have to say, Capt. Sullivan, the Cuban cigar wedding band was a special touch, stud. At least 15 carats.

"Oh Private, it's Reveille," Curly said as his eyes widened. He looked down, looked back up and said, "In the Army, when you get up in the morning, it is called Reveille," said Curly. "And at the end of the workday, it is called Retreat."

"In your case, from Reveille into Retreat is around four minutes," said Doc, as she broke into a laugh.

"There is nothing in this world today to help out the poor guy. Other than maybe someday somebody inventing a little pill to help out the poor normal human guy. Of course, I don't have that problem," said Curly with confidence. "So, in the meantime, Darling, just take one for the team, and quit whimpering about it. You know, after an hour I'm just getting started. Wait until one of them pills comes out," he snickered.

"You're full of horse shit and apple sauce," replied Doc.

"But Honey, when you moan, I've had to stuff cotton in my ears. So, the next time you make the octaves go to a higher rate, the management should kick us out of here for all that noise," said Curly as they embraced among the sheets.

"Shit, it's time to get up and get going Doc. No, not like that," said Curly as they chuckled.

They heard a light knock on the door, "Porter, Sir. I have your uniform cleaned and pressed."

Capt. Sullivan slid open the door. The porter handed him his uniform. "Honey, do you have a dollar for a tip?"

"Ok Capt. Cheap Skate," as she rolled her eyes and reached for her purse.

"I'm famished. You think we can get something to eat?" said Doc.

"Yes, let's go to the dining car, I'm hungry too. It's going to be about a 23-hour trip to D.C.," said Curly.

"Darling, are you going to wire your folks and tell them we are coming up to D.C.?" said Doc.

"No, I like a bombshell," said Curly as he fixed his tie and straightened his jacket. "My mother is from the old country Ireland, and she expects every one of her children to have a very large American-Irish Catholic wedding, and guess who was the first to get married," said Curly as he smiled.

"What time does the train arrive at Union Station in D.C.?" asked Curly.

"At 7 tonight," said Doc.

"Well, Roc, I spent time in the British Army, and they use a 24-hour clock," said Curly. "I wish the American Army would go to this. I use it unofficially and it works rather well."

"So how does this magnificent clock work?" said Doc.

"Let's say we are going to leave at 7:00 a.m.. In the British Army, you say the time all the way up to noon, just like in America. But at 1:00 p.m. here, the British say 1300. At 2:00 p.m. here, that would be 1400, and that would follow the chronological time all the way to 2400 for midnight because it is the start of the day. That's their military way of keeping time," said Curly.

Doc took a draw of her cigarette and flicked her pinky as she listened.

"So Pumpkin Puss, if I said it was 6:15 p.m. What time is that?" asked Curly.

"It's 1815 hrs," said Doc.

"If I said it was 2245 hrs., what time would it be?"

"That would be 10:45 p.m.," said Doc.

"You learn fast," said Curly.

"You have no idea," said Doc, as her eyes welled up.

"Honey, are you all right?" asked Curly.

"Yes, I'm fine," said Doc.

Curly says in his best WC Field imitation, "Sweetheart, my wife for life, and my lover to me. When you are ready to talk, I'll be here for you, my little Mona Lisa." Curly's eyes roamed up and down his wife of seven days, and as their eyes met, he said, "Woman, you're radiant, just like an angel, with an angel face."

The train slowed to a halt and they stepped onto the dimly lit platform.

"Watch your step, ma'am," said the conductor.

They walked silently from the platform to the street.

"So Private; how do I look?" asked Curly.

"Like a West Point Key-det on the Hudson," said Doc.

"Hey Puss, could you please whistle us a cab?" asked Curly. "I know you like to blow—I mean whistle—a cab, Darling."

"Knock it off, Smartass," Doc said as she kicked him.

"Ow! That hurt my shin. I'm still bruised from the last time you kicked me. Why don't you kiss my booboo," smirked Curly.

A piercing whistle went out from Doc's lips right next to Curly's ear, and a cab pulled up promptly.

"How did you learn to whistle like that?" said Curly.

"Remember pucker and blow, pucker and blow," said Doc as she licked her lips. "Here's the taxi!"

"General, where would you like to go to?" said the cabbie.

"I'm not a General yet," said Curly. "Please take us down to Georgetown, 13th and Q Northwest."

"Say Curly, we should look for a little place of our own," said Doc.

"How about around Alexandria?" asked Curly.

"That sounds perfect, Admiral," said Doc.

3. THE FAMILY MEETS

"I might need a new dress, maybe some shoes. Is my hair a mess?" said Doc.

"Darling," said Curly. "You're gorgeous to me. I'm looking you up and down from head to foot. I don't see a thing wrong with you!"

"Thank you very much," said Doc.

"Say Flapper. My mother is very traditional—Irish born and raised there—and she's not quite Americanized yet," said Curly, as he shook his head back and forth.

"Watch out if she gets surprised, but I actually expect her to come unglued. My mother will revert back to old Celtic Irish," said Sullivan. "Complete with the Irish brogue that goes with it."

Curly took her hand and kissed her ring finger. "We might want to take this 15 carat cigar band off and save it," he said gently. Doc nodded yes.

"Pops, he understands Mother because he also was born in Ireland, but raised by the U.S. Army," Curly continued. "My sisters gab with Mom between English and Irish, and we boys can pretty much keep up, too. I will tell you a real family secret," said Curly, lowering his voice to a whisper. "Mom's brother, Anthony Waugh the second, is a known Irish gangster, and started up some kind of an organization."

"Do you mean the I.R...," asked Doc.

"No, not them," interrupted Curly. "She says his gangsters are worse than the I.R.A.. Mom doesn't talk about him much," said Curly as he lit up a cigarette and extended the flame to Doc.

"Mom said, '*Caint an na diabhal agus le cinnteacht sé mian taispeái*,' and made no bones about saying that about her own brother," said Curly. "Which in the old tongue means, '*Talk of the devil, and the certainty he will appear*," said Curly.

Doc cracked the window of the taxi and slowly blew out a long trail of smoke, nodding. Silent.

Curly continued, "Anthony is a very bad man. None of us have ever met the man, except Dad."

"Holy moly, when we younger we got into trouble, Mom's voice would raise two octaves in old Irish, and she would slowly and deliberately direct us to go cut a switch. If she didn't like that particular switch she went out and got one herself; and then we got it twice as hard." Curly sat silent, and looked out the window, remembering Mom's form of punishment. He could still feel the sting of the switch on the back of his legs.

"On top of that, we went to bed with no supper. My older sister, Helen, God bless her heart, would bring us food." Curly looked at Doc and asked, "When you were a naughty girl, what kind of punishment did your folks give you?"

"I was the good child. Never got in trouble, always did my studies," said Doc. "I fell in love with medicine, and decided to go to medical school. I wanted to see the world, helping my fellow man and woman!"

Doc took another long drag of her cigarette and flicked her nails. She watched as some of the smoke escaped the window. Silence hung in the still smokey air.

"My Darling," said Curly, gently caressing her cheek, "Penny for your thoughts?"

"It's nothing sweetheart," said Doc.

"Here we are folks, 13th and Q Northwest," said the cabbie as he came to a stop under a streetlight.

"I'm apprehensive but thrilled to meet my new in-laws," said Doc, as she nervously wiped away a tear.

"Are you sure I look okay?" inquired Doc.

"You're an angel with an angel face," said Curly.

"General, that will be $2.85," said the cabbie.

"Angel, do you have $2.85 I can borrow?"

"Where is your billfold, Marine?" asked Doc.

"I must have packed my billfold away. That mental mistake escaped detection," said Curly.

"There will be the devil to pay," said Doc, as she chuckled. "I also observe that your allocations of finances are diminutive for the gratuities to the hired help are quite odious," stated Doc elegantly.

"What in the name of Webster did you just say?" asked Curly. "Whatever you said, it was quite sexy coming out of your mouth!"

"I said that you are cheapskate, a tight ass, a penny pincher, Sailor boy," jested Doc.

"Yes, I do have a tight ass, but not as tight as yours," chuckled Curly. "But cheapskate? No way. You are mistaken, Little Missy. And on top of that you're full of shit. That's why your eyes are brown, young lady," he said, winking at Doc.

"Well Angel, here we are standing in front of Mom and Dad's place, with the house full of people you've never met," said Curly. They stood in front of the Victorian Painted Lady. Lights flickered in the windows, and streetlights lit the porch that wrapped around the house. A car backfired a block away snapping Doc's head toward the sound.

As they stood looking at the outline of house, the sweet smell of cherry blossoms filled the air. "When you elope with an Irish man, you elope with his whole family. I hope you're ready for this," said Curly.

"Sullivan, I'm a Doctor." She said as she chuckled. "I think I can handle the Sullivan clan."

"Famous last words. If you're not careful, my sisters might dish out a little, or a lot, of their brash humor. Don't take offense; they're just welcoming you into the family."

"Here, let me look at you," said Curly, as he looked up and down at his new wife. "Doc, you are an angel with an angel face. Well. here we go," said Curly, lifting the knocker and slamming it down a couple times. "I adore your knockers!" flirted Curly with a smile on his face.

"You're not too bad yourself, Stud," shot back Doc.

"One of those ten yahoos, minus Mom and Dad, is going to come to that door. You have the pick of six boys and four girls. Hear that?" said Curly as they heard the clomp of shoes hitting the wooden slats of the floor.

"That has to be Shirley," as the door opened. A small girl appeared. The girl looked Doc up and down.

"Hello, who are you?" asked the little voice.

"I'm your older brother, Leonard," teased Curly.

"I know that silly. Who's the broad? I'm going to tell Ma you have a strange lady in the house," she professed in a snotty manner.

"Well, young lady, one good turn deserves another," said Curly.

"What does that mean," asked Shirley.

"What if I tell Ma first, Cinderella?" said Curly.

"How about you give me a sawbuck, Leonard; then I'll go outside like a good girl and play. Your brothers say you're kind of a cheapskape. I would say, you're a whole cheapskape," said Shirley.

"A whole sawbuck?" asked Curly.

"That's the deal. Ten smackers," said Shirley.

"Dr. Kendall, do you have a sawbuck to give to Shyster Shirley?" laughed Curly.

"I sure do, Mr. Capone, here's an Alexander Hamilton," said Doc.

"Now here's your money, highwayman!" said Curly.

"I told you lady, he's cheap," tattled Shirley.

In his best WC Fields imitation, Curly chided, "Now get outta here, ya little brat. By the way, the radio just reported your dolly was riding Fido between here and Highway One. Go on, run after your dog. You could swim the length of the Potomac. You should go join them. Furthermore, learn to swim with concrete flippers on your feet, you little brat." He flicked an imaginary cigar.

"She's a cute kid." said Doc sarcastically.

"Yeah, she's the baby of the family," said Curly proudly.

"Oh boy," said Doc as she rolled her eyes.

"Let's get this show on the road," said Curly. "Down this hall, there's a large dining room that is just off the kitchen. I think everybody is in the dining room—all but Ma 'n Pa," announced Curly.

"Whoa! I don't like the sound of that," said Doc.

"I thought you weren't worried? You said you could handle my sisters and brothers," said Curly.

"Well that was then, and this is now, and you're a big brown cow," said Doc as she elbowed him.

"Just trying to break the ice doll!" said Curly.

"For you or for me?" Doc asked. Doc grabbed Curly's hand and said, "A day of reckoning."

"Honey, you're a very capable Doctor, and I love you very much," said Curly as he turned the door handle slowly and flung the door open to a colossus of drinking, eating, smoking, and jocularity.

Eight heads turned toward them, five men in military uniform at rest, and three nicely dressed young women. They rose, clanging their chairs together, and stampeded toward the couple like great predators circling their prey; all eyes were fixed on Doc.

"Ladies and Gentlemen of the Sullivan Clan, I would like to introduce you to Fedora Francis Kendall Sullivan, my new wife. Close your mouths, you're starting to draw flies," said Curly.

"Fedora is my Christian name, but, all my friends call me Doc. So, who is the oldest?" inquired Doc.

"Well that would be me. I'm Leo," as the tallest man gave her a big brotherly Irish hug.

"Nice to meet you, Leo. You're tall for what I know of the Sullivan Clan so far. Ok, who's next?" asked Doc.

"I'm Harold, and this is my twin sister Helen." Helen, a beautiful young lady with neat auburn hair and piercing hazel eyes.

Helen reached forward and shook Doc's hand. "Very nice to meet you. What was your nickname again?"

"Please call me Doc,"

Harold, a tall, skinny, handsome man stepped forward and kissed her on the cheek warmly. "Welcome to the clan, Ma'am."

"Hi Doc. I'm Raymond." He grabbed her hand and twirled her around. He said, "What is a beautiful dame like you doing with a slug like Crow?"

"Can I cut in, Mrs. Sullivan," said Curly. "I'm next, after Raymond in the family."

"I'm Jack. How'd you like a big fat cigar? It was rolled on virgin thighs," said Jack, with a twinkle in his hazel eyes.

"I'd love a stogie after dinner," said Doc as she stepped forward to hug Jack.

"Hello, my new sister. I'm Maxine," said the elegant young woman, with her curls perfectly in place and a pillbox hat propped neatly atop her head."

"What a lovely cardigan. That pink is beautiful with your hair. And those shoes are cooking with gas," said Doc.

"I have a date with Major Jeffries. He's so dreamy," swooned Maxine.

"I'm Bob. They call me Pearl, as in the gem of the family," he laughed as he shook Doc's hand a little too hard.

"That's quite a handshake you have there. I'll have my darling husband put my shoulder back in the socket later," Doc snickered. "Very nice to meet you."

"Bob's got the reddest hair in the whole family," said Curly. "All the girls think he's the cutest of the lot."

"Nice to make your acquaintance, Miss Fedora. I'm Richard," said the smallest of the brothers. "If you don't mind me saying so, may I say you are very beautiful," said Richard as he held her hand for a moment.

"Hey, watch that, knucklehead," said Curly, messing up his brother's hair. "Go find your own broad."

"Well aren't you a dish. I'm Rita," her dark hair pulled back into a sleek chignon, lighting a cigarette. "Would you care for a coffin nail?"

"You bet, Doll. Thanks," said Doc as Rita sparked her lighter and lit Doc's cigarette.

Doc took a long drag and surveyed the clan. She raised her chin and exhaled her smoke along with her pent-up anxiety.

"She already met Shirley," said Curly. "Cost her a sawbuck!" They all laughed.

"By the way, where is Mom and Dad?" Curly asked.

Helen eagerly shared, "Dad's been downstairs for hours. He's looking for a knapsack that he brought back from World War I."

"So nice to meet all of you. I see where Curly gets his magnetism. With all those Sullivan hugs, it's a wonder my back is not maladjusted, and my hand is not broken," chuckled Doc. "You three girls," said Doc. "We have a lot to talk about."

"That sounds lovely," said Maxine.

"Doc," asked Leo. "Is that a nickname?"

"No," answered Doc.

"So how did you get the nickname Doc?" asked Leo.

"Well Leo, I'm a real doctor," said Doc. "I just walked into Johns Hopkins one day, then walked out the very next day with a medical degree," said Doc chuckling. "All kidding aside, I really do have a medical degree from John Hopkins."

"Well to get a medical degree from anywhere, you have to be pretty darn smart… Even for a woman," said Leo.

"Uh, I'll take that as a compliment, I guess," said Doc smiling.

"In any event that's pretty darn spiffy," said Leo.

"Why thank you," said Doc.

The sisters gathered off to the far side of the dining room, to listen to the conversation, and gossip about their new sister-in-law.

"*Muire Dochtúir,*" whispered Helen. "Lady Doctor!"

"Really?" asked Maxine back.

"I'll bet you that she is *Bean de aosáideach suáilce*," gossiped Maxine.

"So, do you believe she is a *woman of easy virtue*?" whispered Helen. "What do you think?"

"*Sí mian a bheith* na scriosadh an *é*," whispered Maxine.

"You think It will be the ruination of him?" asked Helen. "Does she have a *mion* gréithe de *gearrann*?"

"I have not examined her mouth to see that she has a *fine set of teeth*," said Rita as she shook her head back and forth at her sisters.

"Well," whispered Helen, "Dad always taught the boys that before they bring a girl home, make sure she has a full set of teeth."

"*Tréidlia* Dochtúir," said Helen.

"Why do you say she's a *Veterinarian Doctor*?" whispered Maxine.

"Because look at the jackass she married," whispered Rita as the girls snickered under their breath.

"Crow, you old son of a gun, no one thought you'd be the first one to get hitched, especially to a Doctor," said Raymond.

"You're a lucky stiff, you old dog," said Harold as he shook his brother's hand and patted him on the arm.

Doc looked around the room, playfully pushing the brothers aside. "Is there any Bush Mills around here?"

Leo stepped over to the wet bar and inquired politely, "Neat, Ma'am?" He handed her the glass, as she nodded and smiled.

Doc flicked her pinky and took a drag on her cigarette, then she swallowed the whiskey, and winked at Leo with a nod.

"Ain't she cute as a bug's ear," said Jack as he gave his brother a shot on the arm.

"Where'd you meet?" asked Bob.

"At Union Station," said Curly. "She was a damsel in distress who needed to be saved. I saved her," he said as they all laughed. "Geez. This is quite the inquisition. Ray don't you have a burning question for me?"

"Hey ladies, can you point me to the powder room," asked Doc.

Ray thought for a moment and said, "I take it that you have not told Ma or Pa this news?"

"No, I have not," said Curly, cringing. "I'm a little skittish about that. I'm glad she wasn't here when we walked in. I haven't seen her for three years, so I'm sure that would have been enough of a shock even without me bringing her a new daughter-in-law."

"You know if you would have called Mom and told her first, she would have put the ki-bosh on it," informed Ray.

"Then you would have been all wet," said Harold, as he chuckled.

"Here you go boys," said Richard as he popped around the corner to the dining room. "I bought us all a round of beers. Courtesy of Pops."

"Why, thank you, Dick," said Curly, taking one for him and another for Doc.

"She's quite the cat's meow," said Leo, as he grabbed a bottle beer from Richard. "Thanks, brother."

"Say Helen," said Curly. "Have you seen Dr. Sullivan in the last few minutes?"

"Yes, she's in the little lady's room. Taking a number two," bellowed Maxine as she snickered.

Curly pinched his nose and said, "When she comes out, tell her I got a cold beer and a warm fart for her."

"I'll be sure to let her know," said Helen.

"What if Fredora, turns out to be a dumb Dora?" whispered Maxine to her sisters.

"We'll find out about that one," whispered Helen, covering her mouth.

"But you know girls, our brother has *Bogadh de na inchinn*," whispered Rita.

"Yes, he is suffering from *softening of the brain!*" whispered Maxine as they all chuckled out loud.

"What did I miss girls?" asked Doc, as she returned to the dining room straightening her skirt.

"Just talking about your husband, Captain Romance," said Rita. The girls and Doc chuckled.

"I'm pretty keen about him, too, but he is a bit of a wise guy. You know I mean, a smartass, but in a fun way," remarked Doc. "Excuse me a minute ladies, I think my husband has a beer and a warm kiss for me."

"A beer and something warm and special for ya," laughed Helen, as Doc walked across the room to her husband.

"Sise *tá absalóideach spraic thar!*" whispered Rita

"You are absolutely right," said Helen… "*She does have absolute control over him,*" as the girls shook their heads back and forth.

"Wait 'til Ma, gets home. There will be a Sullivan knockdown, dragout tonight. I feel it coming," said Maxine.

"*Sé ta ar a gairid coniall,*"whispered Helen as she watched Doc through the smoke that had filled the room.

"I agree," murmured Rita. "*He is on a short dog leash,*" pantomiming a hangman's noose around the neck.

"What do you think Pa will do?" said Rita.

"I don't know, but we should definitely make a plan, because there is going to be hell-fire to pay," added Helen.

"Boys, gather around. We're going to toast the brand-new bride and groom with some old Irish wisdom," said Ray.

"Curly. Doc," Ray raised his glass and continued, "As you slide down the banisters of life, may the splinters never point the wrong way."

They all raised their glasses and bottles, and said, "*Sláinte!*"

"Here, I have one," said Bob. "May your troubles be less, and your blessings be more. And nothing but happiness come through the door."

Again, they raised their drinks and gave a hearty, "*Sláinte!*"

"Get outta the way," said Jack, as he playfully pushed his brother aside. "There are many good reasons for drinking, and one has just entered my head." He stood straight and delivered his toast with a flourish, "If a man doesn't drink when he's living, how the hell can he drink when he's dead."

"Sláinte!"

"Thanks, boys. Those were great. By the way where *is* my new mother-in-law?" asked Doc.

"Rita!" shouted Curly. "Where is Ma?"

"She went to the Holy Trinity Church to drop off some clothes and food for the needy!" said Rita.

"Mom," said Helen to Doc. "She just loves that new Cardinal, Timothy O'Leary. Mrs. Smith Jones who lives three houses down said that the new Cardinal has the ability to give a good fire-and-brimstone sermon. You feel you're on the cusp of Heaven," explained Helen, pointing one finger up to heaven.

Rita walked into the hall and opened a door. "General, me darlin', are you still downstairs?" bellowed Rita.

A few seconds passed, and then "Yes I am," he said. The octave in his voice raised, as he yelled to her, "Rita, me darlin', I'm trying to find my black leather briefcase from World War I"

"General, me Darlin'," said Rita. "It's on the third shelf up, in the back."

CHAPTER 4

"Dad, chow is served," said Helen. "You still looking for that old satchel? Come have dinner."

Donald grabbed a step stool, and looked across the length of the shelf. He moved a box labeled "PORCELAIN," and another labeled "BOOTS." In the back, behind an ancient duck decoy, he spotted a buckle and a strap.

"I see it. Come'ere me darlin'," he said as he stretched to reach the strap. He pulled, and the leather bag slid into view. He pulled harder, and it came loose from its home of 23 years, given to him on the last day of WWI, November 11, 1918.

He hadn't thought about it for years, but he received a telegram that afternoon.

"By thunder, this is dusty," said the General as he took in a deep breath and blew across the face of the bag pelting the air with a dust storm that dimmed the bright lightbulb as it swung back and forth above his head, flickering. The strobing light and the din of the cloud of dust in this small area brought back a tsunami of bad memories.

4. IN A TRENCH IN WESTERN FRANCE, NOVEMBER 10, 1918

"Sgt. Sullivan. We cleared the south trench of the dead," said Pvt. Wagner.

"But not the bunkers?" asked Sullivan. "Check for personal items, weapons, and papers, and then roll those bastard Huns outside of the trench," said Sullivan, in his Irish brogue. Wagner stood at parade rest. Sullivan could see that he didn't know what to do. "Pvt. Wagner. I know you're a doggie, so this is our SOP. You're looking for papers, ID cards, maps, code books, and anything else of value to beating these mother fuckers. All and anything you find, gather it up and hand it to me."

Wagner rolled over the first dead German. His sunken face was covered in a thick mass of blood and dirt. Wagner shook the blood off his hands, and reached into the inside pocket of the German trench coat. He pulled out a piece of paper and opened it. He looked at his Platoon Sergeant, "I got no clue on how to read German, Sarg., but this looks like a letter from his sweetheart." Wagner reached into the right-hand pocket of the trench coat. He felt something warm and wet and pulled out a piece of rye bread dripping with blood."

Wagner wiped one hand on the German's pant leg and continued his search. On his belt, he found a six-inch steel blade of a trench knife. The dried blood on the steel made it hard to distinguish from the wooden handle. He held it up to look at it.

"That is what you call a *Nahkampfmesser*, son. In the right hands, this will slice you from stem to stern and you won't even feel it, me boy-o," Sullivan advised.

"Pvt. Wagner, get Doc to look at your arm," ordered Sullivan, pointing at the 12" gash on the right arm of his trench coat, oozing with blood. The dirt and grime hid the deep cut matching the trench coat.

"Oh shit, I didn't know I was slashed," said Pvt. Wagner.

"Boyo, go see Doc now. To the quick march, lad. Congratulations, you just won the Badge of Military Merit. It won't hurt your arm if you can't salute when they pin it on you," said Sullivan.

Wagner walked the trench line looking for doc. Sullivan examined the items they had gathered. He tossed the bread on the ground, and wrapped the other things in a cloth and tucked them in his trench coat.

One. Two. Three. Large blasts bounced off the parapet. Sullivan looked around and found Cpl. Lewis wide-eyed, holding his smoking M-12. The smell of burnt sulfur and cordite filled the trench around them.

"What happened Cpl?" shouted Sullivan.

"They… they came out of nowhere. They popped out of the bunker and ran right into me tryin' to get out," Lewis said. "So, I gave 'em a little slam-fire for their troubles," as he lit a cigarette with a shaking hand. "Holy shit, was that close."

"That's right, me Boy-o," said Sullivan. "Good kill. Go ahead and check those guys for papers and contraband real quick."

Among the dead German officers, Lewis found a Lugar, a map, a few knives, a boot grenade, a tin of tobacco, and a pipe.

"Boy-o, where is the rest of Headquarter section and the old man?" asked Sullivan.

"Sgt. Sullivan, Capt. Hill took them on a leader's recon up the communications trench to the second trench. He gave me orders to stay right here," said Lewis as he tried to wipe the blood and gun powder from his hands. "I was to leave my post only if I saw the enemy, or after 15 minutes. Then he said that I should find the First Sgt. or you if he didn't come back with Headquarter section," reported Lewis.

A tall blonde walked toward Sullivan and Lewis. Fresh blood covered his face, with his striking blue eyes shining through the darkness. "Here we are boys, y'all doin' okay in here, Sir?" asked SFC. Stephen Forthright.

"Good to see you Cowboy. Geez, you look like you've had your face buried in that Oklahoma clay," Sullivan chided.

"Yes, Sir. Just like home."

"Have you seen Top in the last 30 minutes?" asked Sullivan.

"We're fixin to come get y'all," piped in SFC. Decatur Shea as he came up behind Forthright. "We had the First Sergeant," said Shea.

Sullivan interrupted, "You had the First Sergeant?"

"Sir, as per our orders," said Shea. "When we made the breach, y'all took the first right with y'all two squads from first platoon, an' awhat's left of Forthright's second platoon," said Shea. map

Sullivan stepped closer to Shea, "Sergeant, what happened?"

"About 26 of us were afixin' to go to the left with what was left of my third platoon," reported Shea calmly. "And what was left of

Wilson's fourth platoon, went down to that first trench, in about 10 to 15 yards," said Shea, in his Georgia drawl.

Looking over Shea's head, Sullivan saw only the whites of Wilson's green eyes peeking between Shea and Forthright, and said, "Did you get your arse kicked, there Wilson?"

"No, not this time, Bossman. That's when we ran right into a whole bracket of them Heinies paahked in their sleeping quarters, and we smacked em haahd," said Staff Sgt. Mike Wilson with his New England humor and candor.

"Good work, boyo," said Sullivan.

"We ran in, and they came arunnin' out like a congregation a gators was on the attack in Seminole Lake," said Shea.

"We were in hand-to-hand waahrfare with them big, dumb Heinies. We're rolling around on the ground, biting, diggin' out eyes, stickin' em with knives, baashin' them with trench clubs. Then we stahted in stabbing them with entrenching tools, shooting with 1911s, and when we ran outta ammo, we just coldcocked them to make sure they didn't make it to their next living birthday. Took some big balls behind it, and a fine repertoire of cussing," said SSG. Mike Wilson. "It was a maximum effort, Sarg."

"Good job, boyo. In five or six years, you're gonna be promoted to Sergeant First Class," said Sullivan proudly.

Sullivan turned to his squad and said, "Men, Cpl. Lewis has informed me dat Headquarters section with the old man, went on a leader's recon."

"Cpl. Lewis, take Privates Mahoney and South and da Hotchkiss machine gun with what's left of the ammo, and support this entrance so nobody can get it," said Sullivan, adding "I'll try to get relief to you later and, and if at all possible, some food, too."

"Sgt. Sullivan."

"Yes, Lewis?"

"About 10 minutes ago—maybe a little longer—there was machine-gun fire, some grenades, and sporadic single shots coming from that way," said Lewis, pointing toward the number 3 trench.

"Understood, boyo," said Sgt. Sullivan, as he turned and said, "Sgt. Shea, you and Sgt. Forthright clear dis bunker."

"Roger that," said Forthright.

"Then see if there's any rat food and papers in the bunker," said Sullivan.

"Someone get a lamp," said Shea. "I'm sure there's a case of Georgia peaches in this here bunker. I can taste em now."

"Make sure y'all cover up the door good, for light discipline," said Forthright.

"Get this bunker neat and tidy. I don't know how long we can stay here," said Sullivan, as he removed his helmet.

"Kraut looks as fat as a Georgia hog," said Shea.

Shea picked up the feet of one of the dead Germans, and Forthright put his hands under the arms, and lifted the man up to the firing trench. They climbed up to the firing step and heaved him up over the trench side.

Forthright laughed and said, "I'd say he is as fat as an Oklahoma oinker. Two more fat asses to go."

"Why didn't y'all fuckers go crawl away and die, and save my back," said Shea. "Y'all Punkin' heads?"

They removed the other two dead men, found a wooden door and a tarp, and set them up for light discipline. They covered everything that might leak light out.

Sullivan inspected the area, put his hands on his hips and said, "Ah, smells just like unwashed Hun. Did the arseholes leave any chow or better yet, something strong to warsh it down with?"

Shea began looking through the bunker; he lifted up a tarp and said, "Why hush my mouth, full of black-eyed peas and cornpone with a side order of buttered and peppered grits. Mr. Sullivan, your prayers have been answered. Lookie what I found. About three cases of your all-time favorite, Crow; English whiskey from the Ristols dee-stillery."

"Mary Magdalene," said Sullivan. "One good reason why the English love Irish whiskey so much is that they send it to the Old Country to make it right. The Old Country filters it back through their livers in a slow-aged process. Then right back to the English at three times the price. Ireland is the best in the catalog at making Irish whiskey, that's fer damn sure. Make sure all the boys get a bottle of this swill."

Searching on the other side of the bunker, Forthright said, "I have something here. Some hard bread, a hunk of sausage, four German iron rations, and some-a-da finest French iron rations on the market today. And here is nice delicious hunk of dead rat," he uttered as he kissed his fingers. "Mucho Grando! Magnifico!"

Shea yelled across to Forthright, "I got about the same thang over here, a smidge more though." He lifted a trench coat and looked under it, "Well, I'll be a Yankee carpetbagger, you lucky American-Irish bastard. I get lice and a boll weevil stuck up my ass, and you get 10 cases of Bush Mills, served right up on a silver salver."

"Lemme see," said Sullivan as his head whipped around. He lifted up the lamp to inspect the find. "Bush Mills. Ten-year single malt, glory be to the Saints and all those in Purgatory Pub," he said as he picked up a bottle and pointed toward Heaven. "Boyo's, drinking Bush Mills is like a symphony in your mouth. First, it hits the tongue, then it swirls and twirls around, like its dancing with your favorite mistress or your mother, and then it gently paints and reaffirms your throat like the warmth of a good woman," conveyed Sullivan. "Then after that, straight to the kidneys to make more Ristols," chuckled Sullivan. "I'll divvy these up later."

Sullivan lifted a bottle of Bush Mills in the air and said, "In the meantime, raise your bottle of mutton piss to the English for making it. *May we all be alive at this same time next year. Go mbeimid go léir beo ag an am céanna an bhliain seo chugainn.*

"That's a poor rep'esentation of liquor. It'll clear your throat, but ain't as good as my Grandpappy Smith's mash," said Shea. "That man could squeeze a fart outta each kernel of corn to get more flavorin."

"Now boyos, you be drinking a wee little bit at your own risk," stated Sullivan pointing at the bottles of Ristols. "When you drink that English pig swill, it'll eat your guts out. That's why one good swig of that, would chafe the poor brains clean away from the froggy French. That's why them frogs hide behind us American's. So, let's drink to the cows coming home; and may they never come home." Sullivan sat on the firestep, closed his eyes, and took a long drink.

When he opened his eyes, Sgt. James O'Keefe was hovering over him, smiling. Sullivan handed him the bottle and he took a swig. "Hey me boyo. You look like the back end of forward-moving mule, Doc."

"Thanks, Crow." The whites of his eyes were bloodshot and worn, and just a sliver of blue was visible through the thick layer of blood and dirt.

"Doc, I'm glad you could make it to our little soiree. It's not like those fancy medical school parties back in Philly," laughed Sullivan as he lead Doc into the bunker. "What'd you come up with, me boyo? Give it to me straight, what's our dead and wounded count?" asked Sullivan.

"Well Crow, you know we lost the First Sergeant," started Doc, as the remaining men nodded yes.

The men in the bunker got quiet and looked at the duckboard and dirt under their feet. Shea asked, "Doc, do you wanna tell Crow or should I?"

"Tell me what?" asked an inquisitive Sullivan.

"Crow," said Doc, as he took a deep breath. "I thought I'd never have to do this." The words hung in the air. He raised his gaze slowly, as a tear washed a river through the mud. He looked Sullivan in the eyes, "Crow, I had to shoot James O'Flaherty in the head."

"James," said Sullivan as he dropped his head, nodding back and forth, making the sign of the cross. "Bless his soul, and the rest of the boys."

Doc explained, "Them assholes drug him around the traverse by his ammo belt. We couldn't get there fast enough to help him. They went to hacking away on Jimmy with their entrenching tools. He was screaming bloody murder. We moved to the right, so I could get a shot."

Shea cut in, "But I let go of my grenade and it blasted the alligator crap right outta them thar Germans, akillin' poor Jimmy, too."

A moment of silence came, and then they all raised their bottles in a silent toast to their dead comrades.

"Boyos, don't ya let them feelin's fester inside. It was a hard decision in your heart, but you know it was the right thing to do.

Nobody wants to see a friend suffer needlessly," said Sullivan in his sympathetic Irish brogue. "Gentlemen, God will not judge you for a mercy killing. It is the savagery of war—kill or be killed," said Sullivan, as he stood up and put his hand on Doc's shoulder.

"James Jackson is dead, too. He got shot through the throat. Ski, they got him, too. Shot right in the head," said Shea, hanging his head. "My ol' Grandpappy on my father's side, fought in Company D, Doherty's Hussars of Cobbs Legion in the Civil War, ya hear," declared Shea. "After the war Grandpappy bought him some old Razorback huntin' dogs to hunt wild boars. D'ya know the tusk of a boar can kill a man? Poor Billy "Blue Tick" Montgomery, from the quiet cotton fields of Louisiana got one of them French nails right in the eye, just like one of them thar boar tusks," Shea continued.

Shea looked at his watch.

"Y'all, it was a foregone conclusion that his old buddy Alan Blue Lacy, from Texas was acomin' over, afixin' to help out. Blue was jumped by two Huns, they knocked his helmet clean off, an gotta 'im to the ground. Then they took turns acrushin' the side of his skull in with a mornin' star," said Shea. "Them thar critters took a poke at Wilson, who dropped them both with one shot from his 1911."

"Yeah, I shot 'em like Annie Oakley," said Wilson. "Then poor Cpl. Ellison was cleaved with one-a-them Mornin' Stahrs with spikes. They opened the side of his neck with a 6-inch gaysh." He shook his head and ran his finger across his throat. "I smashed into that bast'ed Hun, taking the Mornin' Stahr away from him. Then givin' him the same medicine, back in spades, of course, with all my haht. I told him diamonds were a queen's best friend, I think. I hit again with the Club, splittin' his head open like a French cut diamond."

Wilson cleared his throat. He removed his canteen from the strap, unscrewed the cap slowly and took a drink.

"Ya might want somethin' stronger than water," said Doc, handing him a bottle of Ristols.

Wilson took a long pull, and coughed, "This tastes like mule piss from Georgia." They all laughed.

Wilson continued his report, "Sinclair. Y'all should have seen his head. They crushed his skull in with an entrenching tool. I turned 'round n' saw Shea drop that one. I turned the other way to see James Flannery fall on to the duckboard. Them Germans stripped him of his Brodie, then one bast'ed plunged his trench knife into Flannery's chest. I shot two a them and then ran outta fuckin' ammo. Another shithead German came up, and I bashed his nose and right cheek bone in. I barely reloaded my 1911 and then immediately unloaded into his young darkened face. Then I shot two others that had just come up," he continued. "It was just like the time my dad took me to Coney Island's shootin' gallery, except I didn't win a prize that time, but this time I got me two Heinies. The prize was my life."

Wilson put his index finger up to his lips and blew. He twirled his finger-gun and jammed it into an imaginary holster. "Near forgot to mention that young James McGee was one of the first to go down. He was jumped by three of them. They had him disemboweled with their trench knives in less than a minute. He didn't know what hit him. Looked like a steer under the butcher's knife."

"Shea shot them three som'bitches. Poor bast'eds—they all died ugly," said Wilson.

Shea wiped the mud and blood from the bottle of Ristols and took a drink and coughed.

"Jesus Christ! Crow was right about arottin' yer guts. I wouldn't let my best hog drink this slurry," said Shea as he put his bottle down. "Michael O'Grady got a spiked club to the side of his head, and another to the back of his head. Squirted blood about 10 feet. Anyways, we put down about 42 of them varmints." He added as he took another swallow of swill, "Outta 27 of us who went into the trench, 13 fuckin' men walked out or was carried out alive. The other 14, God rest their souls," he said, shaking his head slowly and making the sign of the cross.

"Boyos, we fared no better," said Sullivan. "I too walked out with 13 men. Jim Wright was beaten to death with a trench club, and Andy Olson had his throat slit. I dunno if he's gonna make it," Sullivan added.

"No Crow, Olson didn't make it," said Doc solemnly.

Forthright piped in, "Robert Dempsey was cut down tryin' to save Patty Keogh. Patty's dead, too. He was stabbed at the base of the neck."

Sullivan looked deep into his bottle of Bush Mills. He took a drink and set it beside him on the firestep. "Big Jim O'Leary, that big redheaded Irishman, saw a potato masher get flung. He grabbed it and tried to heave it out of the trench, but three Huns jumped him. They didn't see the potato masher fly behind them as they ripped Big Jim's Brodie off his head, pounding him in the head. Then the grenade went off killing all four."

Sullivan looked at Wilson and then at his bottle of Bush Mills, then back again. Sullivan warned as he pulled his bottle close to his chest, "I will take your manhood away."

Wilson's eyes grew to the size of saucers. "Yes suh. I remember July of 1918. I would like to keep my manhood if that's okay with you."

Sullivan continued without skipping a beat, "I went to reloading my 1911, n' saw Patty O'Connor get blown to smithereens along with the Hun he was fighting. Patty and the bastard were killed by a German grenade that had a slow fuse. Sean Duffy. They caved in the back his head…"

"Then Anthony Fitzpatrick got his throat cut," interrupted Forthright.

"Crow," said Doc. "Four of them other guys have mortal wounds."

"So, what do you have, Doc?" Sullivan asked.

"Jim Gillespie—half his skull is gone. You can see his temporal lobe," added Doc. "Robert Barnes lost an eye and got a mortal stomach wound, and he wants some water. Worst thing we could give him right now. Benjamin Davidson was also beaten with a spiked club in the head, and Bob Martin got ripped open from the middle of the chest to his crotch. I made them as comfortable as possible. I told the guys to feed them some whiskey," said Doc shaking his head. "Damn. I worked a couple a years at the Omaha Stockyards. This trench is worse than them Stockyards and butcherin' cattle."

"I know you did your best Sgt. James O'Keefe," declared Sullivan. "Me, those men, God, and all the Saints as they watched over you. So do not burden yourself. You know as well as I do, that they will go to a far better place," consoled Crow.

Sullivan stood and looked over his men. "Wilson, Doc, Shea. Tell the rest o' the boyos to dry their feet and socks out and that we will be moving out in the morn," said Crow.

"Anything else, Sgt. Sullivan?" asked Doc.

Suddenly the bunker door opened, "Is there a Captain Robert Hill in here?" asked a voice with hard Irish brogue.

"Who would like to know?" asked Sgt. Sullivan.

"Me. Brigadier General Clancy Clust O'Rourke, Esq. would like to know."

The men snapped to attention.

"Come in, Sir. I didn't know high mucky mucks were visiting," said Sullivan.

"As you were men," said the General. A patch covered his left eye, and a sharp blue eye pierced the darkness. Neat gray hair peeked from beneath his Brodie, and a roundabout surrounded his waist on his trench coat. His presence was a stark contrast to the men in the bunker. He unhooked and removed his Brodie and gloves, and set them on the table. "So, what about Captain Hill?"

"He's not here at the moment, Sir. Right now, I'm in charge. Sgt. Sullivan reports, Sir. Begging your pardon, how can I be *cuidiúil* tonight, General, me darlin'?" asked Sullivan.

"Thank you for being *helpful*, but my orders are with Captain Hill!" said Gen. O'Rourke.

"In the meantime, Sir, may we offer a wee bit of refreshment? Sir, our fighting 69th establishment only serves the finest selection of whiskeys in the trenches of France," said Sullivan smiling. "I'm sure General Darlin', you'd appreciate a good snort or three to clear the French dirt from the throat. To the left, Ristols, or on me right, Bush Mills," presented Sullivan.

"By Saint Michael and all the saints," said an elated O'Rourke, "How did you come across Bush Mills in this godforsaken place?"

"The Huns," said Sullivan. "The boys found an outstanding cachet when they cleared these trenches."

O'Rourke motioned to the Bush Mills. "It's been two years, eight months, 15 days, nine hours, 32 seconds since me lips has tasted that elixir," sung O'Rourke in a happy-go-lucky Irish brogue. "Me boyo, it was mid-1915. I was given orders to sail over to Europe. Never liked sailing," said O'Rourke taking on a more serious tone. "The last time I was going to sail somewhere I decided to walk. After gettin' me orders with the British. I was set up with all me gear. Then after some time lollygagging, they flew me to France in a Handley Page bomber. Then some very bumpy lorry rides to the British front as an observer. By Saint Michael, they put me in the 16th Irish Division, and I arrived right after the battle of Hulluch."

A few men sat down on the firestep, and the others were in the bunker. They continued to listen to the General; eyes and ears at the position of attention. At 68, the General looked strong and imposing, yet his posture and demeanor gave him a charismatic quality.

"In and around Loos, France, the Irish Division got a good dose of gas," continued O'Rourke. He pulled out a monocle attached to a Catholic rosary and put it to his eye. "After the battle of Hulluch," the Irish learned to cut the jugular vein of the Hun in trench warfare."

Doc held out a bottle of Ristols, and the General held up his palm toward it and said, "I will slap you back to diapers."

The men laughed, and the General continued, "Then in July, we moved into the Somme. As a whole, the Commonwealth units on the field in the first day lost nearly 20,000 men. They were killed by something that changed the course of warfare: the use of the machine gun. During the Somme in early September 1916, the 16th Irish Division took the town of Guillemot, about 160 kilometers due north," said O'Rourke with a big smile on his face. "But t'was a cost of many a good lad," added O'Rourke as the smile melted off his face.

Silence filled the area, and O'Rourke continued, "Then to the battle of Ginchy, after a long march. During these two battles, the Division lost over 200 officers and over 4,000 more men. In June

1917, the 16th Division, Irish and the 36th Division Ulster marched into West Flanders, Belgium, to take part in the battle of Messines," said O'Rourke in his Irish brogue. "The British started operations by etonating over 450 tons of gun cotton and ammonal, throughout 21 tunnels. Some said there were pillars of fire and they could be heard all the way to London. Glory be. The two Divisions went on a coordinated attack in the village of Wijtschate, Belgium. They cleared the Wijtschate Wood and Grand Bois." O'Rourke went on, "On the 9th of June, the 16th Irish Division went to the rear for reconstitution. A few weeks later, they threw the boys into the line at Passchendaele, West Flanders. That is the last time I saw the boys from the Emerald Isle."

He went on, "Many a good boy have been cut down by this war," said O'Rourke. "In one year's time, I made and lost many a friend in the 47th, 48th, and the 49th Brigades of the 16th Irish Division," he said as he looked down at the ground shaking his head slowly back and forth.

"Right after that, I got pulled back to the rear and got me new marching orders. Right to Paris," said O'Rourke. "So being a General with high moral virtues, I stayed in the finest chalets," he said as a smile formed on his lips showing arow of white teeth. His blue eye beamed of past pleasures. He turned to Sullivan, "Mr. Sullivan, have you ever fallen into the arms of two French women and had a, *Goirt Comhfhiontar*?"

Sullivan started to chuckle and said, "No sir, I have not had a salty joint venture with two French women. I'm happily married, Sir, to my Darlin' Mary Mags, Mags is short for..."

"Wait a minute, boyo," O'Rourke said, cutting across his words. "Lemme guess, Magdalene. I'd toast your marriage if I had something strong to toast with," said O'Rourke. "All this time you been yakking you haven't offered me Darlin' General a drink. Did I hear you say something about Ristols? May I have your permission to have a bottle of it, please?" asked O'Rourke. "Pop the cork me good man, and slowly pour it right on me hands. G'tting them sterilized like a Darlin' Doctor delivering a newborn," he chuckled. Doc poured a bit of Ristols in the General's cupped hands, who flicked his wet fingers off at Wilson.

Sullivan handed him a bottle of Bush Mills, and O'Rourke lifted it up high over his head, looking at it with his good right eye between him and the lamp. "Next to a Gurnsey's milk," said O'Rourke. "This is God's elixir of life." He pulled the cork out with this teeth and spit it into his hand. "With all your hot yammering breath, that kicks up hot dust, you won't let a man get a word in edgewise around here, and when a man like me gets *tirim...*"

"I can understand! A big strapping, Darlin' General like yourself must be *thirsty*," said Sullivan, smiling.

"One cuts the dust! But two clears it," chuckled O'Rourke. The two men tapped the bottles of fine whiskey together. O'Rourke took a swig of whiskey and gurgled. "Sgt. Sullivan," he said.

"Yes, General."

"Could you stand up very calmly and move to your right?" asked O'Rourke.

"Yes, sir," said Sullivan, carefully standing and stepping to the right.

"There's a very large rat, who is fat as a cat, so fuck that," said O'Rourke. Then came a crack of fire, sound, and smoke. "Gentlemen, that was the mess call. Supper is served," he said as he put his pistol back into his belt.

"Sir, is that a Colt single-action Peacemaker?" asked Sullivan.

"That it is, me boyo" said O'Rourke as he took an elephantine imbibe of Bush Mills. "I have an old friend. said O'Rourke. "These are special hand-loaded 325 grains of propellant, in a copper jacket for the 45 Colt, with 28 grains of tin, antimony, and lead to make the head of the bullet." He took out a bullet and put it up to the light. He passed it to Sullivan.

Sullivan turned it end to end, examining it between his thumb and index finger, "I'd hate to be hit anywhere with this little prick."

O'Rourke continued, "Me friend, he used to work for the Hercules munitions and chemical company. A true craftsman, head of the guild. He made a special cast to me precise specifications. The die is made to concave the head of the bullet in a quarter inch. Look, at the head of that bullet. See the two 1/8" crosscut channels? Those make that bullet explode like a mushroom inside the body." They all gathered around the light to get a closer look.

"For maximum impact, we took me standard Colt single-action Peacemaker with a seven and half inch barrel, castrated it down to four inches, and took out the injector rod," explained O'Rourke. "I don't give a flying fiddlers fuck about distance or accuracy. But this little Michelangelo does an excellent job up close in the trenches, if you don't mind the bloody mess it paints!" He took another long drink of Bush Mills, and put the bottle in his trench coat pocket.

"Well, Maconochie's stew and farts! I'll drink to that," chimed in Sullivan. Sullivan passed the bullet down to Doc, who examined it and passed it down for each man to do the same.

O'Rourke explained further, "The Hague Convention of 1899 banned the use of soft-tipped bullets. Some cairde call 'em dum dum bullets," he laughed. "So, the treaty was ratified by all the powers to be, except for Uncle Sam. He told them to, as they say in the old Irish tongue, '*Bata Sé sa a cranra poll.*' For those of you men who aren't of Irish blood, that means '*stick it in a knothole*,' pull their bloomers down around their ankles. Then they can piss up the tree, and shake it off," said a happy Gen. O'Rourke, as he took another slow, long drink.

"I'll drink to that, too," said Sullivan.

"But in 1907, the US finally ratified the Hague Convention. There's nothin' more effective in the trenches, in me opinion. What blarney they don't know, won't hurt them," said O'Rourke.

"Holy shit, Sir, that would put a ki-bosh on your entire day and night," said Wilson.

"That it would, me boyo," said O'Rourke. "But I'm curious, son? Which one are you talking about? The knothole or getting shot?" he asked as he winked his bright blue eye at Sullivan.

"Sir, I would have to suspect both," said Wilson smiling.

"Mr. Sullivan."

"Yes, General?"

"You have trained your lads well, Sullivan. You're to be complimented, Sir," said O'Rourke. "I see stars pinned all over you if you were to become an officer," he added with a straight face.

"There's a finger over here," exclaimed Wilson as he picked up a bloody, dirty ring finger embellished with a worn gold band. "Better not take that, 'cause that's bad luck." He set it back on the ground in a corner.

"It belonged to one of the Huns," mentioned Sullivan…"Lewis shot two of them earlier this evening."

"He must have been ahidin' in that dark corner," said Shea.

"You just picked up on that Sgt. Obvious?" snickered Wilson, as he took a swallow of Ristols and passed the bottle to Shea.

"Key lime pie and pickled hogs feet, you're da one thata picked up dat finger, rummy dummy—not me," said Shea with a shit-eating grin on his face.

"Decatur Shea?"

"Yes, that's Mr. Decatur Shea from the grand state of Georgia, Michael Wilson."

"Why don't you take that finger and stick it square up your ass, and let it have a go at finding that boll weevil up there," said Wilson.

"Mr. Sullivan?"

"Yes, Mr. Wilson?"

"Mr. Shea is calling me bad names again!" said Wilson as he looked at Shea with a funny "fuck you" look.

"Mikey, me boyo, stick this in your gob. And that's not a suggestion," said Sullivan as he handed Wilson another bottle of Ristols.

"Shea," snapped Sullivan.

"Bossman," said Shea, with a surprised look on his face. "I'm innocent of all accounts as a Southern gentleman, y'all," as he gave back the same "fuck you" look at Wilson.

"Stick this in your gob, too," said Sullivan as he passed him a bottle of Ristols.

"Now that the dust has been cut in me throat, maybe I can get a word in edgewise," said O'Rourke as he belched. "Now that the unruly children o'er there are to be seen and not heard, and have been properly punished, the men can go back to talking," remarked O'Rourke.

"Mid-August, I was reassigned," revealed O'Rourke. "I arrived right after the battle of Pilckem Ridge. The Frogs went into the Third Battle of Ypres. Holy Trinity! You think they would have kicked the Huns arse the first time. They turned me over to the French 1st Army, and I split me time between 1st Army Corps and 36th Army Corps operating in and around the Flanders area," O'Rourke continued.

"Unfortunate wee bit about the Froggy French: They went through commanders like shit through a Christmas goose," said O'Rourke as he took a big pull of his liquor. "The French infantryman is called a *Poilus*—means *hairy one*. Those frogs don't know if they're coming or going. There were mutinies that were basically caused by piss poor leadership," as he took another drink.

"Doc, why don't you climb up and see if you can find out what unit those bastards were from," O'Rourke ordered as he pointed to the top of the trench.

Doc stood and walked over to the firestep. He climbed the steps and over the top he went.

"Now I would like to propose a toast," said Sullivan. "It is 4:00 a.m. on November 10, 1918. Boyos, raise our bottles," they raised their bottles. "To the 143rd birthday of the barnacle battlers, the United States Marine Corps," wisecracked Sullivan. "The only way they can get around is by attaching themselves to ship's arse to remove barnacles. That action right there will make the ship go faster by them thar Marines aswimming. So happy birthday Barnacle Bill, the Leatherneck," Sullivan announced proudly. They clanged bottles.

"And Gentlemen," said O'Rourke. "Do you know why they wear the leatherneck?" The men shook their heads no.

Wilson piped up and said, "Hear it blocks the blood to the brain." Then adds, "Well that's what I heard."

"You're half right me boyo, but three-quarters wrong. It all stems from having no neck, backbone, or brains. That's why they use leatherneck. It keeps their neck up and their pea-sized head in place. It's plain physics. They earn one leatherneck per year just like Dzilla neck rings. Saw one Navy man who's neck was so long he could eat an apple off the tallest limb. And that's no blarney," laughed O'Rourke. The men laughed along with him.

"But when the Marines are being shot at, they crap their pants first and cry for mama to change their soiled diapers. They have Miss Nancy Lilliputian guts! So, they throw their diapered hips side to side dodging bullets. With no spine, bullets miss their small pea heads… or is it their arse? They're about the same, no matter! It's plain physics," he said. He scooted his hips and head side to side, as all the men laughed.

CHAPTER 2

"Sgt. Sullivan?"

"Yes, Cpl. O'Brien?"

"Would like to report that Ugh and Thug have returned, Sgt.," reported O'Brien.

"Send them right in, boyo," said Sullivan.

A thin man with two long charcoal black braids down the middle of his back pushed open the door and stepped into the bunker. He removed his Brodie and set it on the table.

"Thug, welcome to the new C Company CP of 42nd Rainbow, Division 165 infantry regiment. Or as we prefer, the old 69th Irish Brigade," as he swept his arms wide as if to present an elegant French Chalet. "The bar is open, serving the finest rot gut anywhere in France," chirped Sullivan.

"I can't wait for this war to end," said Wilson as he handed Thug a Ristols. "I'll go to the first beautiful woman, in fact any woman, and I don't care what her name is, because I'm gonna call her Erin. Age isn't even a factor, 'cept within law and morality sake," as he smiled and formed the shape of a woman in the air. "Then, I will very politely say, 'Erin go bra less,'" snickered Wilson. "I loved the number 69 since were in the 69th Irish brigade," said Wilson as he licked away his mustache with his tongue.

"Well, ain't you the crust for the key lime pie, skunk boy," joked Shea. "The last time, Mikeyy, you waggled yer lickin' thata mustache thata way, it about got yer damn Yankee head blown off," laughed Shea.

"But I left her a nickel for each ride, that would be $.25," said Wilson.

"Mikeyy, yer as dumb as a blind dentist in a gator's mouth," said Shea. "Think back, Yankee boy. We were afixin to go on pass when we were stationed at Fort Mills on Long Island," said Shea.

"Wait a minute," said Wilson. "Not one time did she tell me in our five interludes that I was the stand-in conjugal visit that she missed with her husband in prison. That last time, her brother-in-law caught us just before the unit shipped out. I don't know how many conjugal visits he had, but I'd probably have to take my boots off to count," he said as he rolled his eyes.

"*Alt cloigeanns,*" nipped Sullivan. "That's right you two knuckleheads," said Crow. "Put on a double bridle. I don't mean marriage, chomp down on the bit, if you know what's good for you," as he gave Shea and Wilson a stern look. "Please continue Sgt. Lightfoot."

"Crow," reported Thug, "I regret to report that Captain Hill, Lieut. Arch, Sgt. Moore, Cpl. Watson, Private Mitt, and Private Beach all bought the farm."

"Oh, Mary Magdalene. No!" said Sullivan, distraught.

"Where's John?" Sullivan asked, looking over Thug's shoulder.

"Right here, Sgt.," said Ugh.

"SFC. Lightfoot, your father tells me some men didn't make it. What about headquarters platoon?" Sullivan said.

Ugh's wirey silhouette leaned against the bunker wall, his long coal-black ponytail braid, hung down the middle of his back to his waist.

"Here boyos," as Sullivan handed Ugh a bottle of Ristols. "Wash down the dirt and tell me what you got. Take your time about it," commanded Sullivan.

Ugh took a long swig and said, "As you know, their second trench line is 143 yards from where we're standing. Commander Hill waited as my son and I reconnoitered the second trench. The second trench is clear now. From there to the third trench is 146 yards. The terrain has a little more incline."

"It was one big fight," interrupted Thug. "Jim Beach, and Sgt. Moore were killed along the way." He took a drink of whiskey and savored it for a few seconds. "They have a machine gun nest to the left and another on the right of the communications trench just past the second trench. As we were moving up the communications trench line, we saw that part of the trench had been bombed out. You gotta make a hop, skip, and jump out of the trench for about 10 yards, then jump back in the trench," he stated. He took another long pull from his bottle.

"The Germans popped a flare and caught Commander Hill and Lieut. Arch in the wire," expressed Ugh. "The first burst took Arch's head off. He's back there hangin' over the barbed wire. The old man, he was torn up, Crow. That first burst killed the Captain in the wire, too. That gunner quit, but that fucking right gunner, he lit up a whole belt of ammo on Capt. Hill," continued Ugh as his voice started to raise an octave. "The fucking asshole was screaming and talking shit in German as he cut Hill in two," Ugh continued as his voice lowered. "His guts dropped to the ground, then the prick tried to blow Bob's head off," he said as he wiped his mouth, hestitating.

Thug interrupted, "Next thing I know, we're out of the trench heading toward the machine gun nest led by my old man and he was out for blood. He wanted to get to that nest something fierce. The Germans were starting to fill in the communications trench. Ugh's screaming in the old tongue, making fucking bloody Hasenpfeffer outta the Germans. It turned into a hell of a firefight."

"Walter Mitt was shot in the head, unfortunately. Mike Watson got it there too," Thug continued. "It was simultaneous and I saw the whole thing.... We were fighting in and around the machine gun nest at the same time Dad swung to the left with a shotgun, and this Heinie used Watson as a shield. Neither of those guys made it."

"Then we started to see more reinforcements coming up. We went and threw some grenades and skedaddled as they took potshots," Thug took a long drink and kicked the ground.

"Boyo, did you at least kill the bastards?" asked Sullivan.

"Crow," said Thug. "They're tits up."

"Too bad about Bob Hill. I met him just before we shipped off for the Philippines. We met in the First Nebraska Infantry, United States volunteers. I'm going to miss the old man, and may God bless him and the other souls," said Sullivan somberly.

"Ugh," said Crow. "I know this is hard, but do you have anything else to add boyo?"

"They're assholes," mumbled Ugh, fidgeting anxiously.

"Thomas," said Sullivan. "Are you okay? Yes or no, are you okay?" demanded Crow.

"No," mumbled Ugh.

"What is in your hand that's all bloody? Did you get hurt? Doc, take a look at Tom," ordered Sullivan, concerned. "Mary Magdalene, Ugh, what did you do?"

"Well hush my mouth full of jambalaya smothered in chitlins! I have never seen a scalp," said Shea, looking at Ugh's hand and the bloody topnotch of a scalp the size of his palm.

"Tom, I was gonna to ask you for a little trim tonight," said Wilson as he rubbed the top of his head.

Ugh turned his head to Wilson shaking it side to side, "Not tonight, Junior."

"Sergeant First Class Lightfoot," said Gen. O'Rourke.

Ugh snapped to attention. "Yes Sir," said Lightfoot

"Please explain what happened," commanded O'Rourke.

"Sir, all I can say is once I saw Bob Hill get cut in two, the fight was on," explained Ugh. "We were in and around the trench and machine-gun nest just as my son said," reported Ugh.

"Crow," said Ugh. "You know me, always kidding about lifting a scalp or two. All I can say in my defense is that it was the heat of the battle."

"Gentlemen, there have been reports filtering through the American sector that someone is taking scalps," said O'Rourke sternly. "Any of you boyos know anything of these reports? Be they true or be they false?" asked O'Rourke.

"Sir, there is no validity to those reports from this unit," said Sullivan, with a what-the-fuck-did-you-do expression on his face. "Other than that scalp which is in Sgt. Lightfoot's hand."

"I'll file me report later. I know what it's like to lift a scalp. Also, counted coup many a good time," divulged O'Rourke. "So, tell me Sergeant First Class Lightfoot. Tell me, boyo, how many times have you counted coup since you've been here?"

"If I was a countin' man, I'd say I just went over 135," said Ugh.

"Thomas! Boyo, what the fuck have you been doing at night?" asked Sullivan sternly.

"Obviously not talking to Richard and his five cousins," mumbled Wilson as he looked down and whistled.

Ugh shot Wilson a hard glance and said, "*Pia papi*. Well, I've been meaning to tell you that while everybody else is asleep, I go out counting coup, recon, and getting intel."

Wilson interrupted, "You and intelligence? Alrighty," he scoffed sarcastically.

"I can't sleep, so I tell the guard on duty that 'I'll be out there,' and then I crawl over the top and head over to the German lines. Scares the holy shit out of the guard first, and the Huns later," said Ugh as he chuckled. "The guard and I; we arrived at a special password," explained Ugh.

"Me boyo, what blarney do you use as the password," asked Sullivan.

"Anything in Comanche," said Ugh proudly. "*Ana kwana* is the password. It means body odor," said Ugh. "What ignorant Hun is going to think of using the Comanche tongue?" Ugh said in a fun-spirited voice.

"So, me boyo, what exactly would you go out and do?" said Sullivan, prying.

"I crawl up to their lines, and wait for one or two to go take a piss together like broads, then I quietly slide into the trench. I politely tap my knife on a German's shoulder," said Ugh. "Scrotumless, of course, turns around thinking it's his buddy. Then he gets my *nahuu*, my knife, up to the hilt in his throat. Then once that's done, I check him for valuables or papers, and prop him up against the firestep. Then I beat feet the hell out of there. Y'ask me, it's a very quiet method. It also shakes up his two buddies to see their buddy's throat split from ear to ear," said Ugh.

"And then, me boyo?" asked a highly-interested Sullivan.

"And then?" said Ugh.

"I think I just said that!" said Sullivan. "And then?"

"All right, I'll come clean," said Ugh. "Then, I cut back the first three inches of his scalp, so he won't have no bangs this year," said a cold steely-eyed Ugh. "No charge; it's professional courtesy."

"Now that we know the facts, let us raise our bottles and toast 135 confirmed counting coup and kills," said O'Rourke lifting his bottle and looking right at Sgt. Lightfoot.

"Tom," said Wilson. "By the way, what is *Pia papi*?

"It means *mentally abnormal*," replied Thug.

"Sullivan, with Hill and Arch both dead, that's your commander and your executive officer," said O'Rourke.

"Yes Sir, I realize that. Sir, what do you recommend?" queried Sullivan.

"We're going to cut through the pomp and circumstance of United States Congress and the U.S. Army. I'm giving you a battlefield promotion to First Lieutenant," said O'Rourke.

"Excuse me, General, me darlin'?" inquired Sullivan.

"Lieutenant, me darlin," declared O'Rourke "Pick your *Optio*."

"And that would be?" asked Sullivan.

"That means, 'pick your *Executive Officer*' in Latin," explained O'Rourke.

"Shea," said Sullivan.

"Wait a minute, old boy, dat dog don't hunt this swamp," said Shea, as he scratched his head.

"Boyo, if I got a visit from Uncle Sam's gonads, I would ask how high and how far Lieut. Shea," said Sullivan, with an official tone. "First Sgt. Forthright," stated Sullivan.

"No, wait a minute! Give that to Wilson," complained Forthright.

"I don't want it, it's too much paperwork," said Wilson, scratching his head vigorously.

"Me boyos, I don't like pulling rank on you, but starting with you, First Sergeant Forthright, and you, Sergeant First Class Wilson," said Lieut. Sullivan. "Do I make myself clear? I don't like this any more than you do. But we have our jobs to do, me boyos, and you've got the most experience," asserted Sullivan.

"Yes Sir," as they both acknowledged his request in unison.

"Well Lieut. Sullivan, now I can inform you that in due time there will be a supply train coming up. Higher headquarters has scrounged 35 troops and a range of equipment and ammunition," said O'Rourke.

"Well, kiss my ass. Some relief column," said Forthright sarcastically.

The bunker went silent as each man took long drinks of their whiskey.

"General," said Sullivan, scratching his head and the back of his neck. "We were sent on a Company-sized recon mission. Originally about 125 men, and now I'm down to less than 30. Sir, now that this mission is complete, we need to reconstitute," said Sullivan. His face was war weary, and his body was exhausted. Sullivan said, "Now you're telling me they just sent 35 men, and may I ask, pray-tell, for what? Did Blackjack Pershing write this order up?"

"Son, the mission has changed, and it's a whopper of a humdinger," said O'Rourke. "Some *comhlíon asal* French General in the Fourth French Army went looking for his units."

"Y'all, excuse me, Sir?" said Shea.

"Decatur, it means you're a *complete ass*," said Sullivan smiling.

"That's what I thought, too," said Wilson.

The men looked at Wilson, and then each took a drink.

"The damn fool took a right at Cheveuges, then drove through the American 42nd Division sector. Then they lost him." O'Rourke added, "Dunderhead General thought he was in a summer tour with the top down in his armored car. I guess some French trollop is traveling with him." O'Rourke paused for a moment, then continued, "They found his driver and two guards shot in the back of the head. The 42nd intelligence musta figured a Hun-raiding party got them and they're trying to take the General across at the Pont Maugis bridge. They think that the General *ainbhiosán* is in this vicinity."

"General who?" inquired Wilson.

"General Darlin' was talking about you, too, Sergeant First Class Ass and one Shave Tail Second Lieut.," laughed Sullivan.

"Old boy, I'm sittin right here, afixin to take off my gear and get nekked to take a mustard gas bath on your every word," exclaimed Shea. The whiskey was making his Georgia drawl even more enhanced.

"The word *ainbhiosán* means ignoramus. Mark another one down on the ledger," said Sullivan grinning.

"Ignoramus. Well an early Merry Christmas to you, Crow," shot back Wilson.

"Lieut. Shea?"

"Yes, Sgt. Wilson?" replied Shea.

"Woe is me, my feelings—my frail, frail feelings you might say. I'm petrified, pulverized, demoralized. I, Michael Wilson, a dirty ignoramus? I want to take a cold bath in a shell crater to clean my Sergeant First Class ass. I don't think I'll be able sleep tonight," uttered Wilson.

"You don't sleep," said Shea.

"No, that's Ugh that doesn't sleep," said Wilson to Shea as they nodded to each other.

"Let me recall what I was saying before the oxygen-thieving *Cabach Tuaitín* opened their gobs," said O'Rourke as he let out a hearty laugh.

"I best not ask what he said," commented Shea.

Sullivan laughed and said, "He said you two are *babbling bumpkins*, and I agree wholeheartedly. And I'll drink to that," as he took a swig and held the bottle of Bush Mills up to the lamp to see how much remained.

O'Rourke continued, "Early this morning, a carrier pigeon came in with the note saying the Germans had picked the French General up in this vicinity, and that they're moving units to this area to help support the bridge. Doc, what unit do those Huns belong to?"

"If I read the Huns uniforms right, they're in the Lehr Infantry Regiment of the Third Guards Division," reported Doc.

"Intelligence told me that those guys are a crack outfit," said O'Rourke.

"There's something foul in the wind and it's blowing right at us," said Sullivan.

"I know that, me boyo," said O'Rourke. "What more could you wish for on your first command? Your mission has now changed to a raid and retrieval of the General!"

"Anything for the little doggie Generals," said Forthright.

"Now you won't be going over *taobhnocht arse nocht*," said O'Rourke. "Battery B 150th Field Artillery with their French-built heavy 155 howitzers and Battery C of 151st Field Artillery with the light French 75 mm," he said reassuringly.

"'Scuse me, General," said Forthright. "What is *taobhnocht arse nocht*, Sir?" as he butchered the pronunciation.

"I said you won't be going in there *bare-arsed naked*," said O'Rourke. "They're going to be southwest of Angecourt with a rolling barrage, tentatively starting at 6 am on 11 November with the First Corps Observation to call for fire. I have an old pain-in-the-arse cousin in that unit."

"Begging your pardon sir, I'm going to step outside, would you care to join me?" asked Sullivan, adding "By Saint Michael, General O'Rourke do you hear that, Sir?"

"Hear what?" asked O'Rourke.

"Silence. An eerily-dead silence," said Sullivan. The two men stepped outside the bunker. "No Jack Johnsons. No whiz bangs. No machine-gun fire. No sound of flying machines. No sounds of men dying," said Sullivan. He shook his head back and forth for the dead, and passed his bottle of Bush Mills to O'Rourke as they sat down on the firestep.

The men listened for a minute more, and Sullivan said, "Sir, I was a gangly boy, born in County Cork in a little thatched-roof cottage near the Lee River in 1882. I gained passage to America, then to

Nebraska where me family settled. I joined the army when I was 15 in 1899. A couple months later, we shipped off to the Philippines."

"Well, by St. Finian the leper, I was born 1850, in County Kerry in Killarney, just a good stretch of the legs from you," said O'Rourke.

"General, me darlin', that means you're 68 years old," said Sullivan.

"Gen. O'Rourke?"

"Yes, Lieut. Sullivan?"

"In the old country, we'd call you a *aois codálaí*?" said Sullivan.

"*Old codger*," O'Rourke chuckled. The men busted out laughing. "No, you're full of blarney and bullshit" O'Rourke looked at Sullivan with a twinkle in his one eye. "I don't feel it, and I don't look it. I have the same American Irish jig as you at twice your age, me boyo. I was 13 when I left Ireland early in 1863. The Port of Call, New York City. They asked for me name, I said 'Clancy Clust O'Rourke Esq.,' So with me diaper still on, they asked me if I wanted to be in the 69th Irish brigade," declared O'Rourke proudly.

He took a swig of Bush Mills, and continued, "I told them, 'No thank you, I don't like to walk.' I had already walked the Atlantic Ocean with two anvils on me ankles," he added. "Plus, I had a steady diet of shellfish and red snapper. That kept me going, so I asked to be put in the Calvary! After me Calvary training, we were put on a train with our horses and all the equipment," he said matter-of-factly.

Sullivan listened intently, and nursed his bottle a wee bit.

"Me troop headed west, then they let us off the train and we mounted our horses along with our equipment. We rode up to a little place called Gettysburg. They used me as a runner, then unbeknown to me, I ran into me blithering cousin, Anus McScrotum," laughed O'Rourke. He continued, "We were put in the Sixth Calvary from that point on. We honed our skills at Brandy Station, Wilderness,

Spotsylvania, and Winchester. Some of the boys went to Appomattox. Then to the Indian wars. Me knucklehead cousin and me, we fought against the Cheyenne, Arapahoe, Kiowa, and the fiercest, the Comanche. Mighty warriors, that they are."

He pulled out a pipe and started to fill it. "I've been to Texas, Kansas, Arizona, New Mexico, and Old Mexico. They would have to resole me shoe if I was to walk that much now," chuckled O'Rourke. He shuffled his hands in his pockets. "By Saint Michael, I can't find me matches."

"I have me a light right here, Sir," said Sullivan as they cupped the flame to cover the General's pipe. "You can keep these matches, General," said Sullivan.

"Thank you, son," replied O'Rourke.

O'Rourke took a swig from his bottle, and said, "I got out of the Sixth Calvary, then had to split up with me cousin, thank God," O'Rourke said, happy as a lark. "Then I was stationed at Fort Leavenworth in 1883. I was cadre at the calvary and infantry school. I had me a grand and glorious time of it." He struck a match, cupped it, and relit his pipe, then took a deep draw.

"I was telling me snot-nosed, wet-behind-the-ears, shave-tail Kay-dets on the Hudson what to do," said O'Rourke. "Taught 'em to play toy soldier. I hope they learned something between beatings about the head and shoulder area and my boot right up their arse," he boasted.

"Then in March 1898, I was reassigned back to the Sixth Cavalry. The Spanish-American War was going on in Cuba, where I was reunited with my drivel cousin. The Sixth Calvary fought alongside the Roughriders at San Juan Hill. That little excursion was done by August 1898. By then I had fallen in love with Cuban cigars. Only one time in my life have I had pure ecstasy of Cuban cigars, a bottle of Bush Mills, and two female persuasions, boyo," said O'Rourke beaming a big smile.

"Then we had time enough to clean our equipment and toast to our horses. Then how large we are, and handsome we are, we get new orders to sail to the Philippines in January 1899. We did not even spend a year in the Philippines before we got new orders to go to China. That was the Boxer Rebellion," explained O'Rourke. "That bloody little soirée ended in September 1901, and in every one of those battles, me, me bumbling cousin, and the boys, as the Zulu say, 'Washed the Spears,'" recounting younger years with a cold hard look in his one eye.

"We sailed back home to clean up and had one for the horse and one for the road," said O'Rourke. "From 1902 to 1913, meself and me cousin, Calamity Jane, went incognito for Uncle Sam. Off we went to Europe, Russia, Africa, and other destinations to keep an eye on U.S. interests as they say."

"Aloysius and I had to deal with spies, traders, and traitors of countries, and, of course, loose women. Strictly hush-hush. If it was to be known that I told you, I'd have to kill you," said O'Rourke relighting his pipe and chuckling. "But boyo, me and Blockhead do have our memoirs all tucked away. Then like all good soldiers, we got new orders to come home just in time to clean me nasty arse, have a quick bottle... oops excuse me, a quick drink for me and one for the horse... and have a good smoke. Speaking of washing me nasty arse and me *Coll Cnó*, I'll be asking your permission for that bottle of Ristols."

"Hey Wilson, the darlin' General has an inkling to wash his arse and his *Hazelnuts*," said Sullivan as he cracked a slight smile.

"Ayuh," grunted Wilson.

"Mr. Wilson."

"Yes, General?"

"Wilson, as a child your parents thought you were mentally gifted and had high expectations for you, like Isaac Newton, Aristotle, or Copernicus. A paragon of brilliance. But a woman with visual impairments could see that your parents overshot their target. Me best advice, son, keep that little pea brain underneath your Brodie," said O'Rourke with a straight face. His one eye winked at Sullivan.

"Now, where was I before you hooligans kindly interrupted me? A man can't get a word in edgewise around here," O'Rourke said. "By Saint Michael, we went down to Old Mexico to fight that slippery Poncho Villa, but instead we ended up chasing our tails. Like I said earlier, these last couple years in Europe, I'm here observing the war," divulged O'Rourke quietly.

"I received the nation's highest honor for an action that happened in November of 1887. We were stationed at Fort Grant with troop, uh, damn, I'm drawing a blank. It's funny sometimes, you forget these things," mumbled O'Rourke. "But I do remember, we left Fort Grant, led by Lieut. Finn. We rode down to the Van-Bronson station. When we arrived at the station, Lieut. Finn gave orders for the men to take their saddles off, cool and wipe down their mounts, then feed and water them. Waited about an hour for the Adjutant General, who crossed more pens than swords."

"The Darlin' General had an escort from Fort Bliss, and from that point on we're escorting General Darlin' the rest of the way. The proprietor, Gertie Van-Bronson, her meals are fit to die for, so long as you keep one foot out of the grave," O'Rourke said as he let out a big chuckle. "Gertie made the best Dutch-oven chicken, biscuits, and her peach and apple cobbler. Then right after lunch, General Darlin' gets up and heads for the little General's room outside. Of course, you know all General Officers have their aides-de-camp, and they wipe their General's arse hexadic times."

"Boyo, I'm older than you and of course wiser. In those days, it was six times. It went two brown cobs, then one white cob, and two more brown cobs, and finally, the last white corncob. That's why men like me are tough arseholes," said O'Rourke as he gurgled his liquor, then swallowed. "Yep, that must be quite a sight to see. So here is a toast to all the West Point military aides-de-camp who did the long brown and white cob line," O'Rourke proclaimed as if it was an official decree.

He and the rest of the boys raised their bottles and took a drink as O'Rourke handed his bottle over to Sullivan.

"Then Aloysius, the boys, and I headed back to Fort Grant with the General in tow," described O'Rourke. "The column got about a half-mile from the station, then we ran into a wee bit of a problem. Blasted hostiles—around 40 that were a mix of Apache, Kiowa, and Comanche. Lieut. Finn was just about to give us an order when his horse was shot out from underneath him. I ordered the men to quickly throw out a screen and skirmish line. Our stagecoach got turned back around to go back to Van-Bronson station. Lieut. got up running. At the same time I went to retrieve him, I saw him get an arrow in the back, but he had strength enough to throw his hand up. I lifted Lieut. darlin' over the front of me saddle," said O'Rourke as he shook his head.

"Miss Gertie Van-Bronson was out there with flour on her face, helping me with Lieut. Finn," said O'Rourke. "We took him off the horse and discovered he'd been shot in the head, too. For the next two days we fought off hostile attacks there at the station. Early the third morning, Troop C from Fort Grant came and drove off the hostiles. I had a different long-barrel Colt Peacemaker then. The old girl had a good workout those two days."

He leaned back and took a drink of his whiskey, wiping his mouth on his sleeve and saying. "But in the meantime, the Adjutant General darlin' comes up to me all happy as a pig in shit and says, 'O'Rourke, for a job well done.' Then, meself, and I don't know why, but *Bod*, my *dick* cousin, was also given a field promotion to second shave-tail Lieut. Aloysius was in the corner cowering with the General, reloading the General's chambers," conveyed O'Rourke.

A big smile came over his face, and he said, "That cousin of mine might have mush between the ears, but he's hell on wheels in a fight," O'Rourke relit his pipe. "The General Darlin' and meself wrote up what I call an after-action review, and sent it off to Washington. The Gen. Darlin' would have hand carried it back to Washington, but a wee bit of a complication came up. The Adjutant took sick, so they convalesced him back to Washington. On top of all that, the paperwork had gotten lost, until 1914, when they found and read the report, and they must have agreed with him."

"With the medal, they pinned a star on me. Then they had the *atáirgeach nádúr* to tell me that this is me last ride," said O'Rourke.

"Gen. O'Rourke?" said Shea.

"Yes, boyo, may help you?" said O'Rourke.

"Whata did you say a second ago?" inquired Shea.

"I told him in so many words that they had the *balls* to do that to me, Clancy Clust O'Rourke, Esq., and I say to meself, *this is not going to be me last ride into the sunset*," said O'Rourke calmly.

"Also, General, what is *Bod*?" asked Shea.

"Bodily, it's your prize possession, Sir Lancelot, and the Crown Jewels, young man," laughed O'Rourke.

"Well, hush my mouth full of Key Lime Pie in a crust of fat back," declared Shea.

"Do you happen to know Bill Donovan?" Sullivan asked O'Rourke.

"No, I know who he is, but not personally," said General O'Rourke.

"Sir, there's a Lieut. Mike Kirby here to see you, sir," said Forthright as he walked toward the group.

"Nice to meet you, Kirby," said O'Rourke, as the two men saluted each other, then shook hands. "Kirby, this is Lieut. Sullivan, Commander of Charlie Company."

"Nice to make your acquaintance, under these circumstances," said Sullivan as they saluted and shook hands.

"Sir, I brought up all the equipment that you requested. Also, General O'Rourke, higher headquarters is still adamant about the 6 am rolling barrage," expressed Kirby.

"Lieut. Sullivan, can you work with the time or do we need to adjust the schedule?" asked O'Rourke with concern in his one eye.

"Gen. Darlin', we will adjust fire on the fly," said Sullivan.

Suddenly, dozens of men climbed down the trench wall—young, clean soldiers lined up and sat on the firestep with their equipment in hand. Two of the men walked toward Lieut. Kirby, saluted, and shook hands. "Sir," said Kirby. "This is my Platoon Sergeant, Staff Sergeant James Worth."

"How many men did you bring, Kirby?" inquired Sullivan.

"About 35. This is Cpl. Smedley. He is with the First Balloon Company. He's here to help with all communications, telephones, and will roll out communications wire where you need it. He also brought a handful of Homers. Also Sir, there is talk of an armistice, but it's just talk right now," reported Kirby.

Sullivan looked into the bunker and said, "First Sgt. Forthright, find a spot for Smedley. Lieut. Shea come over here. I would like to talk to you for a minute."

"Smedley, old man, come right this way. Y'all can sit right next to me," said Forthright. "This here is Sergeant First Class Wilson."

"Nice to meet you," acknowledged Wilson.

Forthright continued introducing the men, "This here is Sgt. Tom Lightfoot, and this is Doc." Each man shook hands.

"Jim Worth," declared Doc as he recognized one of the men.

"Jimmy O'Keefe," stated Worth.

"Jim Worth was two years ahead of me in school," said Doc to the rest of the men in the bunker.

"Doc, how are you doing?" asked Worth.

"I'm here," said Doc.

"Old Jimmy always wanted to be a doctor. I thought you'd be sitting in a big fancy hospital, chasing after a flock of pretty nurses," said Worth and he slapped Doc on the back.

"I would go for the whole herd," chuckled Wilson. Worth went quiet, as everybody looked at Wilson.

"I did two years of medical school before this fucking shit came up. So I did the right thing by putting my medical school on hold, and joined the Army. I have learned more here than I ever would've learned in school. Worth, where'd you get that donut-hole sized knot on your forehead?" asked Doc.

"They were shelling in and around our bunkers last week. The first shell landed close to our bunker. I quickly got up to catch the lamp, but the second incoming arty lurched me forward, and

I smashed head-first right into a crossbeam. It immediately made me go cross-eyed, and I think I pee-peed my drawers," Worth said as he rubbed his donut-sized bruise. The boys all laughed.

"You talk to the Medical Doctor?" asked Doc.

"Yeah, he told me to rub dirt on it," replied Worth.

"Doc, good luck. It was nice to see you." said Worth as he turned to walk away.

"You too, Jim," replied Doc.

CHAPTER 3

"Smedley?" Forthright asked as they moved into the bunker.

"First Sergeant?" replied Smedley. He pulled a chair out and sat down at the table.

"Welcome to the 69th NCO Club and restaurant," Forthright said, spreading his arms wide to present the décor. He waved at Wilson, saying, "Garsony, get this gentlemen a drink."

Wilson says, "You mean GarSUN, don't you? Finest server East of New England, Numbnuts. Corporal, what's ya pleasure? Ristols? Or perhaps our finest wine? It's a little bit vinegary, and it's yellow."

Smedley raises his hand and states meekly, "No, thank you. Never liked it. How about a nice cup of coffee?"

"Sorry sir, fresh out. How about a nice pot roast and boiled potatoes," he said as he drapes a dirty and bloody handkerchief over his forearm and stands like the finest waiter at New York's Delmonico.

"Are you two done now? Smedley, back to our roster. What is your full name?" asked Forthright.

"Ronald Leonard Smedley," he said.

"And what state are you from?" asked Forthright, grabbing a chair and swinging it backwards, to straddle it.

"Nebraska," he answered.

"Smedley, isn't your college football nickname the Cornchokers?" asked Forthright.

"No, that would be the Cornhuskers. We also used to be called the Rattlesnake Boys, Tree-planters, Old Gold Knights, Bugeaters, now the Cornhuskers," said Smedley.

"Mr. Forthright is a Bloomer Sooner from Oklahoma. They should call themselves Rattlesnake Boys with all them rattlesnakes in Oklahoma, right Cowboy?" laughed Wilson.

"Someday the Cornhuskers might just play the University of Oklahoma. It would be historic," Smedley lamented. "Like the game of the century," said Smedley. "Someday maybe."

Smedley removes his glasses and cleans them with a handkerchief. He sits down on the firestep and says, "Not changing the subject, but something big must be going on. I heard through the grapevine they're moving up artillery, something about the Pont Maugis Bridge," said Smedley. "There's some rumors flying around that they're going to assault that bridge."

"What's the word on this armistice?" asked Forthright.

"Again, it's just talk and speculation," Smedley said as he shrugged his shoulders.

"Speaking of chickens!" said Wilson. "Whatcha got in that chicken coop?"

"They're racing Homers," said Smedley.

"Look Top, it even has a name. Homer Beak," said Wilson sarcastically.

"Racing Homer is the breed! Their names are Adeline, Beatrice, Cordelia, and Dorothy. I named them all after my mother's sisters," Smedley said proudly.

"Now Cpl. Smedley!" said Forthright as he sat down next to Smedley. "Let me see your chicken coop. Look at all the colors on those chickens—greens, grays," said Forthright as he inspected the birds in their little cage.

"I like those colors too," said Wilson, as he handed a bottle of Ristols to Forthright and added, "Just so long as there's no yellow stripe down his back. Oops, her back, as she turns her tail feathers around from Fun Hun. Did you get that play on words?" Wilson laughed at his own joke. "Say First Sgt., who has the fatter legs Beatrice or Cordelia?"

"It looks pretty damn close to me. But I'd have to look at the breasts to see who was bigger, more supple, firmer, and rounder," said Forthright as his eyes looked faraway into past pleasures.

"Say First Sgt.," said Doc as he put his bottle down on the firestep.

"You say somethin', Doc?" asked Forthright.

"Never mind," said Doc with a little chuckle.

"Wait a minute, you two are talking like you're going to eat my girls!" said Smedley, a little suspiciously.

"Smedley, you Rattlesnake boy, let's cut to the chase. I've a German Lugar, a fancy Prussian officer knife, and a belt," offered Forthright.

"I'll match that and one up him. I also have a Lugar, a slightly used German trench knife, and on top of that, I have a helmet from a generous and dead Hun. It is very pointy, " said Wilson pointing to his derrière, where he had an old wound from landing on the helmet while fighting the Hun.

"A pickelhaube helmet," said Smedley,

"If that's what you say," said Wilson, wondering if that could be true. "And to tie all this up with a ribbon on top, I have the cream of wheat, cream of corn, or is it cream of grits?"

"Let me guess, fat-headed Yankee Doughboy. Do y'all mean cream of the crop?" asked Shea as he rolled his eyes. "Boy, sometimes your grits are sooo undercooked," mumbled Shea as he cracked a smile.

Thug stood and said, "While you all been talking, I have been studying these four birds. Adeline is the fattest, and when we get back from our mission, I'm laying claim to her," he said seriously looking right at Smedley.

Wilson interrupts, "A while back when we were engaged in and around Champagne-Marne area. That first night out, I had to go back to Division Trains and ran into a French truck convoy that was totally lost."

"Mikey, what did y'all steal that time?" asked Shea, laughing.

"I didn't steal it. It was given to me in gratitude for being a good American soldier and citizen, and helping out my fellow man when I can. Myself and an officer that could speak French got the convoy straightened out. And, by the way my Southern-Fried Chicken-neck friend, and I emphasize Chicken neck, it is not stealing; it is called acquisitions and procurement. Mr. Shea. I got your fat-headed Yankee-Doughboy hanging," smirked Wilson

Shea joked with a look of anticipation, "Don't tell me! You got yourself a personal inn-vite from the Kaiser himself for you to Toddle—r is it Kangaroo Hop across no man's land? Spendin' the day with him, drinkin' sweet tea with your pinky out just right."

"No, it was not an invitation from the Kaiser," said Wilson as he rolled his eyes. "I was given a crossbow! But not just any old crossbow—it came from the Degar tribe from French Indochina. They do all their fighting and hunting in some of the thickest jungle in the world. Their officers called them Annamites, but these old boys were called Montagnards," said Wilson with a slight southern twang. "Crap, there I go again, soundin' like Decatur Real-McCoy

Shea," said Wilson without missing a beat. "Smedley, I named this little gem Daryl and Daryl Montagnard Crossbow!"

"Where the hell is French Indochina?" asked Shea.

"It's right dab in the middle of French Indochina," said Wilson as the men turned their heads and looked at Wilson rolling their eyes.

Shea added...."But if we ever have to go over there, we will send our most secret weapon."

"And who is that?" asked Smedley.

"Smedley, you old Bugeater, it's not a who, it is a what," remarked Shea.

"What does it do?" asked Smedley.

"It consumes all the vegetation in French Inn-doh-china as the Yankee moo cow," said Shea.

"So, what is it?" asked Smedley.

"I can tell you what it's not. It's not a Senior Primus Pilus, a Praetorian, a Duke, a Knight, nor is it the Charge of the Light Brigade, Little round top, or Rourke's Drift. Now to present day, it's Wilson, the human Yankee moo cow, chewing his cud and crapping right through French Indochina," replied Shea snickering.

"Do y'all want to hear this or not? I'm fixin to tell y'all about my crossbow," said Wilson trying to break through the laughter in the trench. "Holy crap, did you just hear me again? Fixin? Anyway, I'm, startin' to sound like Decatur Real-McCoy Shea," said Wilson laughing.

"Alligator mouth! That's right, I'm talkin to you Mikey. I'd rather have a Northerner try to talk like a Southerner, than the other way 'round," said Shea as he passed the bottle to Thug. "That goes together like fishin in the middle of Seminole lake nekked, and 50 gators are aswimmin 'round you and it's matin season," Shea said, ribbing Wilson. "The only bait you have, is that tiny inchworm you call a Vienna sausage."

"Do y'all want to hear about this or not?" said Wilson growing frustrated.

"All right y'all, I'll listen up, Mikey, 'til you put me to sleep," said Shea.

"So anyway, I humbly accepted their gift. I just looked at it and named it Daryl."

"Jehoshaphat! I will name mine Daryl, too; so we have Daryl and Daryl Montagnard crossbows," Wilson carefully explained.

"Do you have it on you?" asked Smedley.

"No, it's in the rear with the gear," said Wilson.

"Just as I thought," said Smedley disappointed.

"Lieut. Shea," said Doc as he started to snicker. "I can't believe, I'm saying this. Dad, oops I mean Crow…," Doc said as he started to laugh harder, bending over and holding his stomach. "Oops, I mean Lieut. Sullivan would like to see the XO ASAP, for a few minutes. Look boys, we have a Southern gentleman, a brand-new shave tail with bars on. That's like a swaddling infant with a full set of adult gator teeth," said Doc, barely able to talk through the laughs.

Doc gained control of himself and scratched his head vigorously.

"I'll be back in a few minutes, y'all gentlemen. Then we can continue this glorious conversation," said Shea, as he left.

Wilson barked to Shea, "When you get back, precious sunshine, there will be yummy Southern Fried Chicken, Pulled Pork, Fried Catfish, Fried Gator Tail, Possum Tartare, Hillbilly Hassanpfeffer, Grits, Hominy, Collard Greens, Dirty Brown Rice, Sweetcorn, Cornbread, Cornpone, Hushpuppies, Biscuits with Honey Butter, all served with ice cold Sweet Tea and Lemonade. And for Dessert, warm Hearts and Farts will be right here waiting for you too, hillbilly boy."

Shea replied without looking back, "I retract my statement, about your grits being undercooked. You have the pepper, but your grits are way overcooked in the sun, son," he yelled as he almost disappeared down the trench. "Also, Yankee boy, two can play at that word game."

"Mr. Shea, you're a man of great conviction, trusting, loyal, a true hero, a man with true grits," shouted Wilson as he waved goodbye to his friend.

Wilson sat down on the firestep and asked, "So, Smedley what about the squab?"

"Well gentlemen, that is all well and good, and they're all very nice propositions, but these are not my pigeons. They're the government's pigeons," said Smedley.

Forthright leaned forward with a serious expression, "Let's look at it in a unique way, Smedley."

Wilson interrupted in a quiet yet serious voice, "Smedley, have you ever gone over the top?"

"No," said Smedley.

Wilson handed the bottle of Ristols to Forthright, who took a long draw, and explained, "The running, dodging, falling down then crawling to get up… your buddy was running beside you one minute and now he is gone, physically gone, because of an artillery shell hitting him instead of you."

Sgt. John Lightfoot joined the conversation, "Yeah, when going over the top, you can try to run over to the Hun trench and fuck one up, and then you die. Or you can take your time and crawl over there, and fuck them all, and live."

Forthright scratched his head and said, "Or you see what's left of bodies after they been hit, then hear that high-pitched scream calling for their mother." He took a long drink of Ristols and looked toward the heavens, silent for a moment.

"Have you ever seen what a machine gun can do to a human body? It cut our commander, Bob Hill, clean in two," said Wilson, suddenly angry.

"Smedley, have you ever had to run a man through with cold steel, a Bolo Knife or trench knife. It makes a bloody fucking mess. Or have you witnessed a man get cleaved with an entrenching tool to his neck? His head flops over still attached with muscle and tendons, with blood squirting out like a fountain," said Forthright.

"Or have a friend's guts fall out right in front of you. Again, I reference back to our commander," said Wilson as he nodded to Thug, who witnessed their commander's slaughter. Forthright took a swig and passed Wilson the bottle.

Forthright shared another example, "Try tumbling into a shell crater, landing on uniforms with the owners still in them. The stench of rotting flesh from the prior years of war, and billions of crawling lice. Rats and maggots coming out of their mouths and every other orifice."

Smedley started to get a little peaked around the gills.

"Then the god-awful miasma. It just makes you want to projectile vomit your morning chow! Which might be a little hardtack and a piece of rat…." said Wilson, adding, "If y'all don't get your puke out the first time, regurgitate that smell and when y'all have it in your stomach, let her fly."

"Oh my God, you are starting to sound just like Decatur Real-McCoy Shea," Doc said, patting Wilson on the back.

"Then if he's not the Decatur Real-McCoy Shea, back yourself up a few feet Smedley, you old Bugeater. Don't smell his breath, you'll keel over dead. Look at them sunken, beady eyes," said Forthright.

"Not only do I have indigestion, but indignation from old Bloomer Sooner, my dear old friend, First Sgt. Forthright," proclaimed Wilson, shaking his head.

"So, Mr. Smedley how long have you been in France?" inquired Forthright.

"Just about 10 months," said Smedley. "Just enough time to be introduced to trench foot, trench mouth, Trudy's cooties, huge rats the guys in headquarters warned us about. I try to stay as clean as possible," said Smedley. "But, it's so mother-ducking hard to keep fresh and beautiful."

"Smedley, you old Bugeater, if mother-ducking is what I think it means, son you're in France," said Wilson.

"I don't cuss, smoke, or drink. I used to cuss and smoke a long time ago, but my wife told me to take it outside. Plus, it gets cold there in Nebraska, so I quit. The funny thing is, I never thought I would be this far up on the front line. They asked for a volunteer, and the next thing I know, my commander is shaking my hand, telling me, 'Good luck, son.'" added Smedley.

"Never volunteer," said Wilson, scratching his head.

"These chicken-hawks might be our last meal," said Forthright, sizing up the racing Homers.

"Last meal, like malice murderers or rapists on death row," interjected Wilson.

"So, Cpl. Smedley, back to my roster," said First Sgt. Forthright, "What did you do before the war?"

"I taught 11th grade English in Lincoln, Nebraska. I could've applied for deferment, but being from Nebraska and very patriotic, I joined the Army where I was put in the Signal Corps. Then I went to Fort Omaha for Signal Training!" stated Smedley.

"Now Cordelia," said Wilson to a pigeon. "When I get back from this little escapade, you and I will come right back here in this bunker, old girl. I'll give you a nice hot bath, and then arrange your feathers," said Wilson as he smiled and showed Smedley and Cordelia his Brodie helmet. "Up in New England, the fancy people call it squab," expressed Wilson.

"Have you ever had squaby chicken-hawk before?" asked Forthright.

"Why yes; it tastes just like chicken, rat, possum, and beaver," replied Wilson.

"So, which one a them tastes the most like pigeon?" asked Smedley, puzzled.

"Depends on the day, time, friends, female persuasion, and how much beer you have consumed," said Wilson, as he counted his fingers.

"You know Mikey, there will be other wars and conflicts," said Forthright, as he looked to the sky.

"Your point being?" replied Wilson.

"I'm afraid someday a couple old dogged foot soldiers just like us will be talking about food, or the lack of it, or the lack of taste in food, and the lack of creature comforts in the countryside of France. Maybe someday our friends Stan and Sam can come up with something. They may be precision snipers, ready to surgically remove high-value targets, but the chow they talk about—well, they call that *cuisine*," said Forthright, gazing hungrily at Cordelia.

"Sure, and maybe today, Cowboy, the Lollipop Guild has strapped themselves on the winged monkeys from the *Wizard of Oz*. They'll fly out of my ass, singing *I'm a Yankee Doodle Dandy*, with an armistice," said Wilson as he patted his buddy's shoulder.

"Then someday the Army will make better food…. Better than the shit that's in the reserve ration or the trench ration," said Thug.

"What they call food, I call a joke. I would like some better meat. And while they are at it, how about some hardtack that won't break your teeth and crack your jaw," said Wilson, rubbing his chin.

"Maybe some beans and weenies," said Thug. "So, we fart better."

Wilson asked, "What if in the future, they decide to feed us wheat macaroni in some God-awful cheese concoction in a can? Yuck."

"Or even worse some type of fish, like tuna mixed with wheat noodles," said Forthright acting like he was puking as his body quivered.

"But there are three things that are essential to any good military campaign," said Thug. "They are cigarettes, chocolate, and silk stockings."

Wilson rolled up a sleeve and scratched feverishly, "Crap, something is itchy on me arm." He held his arm up to the lamp and looked closely in the dim light. "Oh my God, Trudy's cooties are having a cardinal knowledge rendezvous on my arm," he said as he looked in amazement. "It's an orgy of cooties."

"Holy moly, look at that one on the side, she's just lying there— kind of like you, Mikey," chuckled Thug.

"That's not what she said," replied Wilson.

"What do we have going on here?" asked Forthright.

"Looking at a den of iniquity, right here on my forearm," said Wilson.

"Outstanding. I see a way to get me some extra food in my future," said an eager Forthright. "Let's see how far those little bastards go in bloody trail."

"What's bloody trail?" asked Smedley as he wiped his glasses to get a better look at the lice on Wilson's forearm.

"Oh my goodness," gasped Smedley. "You want to have a race with lice? A sex race, if I get the jist of your conversation."

"Mr. Smedley, that's why you're an 11th grade English teacher," said Forthright. "By the way, no, that was last week's entertainment," Forthright said as he scratched his arm, adding, "Let Doc tell you about last week."

"Well, Corporal Smedley, sir. It was an experiment in nature. We wanted to see how fast the female and male cooties copulate in cardinal knowledge fornication, and our findings were astonishing. They're faster than rabbits," said Doc to Smedley.

Forthright stood and announced the coming events like a ringmaster. "Ladies and Gentlemen, this week's race will test how far the little varmints can travel in a bloody trail after they nip you. Gentlemen and ladies—that means you, Wilson—pick your mounts, and name them."

Smedley whispered to Forthright, "How long have you gentlemen been celebrating?"

"Oh, I'd say a bit before you got here," said Forthright as he took a pull of Ristols, and then said, "So, who is post one?"

"I am," said Thug, as he pointed at his choice on Wilson's forearm.

"Valiant steed's name? asked Forthright.

"Big Horn," replied Thug.

"And yours, Mr. Smedley?" asked Forthright.

"Well, I really wasn't going to play, but here goes. I pick this guy right here, I call him The Bugeater," said Smedley smiling and pointing at a real fat one.

"Really, Smedley?" asked Wilson with a quizzical face, "What the fuck is a Bugeater?"

"A Nighthawk," replied Smedley.

"What say you, Doc?" asked Forthright. "Who's your pick?"

"Catheterization?" said Doc.

"Geez Doc, I thought Bugeater was odd," said Wilson. "Alright Doc, I'll bite. What's caterzation?"

"It's a very small round tube that is stuck up your PeePee," indicated Doc.

"Ouch! That hurt my weenie!" said Thug, cupping his privates.

"My wiener doggie just went inside its doggie house," said Forthright, contorting his face.

"I know for a fact that my catheterization is larger than your privatization. You gotta remember how many Trudy's cooties I have picked off your body, Sgt. Wilson," said Doc as he started to chuckle.

"Next, I'll put myself down," said Forthright pointing to Wilson's arm. "I'll take this little doggie right here. I'm going with Saddle Horn. Now you, Mr. Wilson."

"My stud is Needle Dick, the Bug Fucker," said a proud Wilson.

"That gives us a Bug Fucker and a Bugeater. A Big Horn and Saddle Horn. The prize for this event is winner take all. Every owner stake your bet," said Forthright.

"Cowboy, what you are contributing?" Thug asked Forthright.

"Smelly, Heinie-ass cheese," said Forthright.

Wilson pops off, "Dear God, I'd rather smell that cheese than your feet."

"I have a can of yummy French monkey meat that I liberated from a dearly-departed asshole three nights ago," said Thug.

"When you say monkey meat, is that the real deal?" asked Smedley.

"Nah, not anymore, it's what the French Army calls beef and carrots," answered Thug.

"I have some hardtack," said Wilson.

"Mr. Smedley, you old Bugeater, what will you stake?" asked Forthright.

"I will put in the finest trench ration," said Smedley.

"I found some coffee and sugar in my haversack. I thought I lost them, but the little bastards were hiding," Doc said.

"Lucky find. What about the salt?" asked Forthright.

"No Sir, I used it last week when Wilson and I enjoyed a nice fat rat," said Doc, rubbing his belly clockwise.

"Gentlemen, it's post time! Mount your lice," announced Forthright.

Sullivan entered the bunker with the General, "What are me Darlin' children doin'?" asked Sullivan.

"Having a lice race with Trudy's cooties," explained Wilson.

Sullivan announced to all, "Alright then, me boyos, since I've been promoted to Lieut., and I'm here with General O'Rourke, we are no longer in the ranks of the NCOs. That being said, I will now be officiating on all calls, and I am the official timekeeper. In other words, gentlemen, me word is law," slurred Sullivan. "General, me Darlin', let me bring you up to speed. Me boyos play Tag, and Up-and-Down, that's Carnal Knowledge racing General, me Darlin'. It's straight up action—winner take all," explained Sullivan. "Gives me boyos something to do in the downtime, General," Sullivan said as he took a swig.

"I've never played this," said Gen. O'Rourke as he looked at the lice on Wilson's arm with his one good eye. "That is quite interesting, in fact, so interesting I'll have me a drink or two. Is it too late to get me General Darlin' a little action?" O'Rourke asked.

"Sorry sir, strictly NCO business," said Forthright.

"That's right, sir. NCO business only," laughed Sullivan. "Alright boyos, when I say go, you'll have a whole 30 seconds, mind you, to see how far the critters go in a bloody trail. If the Gen. could be an impartial judge that'd be grand."

"Glad to be a help son, like a Priest taking confession," said O'Rourke.

"Get ready, GO!" said Sullivan as 14 bloodshot and sunken eyes homed in on Wilson's arm.

"Get a move on, Saddle Horn," yammered Forthright.

"Move, Needle Dick," said Wilson as he cheered on his louse.

"Catheterization, you're supposed to move, not just sit there," said Doc encouraging his vermin.

Smedley says quietly with his hands forming a megaphone around his mouth, "Gooo Biiig Bugeater."

"Get'cher ass goin' there Big Horn," said Thug.

"15 seconds gentlemen," relayed Sullivan.

"Come on Needle Dick, you are supposed to be a bug fucker, blood sucker," said Wilson, nearing complete inebriation.

"Saddle Horn, ya bastard, y'all think you're important, but yer impotent. Yer just like an injured horse, in your case a bug; I must put you out of misery with my pistola," said Forthright as he started to pull his 1911 pistol.

"Whoa, wait a minute, Cowboy," said Wilson with saucer eyes.

"That's my arm Bloomer Sooner," yelped Wilson.

"Move, you mother fucker, Big Horn," said Thug shoving his helmet back on his head in frustration.

"Bugeater, you're gaining ground, I think," proclaimed Smedley.

"Gentlemen! Halt! Gen. O'Rourke, by your estimates who went the farthest?" asked Sullivan.

"Let's start at the beginning," said O'Rourke. "Thug and his mount, Big Horn, moved but a tiny hair. Mr. Wilson's Needle Dick, The Bug Fucker, did not move a freckle."

Thug said, "I told you guys, Mikey don't move too good!" said Thug as he flung his can of monkey meat at the firewall.

"You are somewhat correct, sir. " Then O'Rourke added, "They equal the same thing. The simple fact is, they stayed in the same spot."

"He or she must've figured, 'Why the hell not? I'll just stay here and get a quick drink of this guy's blood with a good nip of shitty liquor,'" said Wilson leaning back and taking a long, steady pull of Ristols.

Sullivan stood up and said, "Where is Shea?"

"What about Decatur Shea?" asked Shea from the corner. "Tried to take a Kaiser, and wipe my Wilhelm Two, but it was in a static defensive position, sir." The two men smiled at each other, and clinked their bottles together, appreciating the humor.

"Excuse me gentlemen," said the General with a slight cough of annoyance. "I'll continue with my analysis of the race, if you please. First Sgt. Forthright, his mount, Saddle Horn, tried and failed comparable to Wilson's Needle Dick. Doc, after eyeballing between you and Smedley, it's come to my attention that you trailed by half a nit," disseminated O'Rourke officially. "Mr. Smedley, you are the winner by a bodacious two and a half hairs," as he offered a bottle to the winning Smedley.

"Thank you, Sir, but I don't partake," said Smedley, raising his palm and waving no thank you.

"God bless your soul son! More for me," replied O'Rourke.

"Alright, me Darlin' knuckleheads," commanded Sullivan.

Wilson tried to stand and swirled. He sat back quickly, barely navigating the chair underneath. He held up his arm and spoke to the critters, "I've had enough of your shit for the night," and slammed his hand on this forearm, euthanizing the tiny horses.

"Crow,"

"Yes, Mr. Forthright?

"I'm going to change out the guard. Have the rest of the boys bed down, and you get some rest, too," said Forthright.

"That boyo; that's why you're the First Sergeant, and I'm not," indicated Sullivan.

"I'll get you up after a while," said Forthright.

CHAPTER 4

"Me Darlin' Lieut. Wakee, wakee," whispered Forthright.

"Is that you, Mary Magdalene?" said a sleepy Sullivan.

"No, it's Forthright."

"I feel that now!" said Sullivan as he raised his hand, and gently felt for his face, finding Forthright's mustache. "Me wife has a better soup-strainer," chided Sullivan.

"A better one, Crow?" asked Forthright.

"Mustache, boyo. And you should see the hair on her back," as he finished a yawn and looked to the heavens.

"Hmmm, the last time I seen Mary Magdalene; she didn't have bristles," said Forthright as he felt his thick, dirty stubble. "Also, Ugh and Thug are just getting back, sir," said Forthright.

"What time is it?" asked Sullivan.

"About 4 am," indicated Forthright.

"I'm gonna throw me one boot over for another 10 quick winks," mumbled a groggy Sullivan.

After a few minutes, Sullivan stood and stretched, and looked around the bunker. He found Forthright and ordered, "Quietly start rustling up the boys and get Schmidtlap up. Tell him to bring a pencil, paper, and two of his chickens. Get me Ugh and Thug. I have a mission for them."

"Pops, what are you going to do with my chickens?" said Wilson absent-mindedly.

"They're going to get off their feathery arses and get paid as soldiers, so they can be all the feathers they can be, by Saint Michael," said Sullivan. "By the way Mikey, me boyo, these are the government's chickens not yours, so no patty fingers," as Sullivan wiggled his index finger back and forth at Wilson.

"Yes, sir," replied Wilson, rubbing the sleep out of his eyes.

"Crow?"

"Yes, First Sgt. Forthright?"

"It's Smedley," said Forthright.

"Smedley, not Schmidtlap? Powerful sorry about that, son," said Sullivan. Sullivan addressed the group in the bunker, "Men, I know it's a little crowded in this bunker, so bear with me and here's the hand we have been dealt," explained Sullivan. "A French General wandered from the French Fourth Infantry Division area somewhere around here. Look at the grid map and sand table here," detailed Sullivan as he placed the lamp on the ground to show the diagram he had drawn with his bayonet. "The worst part is that the General and his trollop were picked up by the Huns. So now it's our job to find and rescue him. Intelligence reports that they are heading to the Pont Maugis Bridge. Supposedly we will have artillery support. First Sgt. Forthright, read the assignments."

"When I call your name, you go with Lieut. Kirby," said Forthright. "On heavy weapons, Staff Sgt. Wilson, Staff Sgt. Lightfoot, Doc. You're on Hotchkiss machine-gun with 5000 rounds," said Forthright.

"Ooops, Poopsy Pops, I mean Lieut. Sullivan. What in the hell is going on? Why us?" asked a worried Wilson.

"Put on your bridles boys, 'member four weeks ago when one of you put the dead rats copulating in my helmet?" said a rather happy Forthright.

Wilson said, "That's the second time I was asked to put on a bridle. I feel like someone wants me to get married to a horse."

"Well, she'd be marrying a horse's ass," muttered Thug, laughing.

"How about we go with Cpl. Lewis, Smith, and Mahoney on the Hotchkiss machine-gun as well. On the Stokes mortar, Sgt. Fields, Pvts. Newman, Slattery, and Allen. Boys, I know yesterday was a rattlesnake rodeo, but we gotta buck up again today," said Forthright

Sullivan stood for a moment and put the lamp back on the table, he looked over the group, and asked Lieut. Kirby, "Son, tell us what you brought for us to dance with the enemy."

"I brought up 200 rounds for the Stokes mortar. Got two Browning machine guns and 25 cases of lead. Got 10 cases of 30 aught six rounds for the Enfield's. Plus 2 and half cases of .45 rounds. Here's 120 more full magazines of pure lead, and 12 ammo belts for the BAR," enumerated Kirby…. "Also, I got my hands on two cases of shotgun shells for the sweepers."

"Make 'em count, me Darlin' boyos," said Sullivan.

Kirby moved some boxes around and said, "There's also two cases of MK 2 grenades," he pointed out.

"Lieut. Sullivan?"

"Yes Lieut. Kirby."

"Through acquisitions and procurement, I threw in 30 sticks of dynamite, and six Bangalore torpedoes—all with fuses," said Kirby.

"By Saint Michael, bless you, boyo," replied Sullivan, slapping Kirby on the back and shaking his hand. "Two questions, Lieut. Kirby. How did you get up here with all of that lead?"

"Ambulance trucks got us up here, and dropped us off about a mile away," Kirby explained.

"And how are you going to get all that equipment up to the area of the operation?" asked Sullivan.

"We brought up pull carts to get all of our equipment to the front," explained Kirby.

"Sgt. Worth?"

"Yes, First Sgt. Forthright," Worth responded.

"When you get a quick moment, I need the names of the 35 men in your unit," said Forthright.

"I'll get those to you ASAP," said Worth as he walked away.

"Staff Sgt. Wilson, you finally get one?" asked Forthright.

"One what?" Wilson asked with a face of puzzlement.

"A shotgun, and one for Lieut. Georgia Peach, too," quipped Forthright.

"Finally, someone believes in me with a shotgun. I've been a blithering BAR boob, ineffective with the Enfield. I'll call him Duke the lead Sweeper," said Wilson, with a big smile on his face.

"Listen up, Privates Tierney, Lincoln, Hannon, Butler, Smart, and Quinn. You will be carrying the Bangalore torpedoes," instructed Forthright. "Cpl. Webb, Cpl. Wallace, Private Reagan, you're going to tote the BAR. Privates South, Jackson, Lofton, and Foster, you have the assistant gunner's belt," explained Forthright. "In addition, you six are carrying the Bangalores, you're also going to act as ammo bearers, so grab all the BAR belts and disperse them amongst yourselves. Then when Webb, Wallace, or Reagan call for ammo, you get to them, Johnny-on-the-spot," explained Forthright.

"For you gentlemen who have the torpedoes, you know the drill. If not, for you new guys take your bayonets off and put them inside your belt so they are easily accessible. Then sling your rifle onto your back," demonstrated Forthright.

Shea added, "Put your chin strap behind your head or bite on it. Iffin ya don't, they'll pull your Brodie back, givin' 'em a slice-the-turkey way to slit y'all's throat," Shea said, pulling his helmet up and running his index finger across his neck. "One last thing, you six thata are in the back. When the fightin' breaks out, you old boys drop your Bangalores, pull your 45s and your trench knifes, and come arunnin' to support the BARs. You hear, now?"

"Strap up, men," commanded First Sgt. Forthright.

The men immediately got to their feet and started to adjust their straps on their Brodies, positioning their rifle slings across their chests, and filling their clips with ammo.

"First Sgt., you have Smedley," said Sullivan.

"Roger that, Sir," said Forthright.

"Cpl. Smedley," said Forthright. "Before we go on our picnic raid., Sgt. Wilson and I will help you get squared away with your equipment."

"Hey Smedley, I will bet you one month's pay, that you have a soldier's Kodiak camera?" said Wilson.

"Yes, I do, before I shipped off, I bought a vest pocket Kodiak camera and film so I can keep a running journal of the time I spent in France," replied Smedley.

"So, if you were to hold the camera in front of you and take a picture of yourself right now, then look at it," said Forthright, "Would you be ready to go on the raid right now?"

"I think so," said Smedley.

"No Bugeater, you're not," said Wilson as he scratched his mustache. "You are what we call in our profession, soup sandwich. You have your trench coat over your equipment. Think about this rattlesnake boy, when we're running, dodging, and shooting, how much time do you think old Boche is going to give you while you try to tear or fumble at your clips for your rifle, your 45, or a trench knife underneath your trench coat?"

"I see your point," said Smedley, looking at Wilson like a lost puppy.

"So, here's what we'll do. Take off your trench coat. Let's see. Ya got your Roundabout, Field Pack, Haversack, Mess Kit, and right here's your E-Tool," as he opens up the dull collapsible spade, and puts it down with the rest of the equipment. "Mr. Smedley, you overeducated feller. All you can do with this one is dig your own grave. After this, get one of the boys to get you a proper E-Tool."

"Smedley, do you have a full canteen?" asked Forthright. "Got your two gas masks? The French M2 and the British CE mask?"

Forthright quizzed, "Smedley old boy, which one do you put on first?"

Smedley looked at the masks, and said, "I would put on the CE mask first."

"That's not a wise choice Golden Knight," said Wilson. "You want to put on the M2 Froggy gas mask first, which is going to last about 5 hours. That CE only lasts about an hour."

"I see the merit in that," said Smedley.

"Now, stand there let me look at you," said Wilson.

"Well, at least you're dressed like an American soldier," said Forthright as he inspected Smedley's uniform.

"Smedley, you have an almost brand-new pair of boots, puttees, OD trousers, shirt, blouse, and your helmet," said Forthright. "Mustang, let's pretend you're taking another picture of yourself with that there Kodiak. Lookin' at you now, you're missing a couple things.

Wilson hands him a gun and a knife and says, "You'll need this, your 1911. And this, a German Nahkampfmesser trench knife,"

"Also, pick up a couple MK 2 hand grenades," said Forthright.

"I've only thrown one time and that was in basic training," said Smedley.

"It's like ridin' a bucking bronc or a woman. You just gotta know when to hang on and when to let loose," said Forthright. "How is your arm? Did you at least throw the required distance?"

"Why yes I did," said Smedley rather proudly.

"Do you see how this is shaped? The grenade has 40 knobbed squares that act as shrapnel," said Wilson as he pointed at parts of the explosive device. And Smedley, don't pull this pin with your teeth or you'll be eating with your gums."

"Maybe someday they'll make it round like a baseball," remarked Smedley, cradling a grenade and examining it as they talked.

"Yeah, maybe someday, probably in the late 1960s," said Wilson counting on his fingers. "So you like baseball, Smedley?"

"Why, yes I do. I was never very good at it, but a classmate of mine was. He was a senior when I was a sophomore. Born in Howard County Nebraska, near a small town called Elba. Name was Grover Cleveland Alexander. To watch him throw a baseball!" Smedley looked out into nothing, and wound up a pitch, and says, "Yow, what an arm! I can see why he's playing professionally. But as of right now, he is over here in France with an artillery unit," he said shaking his head.

"All right Cpl. Let's get you squared away," said Wilson. "Now put your trench coat on, and get that good 'n buttoned up, now your Roundabout, Field Pack, and your other equipment. Now adjust your two-gas-mask apparatus. So that you will be ready to put your French gas mask on first."

Wilson helped Smedley adjust his belts and equipment. He continued, "Now take that trench knife that I gave you; slide that into your belt, making it comfortable for easy magnetism."

"What did you fucking say?" asked Forthright.

"Magnetism. My word for 'easy pull,'" boasted Wilson.

"I thought that's what you meant, Mr. Roget," said Forthright as he rolled his eyes.

"Now remember this, Mr. Bughusker," Wilson said pointing his thumb at Forthright, "Old Cowboy Forthright... As a child, he used to go cattle punching. The only problem is they punched back—now you look at him. There sits the shell of a worn-out Bloomer Sooner," he said, chuckling. "Have one of the boys get you a .45. Also, there are some extra rounds in the bunker," said Wilson, adding, "10 clips, two in each pouch. Remember this, Mr. Smedley. This is about Cowboy, who is a bugfucker."

"You're going to be in the rear, with the gear, with me," said Forthright as he gave Smedley a friendly hand slap on the shoulder. Forthright turned to the firewall and did a farmer's blow.

"Hey, ya almost hit me, Cowboy. Keep that shit to yourself," Wilson faked wiping off his face and shaking his hand. "You almost snotted on Cornboy's face," he said laughing.

"Now, just before we get ready to go, I will help you strap your chicken cage on to your backpack. The Germans have had four years to strengthen their trenches. They ain't like the ones we normally fight in shoulder to shoulder, at best, and that's a tough road. Most German trenches are more elaborate, much wider, and maybe wider in the communications trench, and for sure wider in the supply trench," Wilson said, taking off his Brodie helmet and scratching the top of his head.

"Their traverses are, well, if you don't know what traversing is, imagine a snake when it's in the serpentine shape," Forthright said, drawing a slithering snake in the dirt. "Also, the traversing makes it harder for the artillery to kill everyone in the trench. If you're not careful, you're dead as soon as you go around a corner. The Germans have made a mastery of night trench raids, but not as good as the Canadians," explained Forthright.

CHAPTER 5

Forthright inspected the men, one at a time, finding everything squared away. As he passed each man, he shook their hand and looked them in the eye, and softly said, "Go fuck yourself," as only a First Sgt. can say to his children.

"Crow, old boy, hush my mouth! Guess who's acomin to dinner. Y'all better set out the extra set of fine Chiner plates," said Shea stepping onto the firestep.

"Who or what in tarnation is visiting me house this fine morn?" asked Sullivan.

"Who's in charge here?" asked a man wearing a French Adrian helmet, stepping into the bunker.

"I am," said Sullivan, standing a little wobbly.

"The name is First Lieut. Augustus Washington," he said as he bent his head down to enter the bunker. His wire rim glasses were covered with a dirty film, and his bald head made his face look even more war weary. "Far cry from the glitz and glamour of Manhattan, but we're all stuck here, ain't that right?"

Behind him an enormous man filled the doorway, not able to stand completely upright in the bunker. His French helmet was tucked under his arm, and his head sparkled with sweat even in the cold. The bunker lamp reflected steam rising from his head.

"This is Sergeant First Class John Henry Jefferson," Washington said. Washington was a large man, but standing next to Jefferson, he looked small. A deep, black scar ran from his forehead down to the middle of his ebony cheek, creating a warrior-like appearance.

"Good morning, gentlemen," his baritone, gravelly, but gentle voice filled all four corners of the room.

"Sgt. Andre Hawkins," Washington extended his palm toward a young man, small compared to the other men. He removed his helmet and wiped his head with a rag.

"Howdy y'all. Everybody calls me Hawk," he said. "On accounta the fact that back home I can see about from Dallas to San Antone."

Forthright stepped forward and shook his hand, "Oh you're from TexAss. Poor guy. Shudda been born in Oklahoma, like yer's truly."

"Sgt. George Storms, sir!" He removed his helmet as well, revealing another bald head. "Call me Stormy, if you please."

Forthright stepped in front of him and shook his hand, "Nice to meetcha. I'm the First Sergeant." He stepped to the next man in line.

Washington said, "This is Sgt. Richard Williamson, hails from the City of Brotherly Love." His face didn't indicate Brotherly Love. "This gentleman is known as Deadeye Dick by the unit."

Sullivan stepped forward and shook each man's hand. "Me name is First Lieut. Don Sullivan." He straightened his posture and addressed them formally. "Gentlemen, nice to make your acquaintance. Let's pull up a chair and get to know each other a little bit," said Sullivan as the other men exchanged greetings and names. "Tell me, me buckos. Did ya come to bring us the skinny that the war is over?" asked Sullivan.

"I wish it was that easy Lieut," replied Washington, as he rubbed the back of his head.

"So how can we be of service to you gentlemen then Sir?" asked Sullivan.

"We just drove up from Sechelt. We are with the 369th infantry, U.S. Army, assigned to the French, Sir," said Washington.

"Yes, I know you gentlemen. The Harlem Hell Fighters, isn't that right. All I can say, Sir, is that your war record precedes you. I'm glad we're on the same side," said Sullivan. Washington's men looked at each other in disbelief.

"Glad someone believes in us, Sir," Washington said nodding at Sullivan. "We been given orders to retrieve a French Gen'ral that came up this way. The assignment was provided by the French intelligence. My intuition tells me that this mission is pretty sketchy," said Washington.

"That, by Saint Michael, is what we're gonna do. We have an idea where he's at, probably with his trollop riding his lap. The boyos and I are getting ready to paint the town red," said Sullivan.

General O'Rourke appeared in the bunker. Sullivan shouted, "Attention!"

"At ease," said General O'Rourke.

"General, me Darlin' Sir, meet Lieut. Augustus Washington," said Sullivan.

"I've heard outstanding things about you and your men," said General O'Rourke. "You're one of the 369th, 370th, 371st, or the 372nd Infantry looking for that Royal buffoon French General and his tart," conveyed O'Rourke.

"369th Sir. Our mission is to retrieve the General," stated Washington.

"I'm glad the French realized if they wanna get a job done right, send more Americans," said O'Rourke, smiling at Lieut. Washington. Washington's men glanced at each other, smiling. "Very good son, you can have Gen'ral Frog Legs."

"Lieut. Sullivan, a pigeon just came in," said Smedley as he removed a miniature tin canister strapped to his back and unrolled a piece of paper.

"Go ahead and read it," said Sullivan.

"Sir, let me get my spectacles on," said Smedley, fumbling with his glasses.

"Take your time, boyo," said Sullivan.

"Whoever wrote this doesn't have a clue about English, spelling, sentence structure, and or punctuation," said Smedley, squinting at the paper. "It's all one sentence, Sir."

"Be quick, man, I'm thirsty. What's it say?" asked Sullivan.

"Lieut. Sullivan, Sir, please don't kill the messenger."

"Go ahead Cpl. Tell me what it says, boyo," said Sullivan.

"*Sir, I must decipher some of this. I think it says, "To the comandin oficer there is a slav shipp ful of naggers comin your wai hav them thar black layz sons a bittches to cleam the trinchs burry the dead and an'thang els you kin thank of so your realy soldir boys can go do al the fightin then they cam akt as stechor bearrs and getin you man back to saffety and whach your posibles as thierr nown thieves and rappists,*" said Smedley as he tried to sound out the message with a look of disbelief.

"Who wrote that?" asked Sullivan with dismay in his face and anger in his voice.

"It looks to be First Sgt. S.J.," said Smedley.

"And what is his name"? asked Sullivan.

"First Sgt. Smith Smith Jones. He's my First Sgt.," said Smedley. "He's as big as a brontosaurus with the brain of a pea. His sword is definitely mightier than his pen."

"When this lil action is o'er, I'm gonna march me arse right down there and pay him a lil visit," said Sullivan. "Gonna stick a loaded shillelagh square up his arse."

"No Lieut.," said General O'Rourke coldly. "You're gonna have to stand in line behind me son. Give me that communique," ordered O'Rourke, as he read with one eye. A look of scorn covered his face.

"Lieut. Sullivan," added Smedley. "Physically, the First Sgt. is humongous. I think the biggest man I've ever seen."

"*Galánta le na galar,*" said O'Rourke, nodding.

"General O'Rourke," said Lieut. Washington, "What's that, Sir?"

"Means the man who wrote this message is *infected with the disease,*" said Sullivan. "Lieut. Washington, I would like to offer me hand to you and your men as an apology, and a swig for the ignorance of men. Top o' the morning to ya," Sullivan said as he handed a bottle to Lieut. Washington, "One day, me buckos, we'll all be together in one Army with our names and 'U.S. Army' right there on our uniforms," he proclaimed. "This ain't no blarney. I'm an ardent believer that the actions, deeds, and the words of a man are what matter…."

"…Not the color of their skin!" interrupted Doc, Forthright, Shea, and Wilson in unison.

"Yessir, actions, deeds and words are the soul of a man, Lieut. Washington," said Sullivan, preaching. "I'm also a firm believer that what a man does physically with those 10 Commandments on Earth every day will reflect spiritually in your soul, then on the palm of God as he judges you. So, tell me Lieut., I've always been curious, why do you think our Army chucked your units under the caisson?" asked Sullivan.

"I never thought of it in that perspective. But you hit the nail on the head. Here's my perspective, if you don't mind. We live in a four-tier society; the Rich, the Middle Class, poor Whites, and the fourth is us, Americans of African descent ," said Washington. "The South, for all its glory, from the first turn of the page of the 17th century to this moment, early in the morning, right here on November 11, 1918."

"The two Great Wars of Southern Independence. One was a failure. The other war, We the People are still paying for every day. Right now, as they say, the years preceding the war when the slaves were their property, the whites had their social order. The slaves had theirs, too. After the Civil War, the South was forced to assimilate to one social order as per the Federal Government, bringing these states back into the union. So, they pigeonholed their new society and ours and anybody else that doesn't meet their social order in industry, law, education, arts, religion, and anthropology. Even monetarily. They are trying, to this day, to disenfranchise our vote by any tool they can implement—unless you have a dollar fifty in your pocket. Then you could vote."

"What if ya only got ninety cents?" asked Wilson.

Washington answered, "Well, if you were white, they'd give you the sixty cents."

All eyes looked at Wilson. "Just asking. You mean you don't getta vote if you don't pay? I've never seen that—in the Northeast anyway. Sorry for interrupting, Lieut. Washington. Please go ahead," said Wilson.

"Who do you think came out on the bottom again on January 1, 1863, when the great Mr. Lincoln issued the Emancipation Proclamation. Then states' rights came about. People actually thought it would go into effect?" pondered Washington. "The only spirit of that proclamation was Mr. Lincoln going to Heaven with it. Then after the war, there was a new war. Black codes," continued Washington.

The men sat silently as Washington spoke. Doc raised his index finger and asked, "Lieut. Washington. What are Black codes?"

"Let's start with convict leasing made possible by vagrancy laws. This way they would arrest more Americans of African descent, then the states could hire out the prisoners to do all the dirty work and hard labor. Also, they have separate courts in some states for Americans of African descent, and most are denied basic rights... and of course, there are a plethora of other laws that were all different in different states," said Washington.

Smedley interrupted, "I didn't know 'bout none of this, and I'm a high school English teacher back home. Thank you for the enlightenment, sorry for the interruption."

"That's quite alright," Washington said, nodding his head slightly to Smedley. "The Reconstruction of 1870, for all its best-laid plans, rendered more waste to our country. It opened up the door to what's going on in the Upper and Lower Chambers of the House right now with corruption and scandal. Put simply, they just buy themselves a seat," Washington added. "Basically, they are political slaves, bought and sold by the people who handle them. The pages check the teeth of the senators and representatives, and some are so old they just take their uppers out and hand them to the pages. More will come, session after session, carpetbaggers, scalawags, the KKK; and they eventually end up in a seat making policies for the Great United States of America. To this day, November 11, 1918, it's still happening," said Washington.

Sullivan stood up and said, "Here, me Bucko, here's a bottle of Bush Mills to wash down some of the bullshit you've had to endure." Sullivan patted him on the shoulder, and sat back down to listen.

"Thanks Lieut. Sullivan. Then came Jim Crow laws back in the 1870s. They covered the South during the Reconstruction and Disenfranchisement. These laws danced all along the Mason-Dixon Line South, down the mighty Mississippi, then straight East to the ocean," said Washington, gesturing a wide circle in the air. "This is Southern society in its glory. It has degenerated because the rebels lost the war, along with their property. Ever since then, they're very bitter. Hopefully one day those feelings will be gone. The Jim Crow laws are solely designed so that Americans of African descent and poor whites will not succeed."

Washington took out a handkerchief and wiped his bald head for a moment. "Hawk, didn't you have some trouble in Texas?"

Hawkins replied, "Yes Commander. Pert'near got myself strung up over just tipping ma hat to a white lady. The Senator himself took a shot at me, and then told his guys 'Round up a posse,' and that's when I ran. Went right from that situation to the recruiting station on our main street and joined myself up that day."

Sullivan shook his head, and patted Hawkins on the back, "That's quite unjust, me lad. Someday things will be different if I have anything to say about it. We're all fighting together for the same thing, even if we don't quite know what that is exactly. Them bastard Heinies killed innocent Americans, and that's all we need to know." Sullivan turned to Washington and said, "Professor Washington, me darlin', please continue with your morning lecture. It's a lot to digest, but please go on," he said directing his attention to Washington.

Washington smiled at Wilson and said, "Mr. Wilson, did you have your hand up for question?"

"Sir, I did not know it was that deep. I apologize. Please, Lieutenant. Please continue," said Wilson, nodding.

"Lemme think, where was I? Oh yeah," Washington said as he stood and faced the men. "The Pole Cats get you on the Poll Taxes. Basically, Literacy Tests, just different wording. They don't want us to vote. They don't want us to have a say. They say equal but separate, but equal so long as you have a dollar and a half in your pocket. That is what the book says," as Washington huffed and shook his head. "They want us to step and fetch—but be quiet. Dance, sing, have kids—but don't get educated, no voting. But there's one thing people need to remember: Security and Education are the KEYS to everything. Security is taking care of your country and your family. Education is the key to getting a much better job, by the grace of God," said Washington, wiping his forehead and looking at each man in the eyes.

"All the basics in life," emphasized Washington. He took a long pull from his bottle of Bush Mills. "I apologize if I sound like a history lesson, but this is something that we as Americans—Black and White or whatever color—should never brush under the manure pile. We have a responsibility to plant a new American standard-bearer somewhere, and hold that line so we can defeat racism," said Washington making a wide gesture with his hands. "Someday, all men will be able to walk and talk together and work this out," preached Washington as a wide smile formed across his face and he nodded.

"When I was a child we traveled north. The northerner's attitude was 'we freed you, but we don't have to feed you,' or 'Go on now,

Darkie. Find the Irish, they will feed you,'" said Washington waving his hand as if swatting away an annoyance. "Again, I must sound like a history teacher instead of a Psychologist," said Washington.

Sullivan asked, "Lieutenant, is it true about a circular sent by the United States Army to the French army and the French citizens telling them to stay away from your units and not be friendly?" said Sullivan.

"You are correct, Sir," said Washington with a huff of disgust. "In fact, I have a copy of it that I keep in the armored car at all times. It was written by Colonel J.L.A. Linard of the U.S. Army. He wrote the secret information called *Concerning Black American Troops*," asserted Washington.

"That is actually the name of the circular?" Sullivan chuckled nervously. "You've got to be kidding me."

"It's true," said Washington. "What it says is that they want the French soldiers and civilians to adhere to the Jim Crow laws of the United States, but that's not what is happening. They treat us as equals," said Washington.

"That is what the U.S. dictates?" asked Sullivan.

"That is right!" explained Washington, Adding, "But it pisses off the United States Army. They want to bring the U.S. norm here to France as well as back home in the southern states."

"Lieut. Washington," said Wilson.

"Sergeant, uh Wilson is it?" responded Washington.

"Lieut., would you happen to have an extra one of those circulars?" asked Wilson.

"No, I do not. Sorry, Sgt.," said Washington. "Why do you ask?"

"That way, Sir, when I take a Lieut. Shea and wipe my Decatur, I'll have that circular on me. In the next night's raid, I can leave it in Heinie's trench as a little gift," said Wilson as the men chuckled a little.

"That gift has been left several times," said Washington with a straight face. "They, as in the American Army, don't want us to have equal footing here or when we get back home. Now, if I was home and Col. Linard was a psychiatric patient of mine and I had to analyze him, I would check his cognitive motivation and give him the Stanford-Binte Intelligence Scales test," said Washington joyously. He continued, "I'd want to know if he is Extraverted, Introverted, or Neurotic. I'd give him the four D's: Deviance, Distress, Dysfunction, and Danger, and observe if he had several neuroses. Or maybe he has Schizophrenia with Oedipus Complex, or perhaps a borderline personality disorder. I call it bi-disorder," said Washington, sounding official. "Then I would see if he was able to manage his anger. Starting last year, a gentleman by the name of Yerkis developed an intelligence test called *1917 Army Alpha and Army Beta*."

"Army Alpha assesses your ability to take verbal commands. You're to follow directions, do basic math, and process information. The test also helps establish leadership positions, kind of like the pecking order at West Point," stated Washington.

"Sir," laughed Wilson. "Don't you mean the pecker order?" Then he added, "Oh my God, can you imagine West Point letting women in someday? That pecker order would go all to shit."

"Maybe not," chuckled Washington. "Your job classification is determined by this test. The other test is Army Beta. The Army Beta is for foreign nationals who want to join the U.S. Army,."

"I would drum that dumbshit Linard out of the Army," said Washington.

Sullivan nodded in agreement.

"So, what I figured out after all my years treating patients is that racism is a mental illness. If someone gets so angry that they must lash out, either through verbal or physical violence, just because the color of a person's skin or some other difference doesn't meet that someone's criteria, there's a problem. But people need to be educated on race. First, they need to look in a mirror and come to terms with the fact they have a major problem with race. But if they are willing to take a leap of faith, not religious per se, but the leap of faith that you're going to make the change of attitude and heart to help defeat it," said Washington thoughtfully. "I know this is true, because I have done my own studies in my practice. I've walked around New York City observing Americans of African descent who are still being treated as steerage. They still can't go into certain sections of the city. They can't drink out of the same water fountains as whites, same as back where my grandparents came from in Grady County, Georgia. But a person who opens their heart and realizes that we're all just people will start feeling better about themselves. It would just melt away, if people would let it," explained Washington.

"Grady County?" Shea interjects excitedly. "I'll have butter and pepper on my grits. I hail from Fowlstown in Decatur County, just a county west of Grady," as he stood up to shake Washington's hand. "I'm a one-a the Shea boys of Decatur County. I got me five older brothers, and three sisters. I'm the youngin'—the runt of the litter who didn't ever get to tag along with his older brothers."

"As I got older, my Daddy and five older brothers, started to takin' me to the once a week special meetins with those fellers who wore the dunce caps and sheets," said Shea. "Daddy, and my brothers dressed like that, too. They made me wear one too. So, I told my Daddy, I didn't be likin' to agoin' to them thar meetins. At first, he just laughed. Then the next week, he didn't laugh. I told him I didn't want to go, and the next thang I knew, I'm pickin' myself up off the ground. He says, 'Get in the fuckin' truck.' So, I done that and, of course my brothers were being right ornery, with them thar rib shots," said Shea.

"We drove about 5 mile outta town. We stopped at a wooded area, and more trucks drove up and it was lookin' to be some high n' mighty folk, likin' our Mayor and other elected O-fficials, some with badges even. Then I watched an innocent black man get strung up on a tree, and set afire," said Shea. "I was right shook up with anger cuz that man never did nothin' wrong. When we got home, I told the old man, that fucker, that I didn't never want to do that again. I was knocked down. But this time I got the tar beaten outta me. My father's famous six-pack straps across the back, a belt buckle the size of a pack of cards first. Then he let my brothers have a go at me. Two held me down likin' a squealin' pig, and then they just took turns putting thata strap to my back like an old mule, 'til I was bleedin'," revealed Shea.

"They shoulda beat your face in instead," Wilson laughed, patting Shea on the shoulder. "I feel for ya, my friend."

"The next mornin' the ol' man took me to school, whisperin' somethin' to the principal about I had fallen on my back on bob-wire. Lord-a-mighty, what a blasted lie," exclaimed Shea. "For the next week, I hadda sit in the corner with the dunce cap on. And for what reason you ask? There wasn't no reason. All them thar kids just alaughin' an amakin' fun a me," said Shea.

"Jesus, Shea, you had a rough go as a kid. Turned out okay as a man, I might say. I'm happy to have you in the trench next to me any day of the week. Whatever day of the week it is," said Doc.

"My pappy passed the baton of racism on to my brothers. I thank God that I dropped that baton and found somethin else. Thata was good old-fashioned love. My lady's name is Alicia Perkeys Shea and she is from Grady County, too. Just outside Cairo. Yah, day we met was a nice sunny day! Saw her walkin down the midway at the county fair and it was love at first sight for me; her too, I'm aguessin'. She's beautiful, as a ripe Georgia peach—radiant, just glorious, an' singin' likin she's the entire choir. That thar woman is undoubtedly the love of my life, and my son is my pride," said Shea.

"You know how hard it is for an enlisted soldier to get married in the army? I do declare, I been in the army over 17 years and most of it's been with Crow," said Shea. "One thang about old Captain Hill, God rest his soul. He was just fine with it, and he gave me permission. But the other officers, as they say, were real southern gentleman. They gave ol' Cap'n Hill all kinds a static over that thar marriage arrangement," said Shea, rolling his eyes. "My wife's people were bought and sold in Atlanta, then they were brought down yonder our way. Alicia's kin ahails from French Creole descent. The real sad part of this story, is the third day after our weddin', her brother William was kidnapped from his own yard. Never found 'im," added Shea, taking off his Brodie and scratching his head.

"The police report stated that five men in white sheets and dunce caps were seen aleavin' the area. It also said in that thar police report, that they stopped ata the Grady and Decatur County line. Another burr in my ass is that my cousin is the Decatur County Sheriff. He swore up and down to the high heavens that he would find them thar varmints of that bastardly, dastardly deed," said Shea.

"I was what they call ostracized, repudiated, from the family, whatever them words mean. Mama called my wife a Black French whore. Then I was told to get the fuck out, and that she an' my Daddy had disowned me. My three sisters banished me from all family activities. And needless to say, I got one good last ass-whoopin' from my brothers. Once I left, I never looked back, Since then my wife, son, and her mother all moved to Lincoln, Nebraska," said Shea.

Smedley piped up, "What part of Lincoln, Sir?"

"Have you ever had a beer at Bob's Tavern in Havelock? They are just over yonder from there," said Shea, pointing over Smedley's shoulder.

"No Sir, I don't drink. Never gotten a beer there, but I know right where it's at," Smedley said, nodding.

"Crow has kin that took my family in," said Shea, smiling at Sullivan and tipping his Brodie. "I can never repay that gift a kindness. Crow is my son's Godfather, an' these are all his ugly Uncles," Shea explained as he handed the picture to Lieut. Washington. "Here's the last picture of the two."

"What a fine-looking family. Your wife is very beautiful, and your son looks big and strong," replied Washington.

"Why, thank you kindly," said Shea…. "It's all thata Nebraska moo cow meat. It don't taste like a piece of alligator tail, an it's better'n possum. Oh, and all thata Nebraska corn, can't forget that."

Smedley agreed, "There's some fine eating in Nebraska, that's for sure."

Wilson chimed in, "Thug, says where he's from they call it *maize*," everybody stopped and looked at Wilson.

Shea, not missing a beat, said, "And thata Nebraska moo cow milk is from Hartington, Nebraska. Right there's a little dairy farm called Burbach's," said Shea, patting his belly. "Sure do miss their milk. Oh, and a big ole plate of pigs feet and collard greens."

"Yeah, I sure miss Louie's hot dogs, down at the corner stand from my office," said Washington. "So, what is your son's name?"

"William Donald Shea, in honor of my wife's brother," said Shea.

"A fine young man," said Lieut. Washington, handing back the picture. "Any of your brothers over here in France?" asked Washington.

"The five scaredy-cat Shea's? Nooooo sir. They all got deferments. Sumthin' 'bout the heels of them thar feet," said Shea, spitting. "Jes like most of the white males in the county. And before I go back to Lincoln, it is paramount thata I pay my respects to my Daddy and my five brave brothers," said Shea, with an antagonistic tone in his voice.

"All of us boys volunteer to help you with your brothers," said Wilson. The men nodded their heads in agreement.

"Right after this war is done," said Washington, "I will get settled in back at home. I'm going to go back to Howard University, and get a medical degree in Psychiatry," Washington said as he loosened the top few buttons on his blouse. "I'm going to write my thesis on the shock of war on mental health," Washington remarked. "What I mean is the soldier's new life after war, how it affected him, and how he is going to react when he gets home into the civilian world. Sleeping habits will have changed; will they change back? I know from personal experience about how nightmares and too little sleep make unsatisfactory bedfellows. A guy wakes up sweating, so he gets out of bed. Is he going to push down a couple shots of alcohol to steady himself?" Washington stood up and stretched his back.

"Some of the psychological reports that have come back in the early years of the war, in a case studied by the British Army, stated that in some instances what British headquarters thought was cowardice, so they put soldiers up against the wall and shot them. It turned out these men were suffering from a type of shock. In those instances, a guy is not going to be the same person. Then how is he going to act as a husband, does he show less loving, caring. Does he enjoy embracing, petting, etc., or does he exhibit violent tendencies and get straight to the point with no emotion?" asked Washington as he took a small drink of whiskey.

"Did he always beat his wife? If he did, is he going to continue to beat her or beat her even more? Or did he not beat her at all before war, and then get home and start to beat her?" asked Washington scratching his jaw line, pensively. "Being a father how are his reactions going to be with his son or daughter. They do or say something wrong, does he jump down their throat or hit them? There might be unpredictable mood swings, both with him and with his family," stated Washington as he wiped his forehead with his handkerchief.

The men looked at each of their brothers in the trench, sizing up and wondering who, if any, of the men might end up suffering like Washington explained. They looked inside to themselves too.

"After a ugly war like this I'll have new patients back home. Are they going to jump into a bottle of alcohol, or find themselves in a pile of pills? Are they going to lose or gain a lot weight? Every time they hear a loud bang, how are they going to react?" stated Washington. "I have asked some of my men to write me after the war on a monthly basis. I want to hear what kind of progress they are making. It has to be honest, and no bullshit. Then I'm able to make an assessment and record it on a monthly basis. I expect to see different emotions each month, and different reactions to those emotions. My plan is to write them back with some helpful information. One day I'd like to write a book about it. Then I'll see if it can help my old army buddies or anyone else with those similar problems," said Washington.

General O'Rourke said, "No blarney, Doctor. You have your hands full, but I like what you are doing for the men."

CHAPTER 6

A brown and grey homer flew into the bunker and stepped directly into its small cage with a flutter.

"Crow, we just got a chicken hawk in," said Smedley as he reached into the cage and removed the small canister from the bird. He opened the canister and removed a scroll of paper; and without opening it, handed the paper to Forthright.

"If that's a message for the commander of the unit, read what it says to me," commanded Sullivan.

"Yessir. It says 'A squadron of Bats will be up to assist you. Signed, Col. Aloysius Finn Gilhooly, Esq.," reported Forthright.

"My cousin Sé tá *á* sciathán sa an clogás-túr," said O'Rourke.

"Means *he has a bat in the bell-tower*," remarked Sullivan, laughing.

Gen. O'Rourke said, "Let's have another belt, boyo." He took a swig, and leaned back to fire his pipe. He took a long draw, and meticulously blew smoke rings, one right through the middle of the other.

"Lieut. Sullivan, another homer just came in," said Smedley, and he removed the canister.

"Go, ahead and read it me boyo. What does it say? Hurry up now, I'm enjoying my smoke," said O'Rourke.

"It looks like this is a follow-up message about the Bats. It says, 'Expect the 185 Night Pursuit Fighter Squadron, out of Rembercourt Aerodrome to support your mission," read Smedley, adding, "I've heard of these guys, the American Army Air Force asked 16 of the craziest pilots to fly at night. These guys fly a Bristol F.2 Fighter, with twin Lewis guns mounted on top. They don't have much combat time, but this is the First Army air squadron ever to do this type of mission at night."

"Yes, I picked up a little information about a new aviation tactic of night fighting. It's the fortunes of war that America's first Night Pursuit Fighter Squadron could meet Germany's first Night Pursuit Fighter Squadron, Jasta 73. The Heinies fly the Fokker D.VII. There could be a great medieval battle in the sky right above us, and their commander is some schmuck by the name of Willie," said Smedley. "Now our 185 Night Pursuit Fighter Squadron is outstanding. They modified the cockpit by making it more commodious for the pilots and radios on those planes."

"Smedley?"

"Yes, Sgt. O'Keefe," replied Smedley.

"What the fuck did you just say?" asked Doc.

"Commodious. It means the cockpit is more roomy. Originally, the plane would hold a pilot and observer, but it's been reconfigured it to accommodate just the pilot and a radio," said Smedley.

Wilson interjected, "Don't that beat all. Even in a flying contraption, they have commodes." The men quit talking and looked at him, then at each other in stunned silence. "Gentlemen, what you fail to realize is that our boys can bomb the shit out of those Germans, with their Heinies right on the Heinies."

Forthright piped up, "I would not want to be bombed by flying crap." The men shook their heads in agreement.

"Another thing to think about. Someday, regular travelers are going to be flying, and they will need to use commodes. One for men and one for women, or just one for both?" said Wilson.

"I've always had a hidden desire to be a pilot, up there flying around, " said Smedley looking up to the heavens.

"Anyway, the Squadron Commander's name is Wild Bill something or another? His wingmen are Dingbat, Bat Crappy, Vampire Bat, and Bulldog Bat—and they are Bat Looney," said Smedley.

"Someone named their aeroplane Bat Crappy?" asked Doc.

"No, it's the other word," said Smedley.

"You mean like Batshit," asked Forthright.

"I got to see them one time taking off from aerodrome south of Paris. The symbol on the side of their aeroplane is quite unique," said Smedley. "It must be a representation of something. It is a yellow circle surrounding a black bat with its wings outstretched. Under those outstretched wings is a fist with just the middle finger protruding up to the bat's head like its body. The other four fingers are brought down to the middle knuckle like she's on a perch," said a slightly confused Smedley. "I understand the bat on the side of the plane, but the one finger—I don't fathom that," as Smedley took off his helmet and scratched his head.

"Rattlesnake boy, are you a teetotaler, Cornchucker?" teased Forthright.

"Yes, I drink tea," said Smedley, lifting an imaginary teacup and extending his pinky finger.

Wilson chimed in, "It's definitely a family affair with those aeroplanes. I'm sure his wife is Dingbat, his kid Batshit, mother-in-law is a Vampire Bat, and the family pet is Bulldog Bat."

"Then why don't they call him Bat Commander or Battyman? Who knows? The Squadron Commander favors his name as Wild Bill. That is all I know about them," said Smedley.

"Lieut. Sullivan get out here quick, Sir!" said Jackson in a distressed voice. "Look to the northeast. An observation balloon just exploded."

"That, gentleman, happens to be John and Tom Lightfoot's handy-work. I'm pretty sure they are light-footing their way back here now." said Sullivan. "All right boyos, stand to." The men stood and readied themselves for battle. Sullivan continued, "Stand to. I think Ugh and Thug each got half of an observation balloon. Be ready boyos. Somebody get Smedley," he commanded.

Smedley approaches Sullivan, "Yes Sir. How can I help you?"

"Get your paper and writing utensil Smedley, and write this down.

Did you observe and get bearings to the observation balloon?

"Smedley, be quick about it, me boyo, and get that chicken hawk sent off," said Sullivan.

A soft voice came from the trench, "Crow?"

"Yes, Decatur?" Sullivan replied

"Them thar Heinie hogs just got first call. Thata balloon lit up the Meuse River like a Fourth of July party on the Mississippi. Son, the hairs on the back of my neck are stickin' straight up like the ass of a porky-pine," said Shea.

"Boyo, I know exactly what you mean, my old friend. I too have a troubling feeling," said Sullivan.

"What's that, Crow?" asked Shea.

"I have a premonition that this so-called war to end all wars is just a smaller audition of war, compared to a much larger war in the future in which we're forced to come back here," pondered Sullivan. "I'm going to figure in about 24 years for the U.S. to be back in greater numbers here in France and around the world."

Shea responded, "Thata thar tree does not fall too far from the nut."

"Yes, you are right. Also, I think using those land ships, aeroplanes, artillery… and then I'd look into the possibilities of what Mr. Benjamin Franklin said in the most elegant way.…

> Where is the prince who can afford so to cover his country with troops for its defense as that 10,000 men descending from the clouds might not in many places, do an infinite deal of mischief, before a force could be brought together to repel them," said Sullivan, quoting Mr. Franklin's writings.

"If we have to come back to France—and we will, me boyo—I'll wager one fine bottle of Bush Mills that in 24 years we'll be right back here. This is no blarney; I feel it in me bones. So all these entities need to be put into one command," said Sullivan. "Let's call it arms combined."

Shea shook his head in agreement and, "That'd be liken a mean ol' b'ar goin' into the swamp with teeth and claws ahuntin' gator."

Sullivan chuckled and said, "I'm just a new Lieut., so that idea and any others that I have, will have to be kept in me haversack, and slowly, but surely, I'll talk to people who will listen or until I get the rank."

"You know what I like about that idea?" grinned Shea. "Thata would give them German bastards two black-eyed Susans in one century," then he added. "Thata would make them thar old boys look like raccoons diggin' into a trash pile for some vittles."

"Lieut. Sullivan," Smedley said. "A return pigeon just came in."

"Go ahead read it," stated Sullivan.

"It says:

"Have bearing. 6 o'clock. Rolling barrage still in effect, waiting further instructions. Gilhooly."

"Crow?"

"Yes, Mr. Wilson?"

"Did you guys hear something just a second ago? I swear I heard something like a motor."

"Maybe it's those bats in your head," said Forthright.

"No, this is different," said Wilson, trying to persuade them to listen.

"No, I didn't hear a thing, me boyo," said Sullivan.

"Either I'm getting old or losing my hearing," said Wilson, putting a finger in his ear and shaking it vigorously.

"Your brain, you're losing your brain," said Forthright chuckling. "If you shake that ear any harder, shit's gonna flop out of yer New England head."

"Crow?"

"Yes Decatur?"

"I'm startin' to fret about our two brothers."

Sullivan replied, "Yes, me too, Decatur. I'm feelin' a little uneasy."

"What iffin they're not back before the barrage starts up?" said Shea.

"You answer that question, Decatur," said Sullivan.

"Well then I'm agoin' ta hunker down like an old tick dug into a white tailed deer awaitin' for my buddies," said Shea.

Sullivan patted Shea's shoulder, removed his brodie and scratched his head. He said, "I'll be right next to you, by Saint Michael."

Washington looked over the trench, and said, "Lieut. Sullivan. Your scouts are back. And they brought company."

"Tom and John Lightfoot, gentlemen, something led you to believe *siúd beirt cloigeanns, ár níos fearr ná amháin*," Sullivan said in Gaelic. "So, the two of you thought that *two heads are better than one*. Doc has always told me that each human has two sides to their brain—the left and the right," he scolded. "So by the looks of it, neither one of you kept up your half of the bargain. Me thinks I should knock the blarney bullshit right out of you two by banging your heads together. Or maybe I'll give ya a great big bear hug 'cause by Saint Michael, he was lookin' out for you two. I told you not to get that close."

Sullivan patted the two men on the shoulder, happy to see them, but both angry and frustrated. "So, gentlemen now that I have your full attention, where did you pick up these two blanket heads?" he said as he pointed to the weaponless, impotent-looking Germans standing behind them with their hands tied in front of them.

"Why is that one limping?" Sullivan asked. "Doc, come here and take a look at this Sauerkraut."

Sullivan turned and looked at Ugh and Thug, "So, tell me boyos and make it quick, 'cause they're goin' to start shelling in about oh so many minutes," articulated Sullivan as he took out his pocket watch and looked at the time.

"Well Crow, after you ordered our mission, we ghosted around in and out of shell craters. If the area didn't have some Germans present, we moved on to the next crater, and son there's a passel of Hienies out there, I don't know how many," said Thug. "As far as the old man could tell, that middle trench is clear. Then we hooked around on the left-hand side of the third trench, and we caught a little crack of light. So we put our heads together and figured out that's probably where the General is."

"What about the Observation Balloon?" asked Sullivan as he cracked a wide smile.

"We came within a bow shot of it; then we maneuvered our way around, and crossed over a road," said Thug. "Close enough we could hear and smell the Meuse River. Crow, if you look on the map, it's that place on the river that looks like a sore thumb. That would be the city of Brassiere. Then we heard horseshoes clanking—the kind that pulls artillery around," said Ugh.

"So, we go about another 10 to 20 yards," explained Thug. "And there we sighted the Observation Balloon. There was a Sauerkraut officer in the gondola, the Observation crews were working like hell trying to get him up in the air.

Gentlemen, you know how polished I am. I nocked my arrow, drew my bow, my flame was good to go. I let loose and missed the balloon, but I hit the Observer in the chest! The luckiest shot I ever made. He stood there for a second looking at the flaming arrow in his chest. Then the old man quickly lit his arrow, nocked it, and shot it straight into the Balloon. The old man shook his head at me as if to say I make those shots, punk. We hightailed out of there, and next thing you know, the sky lit up," said Thug proudly.

Wilson piped up, "That gentleman in the Observation gondola would be a well done to overly crispy Shish Kebab and Wiener schnitzel," he said as he looked at his buddies.

"We crossed the road to circumvent a patrol. The old man said, 'Follow me,' and we slowly made our way in and out of the shell craters," said Thug. "Stumbled on this asshole, with a wounded ankle."

Sullivan cut off Thug and asked, "How did that happen?" inquired Sullivan pointing at the German's blood-soaked puttee.

"We crawled into the crater, and got the drop on these two. We tussled for a few seconds," said Ugh as he grabbed a bottle and took a drink of whiskey.

"We got the situation under control, so we lit out of the crater. I was watching this guy before his ankle was discombobulated, and the old man had the other guy front of me. Then one a them Mustang manure assholes started to flop around like a trout caught jumping in the air right out of the stream. He started making a ruckus, so the old man grabbed his prisoner and flung him around into mine, tripping him. I let go of mine," said Thug, adding, "He fell into a crater and in one swift motion the old man cups his mouth, draws his knife, then plunges it into the Heinie's ankle. I love watching my old man go to work."

"I'll say he did," said Doc, looking at the man's ankle. "He sank right between the Calcaneal tendon and the Calcaneus. There is one oddity though, somehow 3 inches has been cut out clean," divulged Doc, leaning back, wiping his brow, and scratching his head.

Thug added, pointing to the other German, "This other bastard. The old man pulled out his stone-headed tomahawk and caved in his upper two teeth. Then he pulled his trench knife and dug them out. A nice piece of dental work, and I would charge the Heinie double. Figured he wouldn't talk shit if he had a mouthful of sock. Oh shit, he does have an old stinky sock in his mouth."

"Take the sock out of his mouth," said Sullivan.

"Sgt. O'Keefe?"

"Yes Lieut. Washington. They call me Doc."

"May I speak to you for a minute in private?" asked Washington. "Lieut. Sullivan mentioned to me that you shot a close friend."

"Yes Sir, I did," replied Doc.

"I'll tell you what we'll do right now. Say we're not in a trench in France close to the Belgian border. Right now, we're in New York City and you walked up and knocked on my door. Gwendolyn, my secretary of many years, comes and gets me. We would sit down, and you would make yourself comfortable. I would offer you some coffee. Then you would start talking about what is bothering you," said Washington. "It would be foolish of me to ask you how you feel about what happened," said Washington. "But the psychologist in me says, I have to ask."

"Sir, it's the worst thing I've ever done or felt in my life. I can't get it out of my head," said Doc as he wiped a tear from his right eye.

"Unfortunately, that is the ugliness of war. The images, the still pictures and all the moving parts, leave scars in your mind and body for life," said Washington. "In your mind's eye looking back, when you looked at your friend's face, did everything slow down? Did the look on his face, for that split-second, show that it was okay, and I forgive you, please take my life."

"Yes, sir. I'd say that's pretty descriptive," said Doc.

"Even though Lieut. Shea threw the grenade that killed the two Germans and your friend," said Washington, adding. "You'll be a great Doctor because you have that thing. The caring gift of a doctor, the Hippocratic Oath—to do no harm. It's not just words on the paper, you do not want to see anybody in pain. Talk about it; but for God's sake, don't bury it. Like I told Lieut. Sullivan, write to me," said Washington.

"Thank you. Lieut. Washington, what do I owe you?" asked Doc.

Dr. Washington replied, "Zero, Sgt. O'Keefe, I mean Doc; trust me, I know what I'm talking about," said Washington.

Washington and Doc walked back toward the men in the trench. Forthright walked up to the German and removed the sock from his mouth. The German, spit out a long line of bloody slobber, and in lateral lisping yelps, *"Diese gemeine, grausame amerikanische Indianersquaw zog mir meine zwei Zähne heraus,"* spat the blathering German.

"Confounded, what is that Hun blubbering about?" asked Sullivan.

"He said That vile savage American aborigine squaw pulled my two teeth out," said Smedley, translating as he wiped away the German's spittle from his glasses and face.

"Mr. Smedley, tell him to point to the American dentist that supposedly pulled his teeth out," said Sullivan.

Smedley asked the German, *"Du Blöder, welcher amerikanische Zahnarzt hat dir deine Zähne herausgezogen?"*

The German glared and pointed at Ugh.

"I asked Stupid, 'Which American Dentist pulled your teeth out?" said Smedley. "Lieut. Sullivan, the German said, '*Das hässliche*

amerikanische Indianersquaw Miststück mit dem Pferdeschwanz.'"
The line of spittle continued to drool from the German's bloody
mouth to a pool below him.

"What did the Hun actually say then?" asked Sullivan.

"'The ugly one ponytailed, American aborigine squaw bitch,'"
said Smedley.

"Ask him his name," Sullivan ordered.

"*Wie heisst er?*" asked Smedley. The German, looked at Smedley,
and sent a cannon fodder of scarlet droplets that permeated into
Smedley, as Smedley stepped back.

"Sir, the German said, '*Mein Gott, es ist nicht nur, daß ihr
grausame Indianerinnen habt. Ihr habt auch amerikanische Neger,
die eure Schützengräben säubern,*'" as the German started to laugh
harder.

"Smedley, old boy," said Shea, "What'd that old dog bark?"

Smedley replied, "He said 'My God, not only do you have
female savage aborigines, you have American niggers cleaning your
trenches.'"

As Smedley translated, the German turned his head toward
Lieut. Washington. and lisped with a cold heart, "*Lasst so schnell
wie möglich die Neger zu unserem Schützengraben kommen und ihn
säubern und lass die hässliche Squaw auch rüberkommen und für uns
tanzen,*" as he was wiped away his blood and saliva.

"So, Smedley me boyo, what did our toothless arsehole just say?"
asked Sullivan.

"He said 'As soon as possible, have the niggers come over to our
trench and clean it out too, and have the ugly squaw come over and
dance for us,'" explained Smedley.

The German stared through Lieut. Washington with cold, dead eyes, and spittled, *"In diesem Augenblick ficken drei deutsche Juden deine Frau. Hör zu, du Neger Affenjunge, mein Vater war im Krieg in Sudwestafrika in der Herero Kampagne von 1904 bis 1908 und wir haben schwarze Untermenschen wie dich in die Konzentrationslager geworfen und für Sklavenarbeit verwendet, bis sie starben. Sie haben medizinische Experimente durchgeführt, und wenn ich die Entscheidung hätte, würde ich dich und alle deiner Art sterilisieren, zusammen mit dem abscheulichen Indianermiststück."* He gathered spit and blood, and spat on the ground.

"Smedley, balbhán?" asked Sullivan.

"Sir, what I got from his spittlebug translation was. 'At this very minute three German Jews, are fucking your wife. Also, nigger monkey boy, my father was in South-West Africa in the Herero campaign from 1904 to 1908, and we would put black sub-humans like you in concentration camps to be used as slave labor until you die. They performed medical experiments, and if I had my way, I would sterilize you and all your kind, along with the hideous woman aborigine bitch.'"

Lieut. Washington immediately stood and drew his French issued Mle 1892 pistol, and proceeded to shoot the German in the kneecap. He pistol whipped the side of the German's head. As the German lay on the ground writhing in immense pain, a boot to the jaw from Washington rendered the German unconscious.

Doc said with a slightly ornery grin, "Whoa. Sir, I wasn't done with his ankle."

Sullivan whispered to Washington as he was holstering his pistol, "I thought you were a psychologist?"

"I thought so, too," replied Washington, as he removed his glasses and calmly wiped them with his handkerchief.

"Doc, Darlin," said Sullivan, "You better check out the toothless wonder. Seems like he fell," ordered Sullivan, winking a green eye at Doc with a little head nod in the German's direction.

"Well Lieut. Washington, you blew off his patella, thus, the sesamoid bone is ripped from the patella ligament, and got some muscle, too. Also looks like Jerk Weed lost a couple of back teeth," stated Doc.

"Doc," said Wilson "Explain that for the sick, lame, and lazy, dumb, fucked-up, and crazy," jabbered Wilson.

"What this means, his kneecap is hanging by the skin and ligament," said Doc, adding, "Mikey, you don't want this," Doc said as he threw the kneecap at Wilson.

"Will balbhán be able to walk?" asked Sullivan.

"I found some first-aid supplies, a couple pair of crutches, and some stretchers in one of the bunkers. I'll revive him and patch him up. I'll put a splint on so he can walk with the crutches," stated Doc. "Come on douche bag, wake up!" he said as he kicked the German in the foot.

"Smedley," said Sullivan. "Balbhán means dummy," he explained, laughing.

"Hey, Tommy," Wilson said as he approached Thug in the trench. "First of all, Spittle's the Dumb Fuck wants Lieut. Washington to clean their trench. Then Numb Nuts over there wants your Dad to dance for them. I've seen your Dad dance. He has stomped on more toes than a French feller squishing grapes," he said as he and Thug nodded yes to each other.

"Crow, 3 inches of Achilles tendon is gone on this one, and Spittles is missing two front teeth, a kneecap, and I also noticed he has a cracked maxilla between the teeth he lost when he got the boot across the jaw," said Doc. "Say Crow"?

"Yes, Doc."

"The cuts on those tendons, look straight, like they have been cut by wire cutters," said Doc.

"Will these arseholes be fine for the negotiations later?" asked Sullivan.

"Yes Sir, they will," replied Doc.

"Mr. O'Keefe?"

"Yes, Crow?"

"Put the dirty sock, back in his mouth, and also, who the hell is Max?" said Sullivan.

"Maxilla is the upper jaw," replied Doc as he put bandages around and up and down on the German's head, stopping the bleeding. Then he bandaged the knee first, put splints on, and secured them in place with bandages. He gave both Germans a pair of crutches.

"John," said Sullivan. "Where is it?"

"Where is what?" replied Ugh, as Sullivan looked right at him.

"The piece of tendon, me boyo," said Sullivan.

"I cannot tell a lie," said Ugh. "The butler did it. That is my report and I'm sticking to it, Sir," said Ugh, as he puffed his chest out and looked proudly at Sullivan.

"Hmm, no butler is here with us," replied Sullivan, looking around.

"Well, I'm still sticking to my report," said Ugh with a shit-eating grin on his face. "I suppose fuckhead wants it back," he quipped.

"What in tarnation did you plan on doing with it?" asked Sullivan.

"I decided at the last second not to shove that tendon up his ass. But I am going to wear it around my neck," said Ugh with the cat-ate-the-canary look. He added, "I'll wear it so that I won't tendonot to forget things. Then I almost forgot you wanted prisoners, so I brought you an early Christmas present."

Ugh looked at the prisoner and said, "Taama anaa Fuckface?"

Thug looked at Smedley, "Means teeth ouch Fuckface?" said Thug as he pointed to his own teeth.

"Delay that a second," said Sullivan. "Again, Smedley, ask him his name."

Ugh laughed with a cynical grin and said, "Don't forget to ask him, if his teeth ouch."

Smedley removed the sock from his mouth and asked, "*Wie heisst du, und auch wie fühlen sich deine beiden Vorderzähne?*" said Smedley explaining to Sullivan, "I just asked him, 'What's your name, and how do your two front teeth feel?'"

The German prisoner replied very slowly and deliberately through his lateral lisp, "*Du Dorftrottel, was denkst du, wie es sich anfühlt, wenn eine wilde Squaw auf deine beiden Vorderzähne mit einem Steinbeil haut und sie dann mit einem Messer rausgräbt?*" as he winced in pain, wiping away spittle and blood from his mouth.

"Lieut. Sullivan?"

"Yes? Smedley," Sullivan chuckled.

Smedley translated, "You village idiot, how do you think it would feel to have that savage squaw bitch take a stone hatchet to your two front teeth, and then dig them out with a knife?"

Wilson said to Thug, "Little does that Hun know that Cpl. Smedley is an 11th grade English teacher, not the village idiot." Wilson and Thug shook their heads in agreement.

"Shea, Sgt. Jefferson, and Smedley, I want to talk to you over here for a few minutes please," said Sullivan. "Smedley write this down. It's long. So, bear with me."

"To the Observation Officer: By the time you have read this, we will be securely in the middle trench and trees. Cease-and-desist 6 am rolling barrage. Two scouts report hearing horses, metal clanging of artillery between the road and River Meuse. Grid map 028/226 is my best estimate. Going to try a stratagem on the artillery. You will know when it happens. Need French 75s to shell trench line of third trench and trees East of our position. Germans spotted in grove of trees. Look for smoke and dirt plumes of the stokes mortar. There is a man-made bunker, middle part of third grove of trees nearest back. Believe General is in bunker with known trollop. Have the Bats observe and strafe any enemy infantry personnel in shell craters.

Lieut. Sullivan, Charlie Company, the 69th Irish Brigade, 42nd Division."

Smedley wrote feverishly, trying to keep up. He finished writing, and read it back to Sullivan.

"Right Smedley. Get that off quick with your fastest chicken hawk, me boyo," ordered Sullivan.

CHAPTER 7

"B-Battery Sgt. Smith," a deep voice answered the phone

"This is Col. Aloysius Finn Gilhooly, Esq.," he explained to the voice on the phone. "I hear you loud and clear. And I can see you with me one good, clear eye," he said as he ran his hand through his reddish-grayhair, and adjusted the black patch covering his right eye. His one bright green eye surveyed the battlefield. "I need to talk to Capt. Martin, right now."

Smith handed the phone to Martin and said, "It's the Colonel, Sir."

"Tell me Capt. Martin, is the fire control up," Col. Gilhooly said, with his distinct Irish brogue.

"Yes Sir. We have our tables with maps, fire and plotting charts, and aiming circles are good to go," said Martin adding. "We have our commander's telescope up and our rangefinders."

"Capt. Martin," said Gilhooly. "Make sure you cover up all maps and charges. We can't afford to have any short rounds on this mission."

"Sir, got a second pigeon from the 42nd. A message just for you, Sir," said Martin, his salt and pepper hair and brown eyes might have been more suited for the silver screen than the battlefield.

"What do you have, me boyo? Go ahead and read it, Kentucky," said Gilhooly.

"Sir, the message states:

Aloysius, this is your cousin, Clancy. Me arse is here, too; but I don't care about that. What I do care about, is that me arse is sitting on a case of Bush Mills whiskey. Cousin, make the Clans O'Rourke and Gilhooly proud, and shoot straight, accurate, and far," read Martin.

"And a follow-on message, Sir. It says,

P.S. Then there will be a nice bottle of this for you when this little boondoggle is over. Clancy," said Martin, as he folded the message and put it in his pocket.

Gilhooly mumbled, "Fuck me of all places. Me cousin is back. Nancy Clancy Clusterfuck O'Rourke, Esq., that's me typical cousin. He drinks your bottle first, then he'll expect you to go buy the next one. He's always been *greamastúil.*"

"Col., did you say something?" asked Martin.

"Yes, I said me cousin is tight-fisted," said Gilhooly shaking his head, adding, "When we were kids, we would go fishing, I stood on the opposite bank. Clusterfuck would walk to the other side, then belly flop in the Lake, which would create a large wall of water, just like a tidal wave. Thus, forcing the fish to me side of the bank. One or two minutes, we had our fill, me with my pail, him with his fat gullet. And Mr. Martin?"

"Yes Col.?"

"You've never been around me cousin. You're lucky. If you have to stand next to him, you're going to have to pull on your gas mask luath, that's speedy and quick, because of his arse breath, and the constant prattling with that man. He never, ever lets a man get a word in edgewise. He steals your breath away," explained Gilhooly.

***

Back in the trench, Sullivan was getting ready for the mission. "Lieut. Kirby, Sgt. Worth. You know your assignments. Hold down the right flank, you will have artillery, mortar support, and air support," said Sullivan.

"Lieut. Kirby?"

"Yes, Cpl. Smedley."

"Lieut. Kirby, I gave Privates Davis and Smith Jones a quick class on communications and they're good to go. I instructed them on how to set the wire and rig the phone for your operations," said Smedley.

Sullivan approached Forthright who was keeping an eye on the German prisoners, and asked "First Sgt. Forthright, do you have Schnickelfritz and Wienerschnitzel all dressed and gagged?"

"Just like you asked, boss," said Forthright.

"Yepper," confirmed Wilson.

"Me boyos, keep a close eye on these two Heinies. You'll be in charge of them until it's time for them to go and do their part of this mission. Get 'em up and goin'," Sullivan instructed.

"Lieut. Washington," said Sullivan. "Can I see you outside for one moment, please."

"Yes, Sir?" responded Washington. "How I can help you, Sir?"

"I was thinking… with signs of an armistice; this might be our last go around with the Germans. So, me and the boyos would be honored if you'd like to exchange those French Adrian helmets for American Brodies," said Sullivan. "When we go on this trench raid, we will all look like Americans, fight like Americans—and if the worst comes—die like Americans," said Sullivan in a commanding voice, extending his hand to Washington's hand.

"First Sgt. Forthright," Sullivan called into the bunker.

"Yes, Sir," replied Forthright.

"First Sgt. Forthright, please go to the bunker where our brothers are temporarily resting, and retrieve their brodies. God rest their souls, as these will be used for another good cause," said Sullivan.

"Sgt. Jefferson," said Washington. "Please go with the First Sergeant to get the American brodies. Leave the French pieces of shit here in the bunker. We're not going to need them anymore," said Washington.

"Lieut. Washington, me friends call me Crow," Sullivan said as he extended his hand to Washington.

"I have noticed that. They call me Gus," replied Washington back.

"Very good, Sir!" replied Sullivan. "So Gus, what kind of firepower are you carrying on your armored cars?" asked Sullivan.

"The French white ac model 1918. It has a six-cylinder gasoline motor; on the road she goes about 45 miles an hour. We carry five-man crews, including myself or a commander, the vehicle driver, one gunner, one loader, and a machine gunner," stated Washington. I am a psychologist by trade, not a mechanic or an engineer, so I asked them what was going on. Didn't say much then, but they came up to me five days later and told me they worked on the turret, making some modifications on it. They said something about sprockets, chains, and something about a non-synchronization transmission. They also hooked up some kind of a rod system that runs the carburetor, transmission, and then right through the cab. It's hooked up to a foot pedal, and is run by the gunner. Also, gunner runs the clutch and the gearshift of the vehicle," said Washington.

"No blarney? That's genius. American ingenuity at its best," Sullivan said, listening intently.

Washington continued, "Yes Sir, you are correct. Then when the gunner goes into drive, the turret turns to the right; when he goes in reverse, the gun turret turns to the left. Somehow it shifts out of that and drives down the road. Half that crap, I don't understand," said Washington. "The crew took out the 37 mm Puteaux gun that shot 10 to 15 rounds per minute, and mounted a Cannon the d'Infanterie de 37 modele 1916 trp. I think I'm pronouncing that right," said Washington, shaking his head. "This gun's faster and it will sustain a rate of 35 rounds per minute. That's all I really need to know."

"Sounds good. What else is on that vehicle, me good man?" Asked Sullivan.

"We also carry two Hotchkiss machine guns. SFC. Jefferson has trained the men well on a heated exchange with my lefties and my righties. That's what I call them. They can and have put up 40 rounds per minute," said Washington convincingly.

"What are lefties and righties?" inquired Sullivan.

"As you're sitting with the gun looking into no-man's land. The loader is on the right side of the gun, the gunner is on the left. They modified the floor by cutting a door in the floor. With the door raised up, the shell casing hits the backside of the door falling underneath the car," said Washington.

"Once the men get rolling, it's Katie bar the door. Before we came up here, we ran into some French tanks. They were more than happy to give us six cases of the 250-round belts for the Hotchkiss machine gun, and all the 37 mm rounds we could carry," said Washington.

"Thank you for that report. Designate one of your vehicles to support the left side of number two trench. According to our scouts, there's a few places they can hide," explained Sullivan.

"Yes Sir!" said Washington.

"Sgt. Williamson, take your crew and set up on the left side of the number two trench. I have been informed that you'll have places for cover and concealment. Have Pvt. Page drive, and get Cpl. Ford on the 37 mm. Private Bolt will be with me," ordered Washington.

"Yes Sir," said Sgt. Williamson.

"Lieut. Washington, I have my men on the machine gun crew. Cpl. O'Brien, and our own Pvt. Williamson, and Pvt. Wagoner will help support your vehicle on that left side," said Sullivan.

"Yes Sir," said Sgt. Williamson.

"Men, follow me," ordered Sullivan.

The men left the bunker in the third trench and quietly walked along the communications trench. Lieut. Kirby and Sgt. Worth made their way down the second trench to their assigned positions.

"First Sgt. Smedley and General Darlin', set up your communications at the second trench line. Do it well, boyos. This is it," said Sullivan in a loud whisper. "Shea, Sgt. Jeff, you two stay in step like you're dancing." Both men nodded yes.

"Sgt. Jeff, follow me," whispered Shea as they walked south a bit. "So, what did you do prior to the war," whispered Shea.

"I boxed, sir," whispered Jefferson in his low, commanding voice.

Sullivan continued his instructions, "Smedley, when I'm done with you, scamper back and get with the First Sergeant. John and Tom, you know what to do, me buckos. Go carry out your orders."

"Yes Lieut.," nodded Thug. The men crept closer to the third trench through the communications trench.

Sullivan whispered, "Alright boyos, here we are. Right here is where Capt. Bob Hill and Lieut. Arch were killed. God rest their souls. Looks like we'll have to go up top to get past this mess, but it's a hop, skip, and jump to get back into the trench."

Sullivan peered over the top of the trench slowly to see how far the blown out portion of the trench went out ahead of them. He came back down, and whispered, "So, we're going to have to move fast, me boyos. We'll move out one at a time. I'll lead. Any questions before we leave?"

"Crow?" whispered Wilson.

"Yes, Mr. Wilson," whispered Sullivan.

"I just took a shell crater bath and my hair is wet. If I don't have time to dry it, it'll frizz on me," joked Wilson.

"Mikey, me boyo, have blowhard Shea whisper sweet nothings at your hair. By the time we arrive, your Bijou Billboard hair will look and feel réal síodúi," whispered Sullivan, in a sardonic tone. "By the way, boyo, that means real silky."

Sullivan readied himself and hopped out. He ran along the trench line, right past the upper torso of Capt. Hill entangled in the barbed wire. His legs lay below him on the ground. Lieut. Arch's headless body was also enmeshed in the barbed wire, with his head at his feet. One by one, the men's faces expressed both anguish and anger as they passed the bodies of their fallen comrades.

"Crow, old boy, them Heinies musta moved that thar machine gun, 'cause we ain't gettin' the same greetin' as Capt. Hill did," Shea said, as Sullivan acknowledged his statement.

"We're coming up on a traverse," whispered Sullivan.

"Sgt. Jefferson, how good are with your rifle grenade?" whispered Shea.

"I haven't missed yet, Sir," whispered Jefferson.

"Please don't start now," mumbled Shea.

"Don't worry, Sir. I have two rounds loaded in my Tromblon cup," whispered Jefferson.

"Fuck," whispered Shea.

"What's the problem?" whispered Sullivan.

"I have to take a Mikey, and wipe my Wilson," whispered Shea.

"Blasted, Lieut.," whispered Sullivan, disgusted.

"I gotta take a number two," whispered Shea anxiously.

"You're full of blarney and bullshit," whispered Sullivan.

"Guilty. I am full of blarney, but I'm also full of real shit. I'm a gonna have the rizzling' shits. I really have to go, my bungster is so tight right now. The only thang holdin' that dike back, is the lice and them thar boll weevils. Somethang finally busted loose, Sir. When you got to go, you gotta go," whispered Shea louder.

"Decatur, you have two minutes. After that I'll come get you meself, and I will wipe your arse with me boot," whispered Sullivan.

"Crow, it's been about 4 days. Iffin I get hit now, I'm nothin but guts, blood, an old Shea shit. I don't want to go out with so much shit in me," whispered Shea, continuing, "Y'all boys will be the ones ahandlin' me, and you'll be covered in Shea shit," he snickered.

"Understood boyo," whispered Sullivan, adding. "Smedley you still with me, boyo?"

"Yes, sir," whispered Smedley in a meek voice.

"Does anybody have any paper?" whispered Lieut. Shea as he crawled along the line on his hands and knees again asking in a loud whisper. "Does anyone have any paper?"

"I do sir. I have this JC Penney catalog," whispered a private.

"Why thank you, Son. Ah, page 22. Pert near better than Uncle Billy Ray's silk from the corncobs. I'll bring this right back to you," whispered Shea.

"No sir, you go ahead and keep it," whispered the private.

"Do you have more for yourself?" asked Shea.

"No Sir, I do not," he said, "I just have that feeling. I'm not going to make this one, Sir," whispered the private.

Shea sat down next to the private, and said, "Peter is your first name, right? Peter Quinn," whispered Shea. "I understand what you're asayin', son. You're notta alone in this. It's natural to be ascared. I'm pert near scared shitless, too. That's why I gotta go to the crapper.

"Sir, is this for reading or for other purposes?" the private asked Shea.

"It's for both. Twenty-three and a half hours a day, you're areadin' the JC Penney catalog like it's a girlie magazine, and the other thirty, you're in a bloody mess. It's either kill or be killed. So, all I can do is tell you these few things," Shea continued. "Remember your security trainin', don't forget nothin'. Always move the furthest with the mostest. If there are obstacles, think on the run. You gotta get around 'em or defeat 'em; and once your objective is achieved, then we'll go back and get our buddies. We don't leave no one BE-HIND. But sometimes there are those cases, where you do have to leave 'em, 'cause a circumstances. But they'll be retrieved," whispered Shea. "So, don't worry about it, you never know when it's gonna happen; but you can always get back to them thar girlie magazines and idle chit-chat in between firefights."

∗∗∗

"Well, did you get your rumpus all nice and clean, then a nice wash of your wee hands," teased Sullivan with a little cynicism. "Tell me, or better yet, let me tell you a story. The lice jumped on the back of one of your boll weevils and then they jumped in a barrel and came out your Niagara Falls Arse. Then there were fireworks with lemonade, oatmeal raisin cookies, ice cream, and maybe one day seedless watermelon," whispered Sullivan. "Then the boll weevil-ridin' lice broke out of the barrel and stole a bottle of Bush Mills. They had a drink making their great escape. Then they had two more drinks and a military parade for themselves as they sashayed away laughing at Thee," whispered Sullivan, flipping Shea a little shit.

"No, but that paper did hurt pure-tee rough, ana kinda coarse. But, it pert near beat Uncle Billy Ray's silk from them corncobs," whispered Shea, snickering.

"You Darlin' boy," whispered Sullivan as he rolled his eyes. "I'm going to cry *crogall stróic* down my outstanding cheeks," whispered Sullivan, adding, "That means crocodile tears."

Shea got behind one of the German prisoners in tow, and whispered, "Jerry, an' I don't mean my fuckin' asshole brother," whispered Shea. "If you don't quit ashakin an' asquirmin, I'm gonna to stick my trench knife up your ass, or as the main man says, your arse."

"Okay, boyos. Now!" whispered Sullivan.

Shea and Jefferson pushed the injured Hun with the cut tendon out in front of them, at the same time Smedley yelled, *"Die Amerikaner laufen in eure Richtung. Tötet sie."*

At almost the same instant, a middle bunker door opened on the right side, just before the second right traverse. A German popped into the doorway and started shooting at a high rate of fire at the German prisoner dressed as an American. Another German appeared from a secret doorway in the left traverse with a flamethrower, hitting the igniter and shooting a stream of devil's spit right in the German's face. A high-pitched scream rose from the trench. Shea and Jefferson stepped to the left and expelled their ordnance. Shea unloaded half of his clip from the Browning automatic rifle center mass of the German's chest, blowing him to the back of the bunker.

Sgt. Jefferson expended his rifle grenades into the bunker. The ammunition in the bunker was hit, and the resulting explosion lifted

Shea and Jefferson off the ground, and hurled them back 8 to 10 feet. Shea flipped asshole over heels, and both men landed near the first traverse. Dirt, sandbags, pieces of lumber, splinters big and small, body parts in German uniforms, blood and guts were strewn about the middle of the trench.

"Sgt. Jeff, are you okay?" Shea asked as he wiped away the dirt from his face.

Sgt. Jefferson saw Shea's lips move, but could not hear his voice. "Sir, if you asked me if I was okay, then yes Sir, I am; but I can't hear too good," said Jefferson.

"Thata makes two of us," Shea said as he shook his head to clear his ears. "Hells bells. Lookie here," whispered Shea holding up part of the German's arm still holding his gun. "Sgt. Jeff, please help me get this Heinie off me. Oh shit! What's fuckin' left of him anyway?" whispered Shea to Jefferson as they pulled up the top half of a torso with his blue eyes still wide open from the shock.

"You boyos okay?" asked Sullivan.

"Yes, just like a couple of freshly cut hog oysters, beaten eggs, slapjacks, and freshly squeezed orange juice," whispered Shea.

"Must have been some stored-up ordnances," whispered Sgt. Jefferson.

"Crow, I got that fucker's fan-cee gun. I never done seen one like it in all my days," whispered Shea.

"Either have I," whispered Sullivan.

"What in the fuck did old Smedlee say?" whispered Shea.

"What? Oh he said, 'Americans running your way. Kill them.' We figured they'd shoot the first American uniform they saw. Poor son-of-a-bitch Heinie thought that his cut tendon was the worst thing that could happen to him. If he was a rabbit, he'd make a tasty

Hasenpfeffer, don't ya think, me boyos?" Sullivan snickered. "Plus, we don't want our precious Georgia peach and cream gettin' hurt so close to an armistice."

"Well ain't you kind. Don't let your alligator mouth overfill your tadpole arse," Shea chided back.

Sullivan looked around at the carnage they were in. He asked, "What about that fucker with the flamethrower, what's he doing."

"I'll crawl back around, an' take a gander. Iffin I don't get shot first," mumbled Shea, looking around the trench and spotting the German with the flamethrower. "Pretty sure he's dead Crow, but what a way to go, I do declare," whispered Shea. Sullivan crawled around to look. "He's got about a 2-foot splinter through his throat, a 3-foot piece that smacked his whack, an' he's about 2 -foot offin the ground, impaled to the door."

"Better him than me," whispered Sgt. Jefferson indignantly.

"Grab that flamethrower," whispered Sullivan quietly. "Watch out, boyo's, there's still a reception committee up this trench."

"Doc," whispered Crow. "Is everyone okay down the line?"

"NO!" Doc said, in a loud whisper.

"Why, what happened?" asked Sullivan grimly.

"It's Private Quinn, when that bunker blew, shrapnel come flying over this right traverse just missing Wallace's head. Quinn on the other hand has quite a large perforation in his chest; God rest his soul," whispered Doc.

"What hit him?" asked Sullivan.

"An unexploded mortar round pierced numbers five, six, and seven, left-side true ribs, piercing his sternum. Shattered the manubrium, corpus sterni, and xiphoid process, and it looks like a part of his heart was pierced, too," whispered Doc as he looked closer.

"Say Doc," whispered Wilson as he kicked his hat back and scratched his head. "All I understood, was something about a Man-bra, and what's the Ziphoid processing."

"So, Doc, for us nonmedical types, what happened to me boyo?" whispered Sullivan.

"The mortar round hit him square in the chest; in fact about 8 inches of the mortar are still sticking out of him," whispered Doc, adding. "If it had gone clean through him, a few more of us could be dead," whispered Doc.

"Fuck me!" whispered Shea to himself. He sat on the firestep in disbelief.

"I have the Bangalore," a voice came up from the rear.

Shea turned around and saw a young man carrying the Bangalore. Shea said, "Thanks y'all. I'm Lieut. Shea, executive officer. Thank you for volunteering. What's your name, Private?"

"I'm new to the unit Lieut.; name is South."

A muffled sound came from a distance.

"What is that noise I hear to our front?" asked Lieut. Washington.

"That's the same noise I heard earlier, Sir. Even after all this time shooting, I knew I heard something," whispered Wilson.

"Okay boyo's, anytime soon Ugh and Thug will get things going, and then we'll have a barnburner," said Sullivan. "Hey Smedley, me bucko?"

"Yes Sir?"

"Take the sock out of the German Boy Scout's mouth, boyo, and ask him what we're up against in this third trench? Also tell him if he does not talk, he'll get the same treatment as his Fried Wienerschnitzel buddy. Ask him his name," whispered Sullivan.

"*Was ist Ihr Name, was Rang sind Sie welche Einheit sind, Sie in welche Gefahren erwarten uns in diesem Graben.Und wenn, Sie nicht unsere Fragen du am Ende wie Ihr, fried Wienerschnitzel Freund beantworten,*" whispered Smedley to the German.

"Lieut. Sullivan, I asked him, 'What is your name, what rank are you, what unit are you in, what dangers await us in this trench.' Then I told him 'And if you don't answer our questions, you'll end up like your fried Wienerschnitzel friend.'" Smedley got a nod of appreciation from Sullivan.

The German remained silent glaring at Smedley.

"Cpl. Smedley ask the Hun what his name is again," whispered Sullivan.

"Wie heisst du?' asked Smedley forcefully.

The German in a Stentorian lisping voice punctuated, "*Ich bin Private Stephan Herzog Wettin. Ich bin mit dem dritten Infanteriebataillon, Lear Regiment,*" spattered and bellowed the German.

Shea slammed his helmet right on the bridge of the nose, a gush of blood came from the German's nose. "Decatur, I think you broke his nose," whispered Sullivan.

"He needs to be awhisperin'," said Shea in a growled whisper. "Smedlee! Tell rat dick, down here in the trenches that we whisper. Smedlee whata did the cow feller beller?"

"He said, 'I am Private Stephan Herzog Wettin, I'm with the 3rd Infantry Battalion, Lear Regiment,'" reported Smedley.

In a slow, concise voice, the German expressed to Smedley, "*Greift den dritten Graben mit euren 45s und aufgesetztem Optimismus an, und da ihr alle sterben werdet, würde ich zu der östlichen Baumgrenze hinschauen, wo wir unsere Soldaten mit Maschinengewehren,*"

Granaten und Artillerie in den Schützengräben haben, sowie Flugzeuge am Himmel." As the German spoke, he lisped a mist of blood pulsing from his mouth. Again, Smedley backed away.

"Smedley, me boyo, what did the arsehole say?" asked Sullivan.

"Sir, his bullpoopy translates to, "Assault the third trench with your 45s and false bravado. And since you all are going to die, I would look to the East tree line where we have our soldiers in the trenches with machine guns, flamethrowers, mortars, artillery, land ships tanks, with aeroplanes in the sky."

"Does this mean…" Sullivan began.

"Tanks," finished Washington.

"I would eat my Brodie if there was one tank in them thar woods or two in that trench line," whispered Sullivan. "Smedley, ask the Hun about that fancy weapon."

"I'll be real in-te-rested in thata one, too. Just like a gator aviolatin' a deer takin' a mornin' drink at the waterin' hole," emphasized Shea.

"Welche Informationen kannst du mir über diese Waffe geben," whispered Smedley. "Sir, I said, 'What information can you tell me about this weapon?'"

The German whispered incoherent sentences, drooling blood, *"Da ihr sowieso sterben werdet, werde ich euch etwas über dieser Waffe erzählen. Sie ist ein MP 18.1, sie feuert 9 mm Parabellum, basierend auf einen Rückstoß Ladesystem, mit vollautomatischer Schussfolge von 400 bis 500 Umdrehungen pro Minute, mit einer 32ger Magazinfüllung, mit einer Gesamtlänge von 81 cm und einem Gewicht von kaum mehr als 9 Pfund. Also, wie Sie sehen, meine Herren, sie ist leichter und schneller, und mit dieser Waffe werden wir das Blatt des Krieges wenden,"* spittled the German.

"Lieut. Sullivan," whispered Smedley. "This is his translation. 'Since you are going to die, I will tell you about that weapon. It is an MP 18.1. It fires a 9 mm Parabellum round, and it runs off an open-bolt blowback system with full-automatic rate of fire 400 to 500 rounds per minute, with a 32-round snail-drum magazine. Overall length is 32 inches, weight is a little over 9 pounds.'" Smedley continued, "Then he says, 'So as you can see gentlemen: it is lighter, faster, and with this weapon we shall turn the tide of war.'"

Then Shea whispered to Sullivan, "Well put me on a drum and snail-fuck me. That thang was barking out bullets like old Jezebel, hot on the trail of a razorback!"

"*Er sagte, dieses MP 18.1 wird den Krieg gewinnen,*" slathered the German.

"He said this MP 18.1 will win the war," whispered Smedley.

"*Wir werden zurückkehren. Unsere Sturmtruppen werden diese Schutzengräben erstürmen,*" lisped the German, showing his growing agitation.

"Lieut. Sullivan, he said, 'We will be back! Our stormtroopers will clear the trenches,'" Smedley explained.

Smedley pulled out his handkerchief and slowly cleaned off his spectacles, thinking.

Shea whispered to Sullivan, "Say there old boy. Iffin one gun can do all that, just think iffin you turned loose a whole company in them thar trenches." He shook his head at the possibility, and continued, "Look at our Browning Automatic Weapon. It is about 7 pounds heavier, and 15-inches longer. Plus, they have somethin' called the snail-drum magazine that holds 32 rounds with a quick reload. We have a 20-round box magazine for the BAR, but we fire the 7.62 compared to their 9 mm. There's one drum in the MP 18.1 , and the dearly de-parted was atotin', four more drums with that little extra fire power. We might be able to cut them thar odds down. This thang shouldn't be too hard afigurin' out."

"Boyo, I understand what you're saying, it could indeed turn the tide of war," whispered Sullivan. Then he turned and addressed two men, "Privates Jackson and Lufton, if you could, please do some babaí suí on our toothless princess. Keep him company for right now, boyos. I will call for the three of you to come up later."

"Roger that, sir," whispered the Privates.

Sullivan added, "In the old tongue that meant babysitting. And boyos if he drools wrong, put a bullet in his head."

CHAPTER 8

"Col. Gilhooly? How do you hear me?"

"Yes, Capt. Martin. Roger," answering into his radio phone.

"We are picking up broken voice transmission. Sir, do you have your radio turned up?" asked Martin.

"Roger," said Gilhooly.

"Squelch Col. Squelch ho squelch, oly squelch, squelch, squelch, motherfucking radio," said the pilot as he chewed on a fat cigar.

"Col. Gilhooly, do you understand and receive?"

"Yes, Martin,"

"That transmission is coming in south by southwest, Sir," said Martin, adding, "I think it's the 185 Night Fighter Squadron, the Bats."

"Gil squelch hooly Col squelch dammit. This is Lieut. Wild Bill Kel squelch. Are squelch you squelch my trans squelch?" His white scarf blew into his face in the open cockpit. Taking the scarf in his fist, he cleared the mist from his goggles while puffing on his cigar.

Gilhooly took a moment to decipher his frustration, and spoke into his radiophone, "This is Col. Gilhooly. Use proper voice radio propagation and proper radio receiving propagation."

The pilot smashed the phone against the radio and muttered to himself, "I need communications not a fucking thesaurus class. Cocksucker, just as I thought. Built by American Telephone and Telegraph Company. What a piece of shit." Wild Bill chomped harder on his cigar as he signaled by hand to the dingbat to his right. That pilot passed it on to Vampire Bat to his right, Batshit. Wild Bill then signaled to the dingbat to his left, and they passed it on to Bulldog Bat. The signal they passed on to each other indicated that all was not well. All pilots gave thumbs up.

"Wild Bill. This is Col. Gilhooly; this is Col. Gilhooly. How are you hearing me now?" asked Col. Gilhooly.

"This is Wild Bill squelch, you squelch, hear squelch, communications squelch, not squelch, read squelch, communications, I am a little above squelch, level about squelch, minutes out squelch. Shit! squelch." The transmission faded away.

"The name is Col. Aloysius Finn Gilhooly, Esq. How do you hear me now?" he said with a stern voice.

***

"Doc?"

"Yeah, Mike?"

"Do you hear that to the northeast?"

"I hear something," whispered Doc.

"Lieut. Sullivan? Private Lincoln just brought this in, Sir."

"Smedley, go ahead and read it," whispered Sullivan.

"It's from the Commander. Military Intelligence," Smedley paused as everyone had a muffled chuckle. "It has been reported that Germans have invented an automatic pistol, called the MP 18.1, with a 32-round magazine called the snail drum. They said to be on the lookout for it. Also, reason to believe captured British Mark IV tanks north of your position. Intel also reports that Jasta 72 is coming in from Northwest to Southeast, and Jasta 73 is coming in from Southwest to Northeast."

"What's a Jaster 72?" asked Wilson.

"That would be a fighter squadron, coming our way," whispered Smedley with trepidation.

"They are also flying in this foggy shit?" asked Doc.

Tell me, me bucko, something I don't fucking know, whispered Sullivan to himself. "*Siúd tá a ciceáil sa na Cadairne.*"

"Say again?" asked Doc.

"It means quite simply, that's a kick in the scrotum,. By all that's holy, we're having a festival, a fine festival, there'll be a grand social gathering, high society right in the middle of no man's land, by Saint Michael," Sullivan said as he looked to the heavens. "I'll bring a dessert—exquisite Chocolate Tally-Ho ice cream sundaes for all," whispered Sullivan angrily. "I will shove those sundaes up me arse to keep them good and cold, then the Germans can come over and pull my pecker, and I will yell Tally-HoHo! Then all the Huns can eat shit and…"

"Say Crow," interrupted Wilson. "After you eat your big piece of shit chocolate Tally-Ho Sundae concoction, then take a big bite of your Brodie helmet, but don't get upset if I don't take a bite. I'm still a little full of hardtack and last night's rat," whispered Wilson.

"What in the fuck you are talking about Mikey, me boyo?" inquired Sullivan.

"You said that you would eat your Brodie if there are no tanks. Not only is there one tank," Wilson put up his middle finger slowly like a cameraman taking film, and continued, "But there are two tanks," as he slowly cranked his index finger up.

"Boyo, you're a good man to have around in a brawl," whispered Sullivan, cracking a little smile.

"I won the pool!" whispered Wilson.

"What pool?" asked Sullivan.

"That you would be wrong about something," whispered Wilson, laughing.

"Mr. Wilson…?" whispered Sullivan.

***

"Are you about ready, old man?" whispered Thug.

"Son, on my worst day and Shea's boll weevil stuck up my ass, I could still outdo you," said Ugh. "Are you ready, son?"

I think I just asked you that two seconds ago," repeated Thug.

"Then light it up and let's get the hell outta here, *kwita maropona*," chided Ugh.

"Pops. I love when you call me dung beetle."

***

"Squelch Gil squelch Col. squelch. I need this shit like I need another hole in my fucking head," said Wild Bill wiping his goggles off with his scarf again. "Col. squelch you squelch dic squelch, do you squelch. Shit! squelch," transmitted Wild Bill.

Suddenly, the morning darkness was illuminated, followed by six large booms from cannons that had just hit the first trench line. The large rounds made a howling sound as they seared through the air sending massive plumes of dirt, followed by a hail of branches, wooden beams, corrugated steel, and bodies.

***

The radio came to life in a field south of the trenches. "Martin, this is Gilhooly. Fire mission, adjust fire. All right boyos, on the QuickTime; get me up there," commanded Gilhooly. The men steadied the ropes, and watched the winch pull Gilhooly up, ascending to the heavens.

"Martin to Gilhooly. Martin to Gilhooly. Come in Gilhooly. Range?" informed Martin.

"Gilhooly to Martin, Roger, Martin. My best estimate on range is 1900 yards, direction 45 degrees, five rounds recalibration. You may fire when ready," answered Gilhooly.

***

"Boyos, they took the bait. Good job boyos, they took the bait," whispered Sullivan to Ugh and Thug as they knelt down, huffing and puffing from running inside the trench.

"I hope that fire is big enough for you," whispered Thug.

"Crow, I heard the first three rounds coming from the northeast," whispered Wilson as he pointed. "But those other rounds came from that large grove of trees to the east."

***

"Col. squelch, you have new dic squelch, shit squelch."

Then silence.

"Col. Gilhooly," Martin called on the radio.

"Yes, Martin. I receive and understand."

"I think the Bats are trying to contact you. Did you hear them, Sir?" asked Martin.

"No, didn't hear a damn thing," replied Gilhooly in his deep Irish brogue.

In the distance, German artillery could be heard firing. Closer, the men heard the flash bang and felt the rumble of the earth as artillery blasted plumes of dirt.

"Lieut. Sullivan," said Washington.

"Yes, Mr. Washington."

"Sir, look to the northeast. See those five dots coming in low going into the soup? Now look a little to your right, due east. It looks like the other five aeroplanes are going to try to flank the Observation Balloon coming in from east to west," added Washington. "Bolt" whispered Washington.

"Yes Sir, you hightail your fanny pack back to the gun crews." whispered Washington. "You tell the boys; we have a new mission. Tell Sgt. Hawkins, Gathers, Smalls, Moffat, Sgt. Storms, and Privates Downs and the others," murmured Washington. "Lieut. Sullivan, I have an idea?"

"Lieut. Washington, Sir, at this moment my command is subordinate to yours. You know more about the workings, with your armored cars and troops than I do. Whatever it is, it sounds like a damn fine plan, carry on," whispered Sullivan.

"Bolt, you tell them to go back to the main road. There is a fork, stay left on that road. Follow along a slight elbow; then keep on that 'til you come to a left curve. You come upon a wooded area. Go halfway up, then take an immediate left off the road and into the woods. Keep going until you get to the highest point. Hide right there in the trees. The Jastas will fly right by," whispered Washington. "You'll support the Observation Balloon which will be to your right. Don't forget to tell the crew to lead for speed," whispered Washington. "Be careful. Tell your men Godspeed," whispered Washington, saluting Bolt.

Bolt returned the salute, turned, and hightailed down the trench to pass on the message and to perform their mission.

Washington pulled out his pocket watch and checked the time.

"Lieut. Washington," whispered Sullivan. "What is the meaning of 'lead for speed?'"

"When trying to hit a moving target, you do not want to point directly at the aeroplane in flight. You want to lead the fire out about 50 yards or more. You're used to shooting at a person. Aeroplanes are motorized crafts that do 80 to 100 mph at top speed," whispered Washington. "So, warfare is rapidly changing and for the worst, I'm afraid."

"I know one thing for a fact," added Washington. "I have a Private Smalls in my command, but his nickname is 37 mm."

"I don't quiet follow," whispered Sullivan.

"Sir, think of a 37 mm shell. Girth and length equals 1 pound of human anatomy—his penis."

"All that's holy," whispered Sullivan as Washington chuckled quietly.

"Sometime back, we were in the rear getting reconstituted and R&R after a week. The French called for a Short Arm inspection, since prostitution is legal behind the lines," Washington added chuckling. "The French doctor told them to drop their drawers. Small's monstrosity flopped out to the astonishment of all. The Doctor backpedaled, almost falling down. He yelled, 'tu Beaucoup!' Most all the officers started to draw their pistols. Men ran for their stacked weapons. The Sgt. of the Guard was almost called out. I looked at it, and said to myself. 'That some crazy shit!' Then I turned around and walked away laughing." whispered Washington, laughing hard as he wiped a tear from his eye. "So, I would hate to be the first female to quench his thirst."

"Holy Saint Michael," snickered Sullivan, as he looked to the heavens.

"Then at the other end of the spectrum, we have Sgt. Hawkins in the unit. They used to call him 10 mm. As you can see there's quite a discrepancy," snickered Washington. "So every once in a while Hawkins gets kind of ornery with Smalls. In my professional opinion, in Sgt. Hawkins case, it's just plain old jealousy. Rumor has it in the unit that the men have called Hawkins Sgt. Shrink. Better him than me, I guess. The men hung a nickname on me too, Capt. Psychologist."

***

"Martin. Come in Martin. Correction, right 200, add 400," said Gilhooly.

"Roger, Col."

"Martin. Look to the east on this side of the Meuse River. They're shooting their pom-poms and other anti-aircraft at the Hun squadron," said Gilhooly. "They said in earlier reports, they would move up some anti-aircraft, so that must be them," said Gilhooly.

***

"Lieut. Sullivan," whispered Lieut. Washington. "Over to the east. The anti-aircraft has gone up."

"Where is our flyboys? Sonofabitch. That's bullshit blarney," grumbled Sullivan.

"They must be in and out of the clouds," whispered Washington.

The crack of German artillery sizzled through the air, and more pieces of corrugated steel, barbed wire, and tree limbs were blown into the air from the first trench.

***

"Gilhooly to Martin. The 75s, two rounds fell short 200 yards, the third went left 200 yards. Gilhooly to Martin, the 75s only. Add 200, right 100," said Gilhooly.

Artillery pounded the earth as fire and smoke rose in the distance. Gilhooly fixed his spotting scope on the area where the artillery fire was coming from.

"Martin," said Gilhooly.

"Yes Sir."

"Put the 75s on their east battery. Martin, do you hear?"

"Roger, Col."

"The 155s. Add 1000 yards, and right 200 yards. Five rounds, recalibration," ordered Gilhooly. "It's getting tough to see up here," he snapped.

Respectful dins of cannonade were sent to the Germans. The 155s and the French 75s cut loose more of their ordnance. Rounds were spent on that misty morning, November 11, 1918.

"Holy shit. Anti-aircraft just took one down to the east. I can see the flames," whispered Wilson to Washington, handing him his binoculars.

"Let me look," whispered Lieut. Washington, as he lifted the binoculars to his eyes.

***

"Strike one up for the artillery, Sir. We got one of the German planes," reported Martin.

"I see nothin' but the ball of flame, boyo. Nor did I see any rounds land. Are you daft, man?" said Gilhooly.

"Col. Gilhooly. Come in, squelch Gilhooly. This is Wild Bill squelch."

"I hear you," said Gilhooly.

"Requesting new instructions squelch. Where do you want the squelch?" said Wild Bill. "Reports have Jasta 72 coming this way squelch," as his voice faded away.

**

"Gen. O'Rourke," whispered Forthright. "All the field phones are squared away. Acept'n when that old boy Smedley gets back, I'm agonna give him a ration a shit. This phone wire just fell down." whispered Forthright.

"Young Forthright," whispered O'Rourke.

"Yes Sir."

"I watched Smedley tie that off like a boy scout," whispered O'Rourke.

"Sir, are you athinkin' what I'm athinkin' is happ'nin?" whispered Forthright.

"Peckerhead Huns. They're in the trench somewhere," O'Rourke hissed. "Hunker down against the wall son, and get ready."

Four Huns entered the trench intersection. Forthright and O'Rourke made their play. O'Rourke to the right, Forthright to the left. One of three Germans coming at O'Rourke looked young, the other two were veterans of trench warfare. They came at him with spiked clubs and their entrenching tools. O'Rourke, promptly grabbed the youngest one, throwing him against the trench wall to shake him up. Then he pulled him back, using him as a shield. A Hun plunged his entrenching tool into his young comrade's neck and the other Hun swung a club, splitting the young man's head in two. O'Rourke grasped the handle of his tomahawk from his belt on the left side, and arched it across the eye socket of the second German. A spray of blood covered the trench wall.

O'Rourke threw the young German at the third Hun and in one swift motion, pulled the German's helmet back and crushed the back of his knee with his foot, forcing the German to his knees. O'Rourke pounded his neck with his tomahawk causing blood geysers to flow out of the huge gash. The General saw that Forthright had gained the upper hand over the other Hun, and was quickly and silently slitting his throat.

Suddenly, they both looked up and got a big surprise—a huge Germanic warrior was drawing a bead with the MP 18.1. They heard him shout, *"Ich werde euch beide töten, dann werde ich auf...."*

Out of the morning mist, the men heard the pound of footsteps running on the duckboards. Then, like a lion in the Serengeti, Cpl. Smedley pounced on the German's massive back, surprising him. Smedley pushed the Hun's head forward with his hand, and drove his Nahkampfmesser trench knife through the back of his neck and out the front of his throat. Smedley rode the large German down like a water buffalo, pulling the trench knife out, and raising it in victory. He looked at the blood dripping off the blade and asked, "Did I really fucking do that?"

"Yes, you did, boyo." General O'Rourke said as he grabbed Smedley's knife, wiped blood from the blade with his thumb, and smeared it across Smedley's forehead, saying, "You have just been indoctrinated."

"Is everybody alright?" whispered Forthright. Smedley and O'Rourke nodded yes.

"Smedley!" whispered Forthright, giving him a pat on the shoulder. "I knew you had it in you; you over-educated Bugeater."

"I don't think any more fucking Boche knuckleheads, are comin' this way. In that case we'll have a wee drink, maybe three, then a wee pee." He pulled out a flask from his trench coat, "I have one last Lonsdale Cigar. It might be named after some damn Englishman, but it's pure Cuban," O'Rourke whispered as he relieved himself on a dead German's boots.

O'Rourke leaned against the wall of the trench and took a drink from his flask. "This'd be an enjoyable time to fire up that little Darlin', as long as we cover our light," he whispered.

"Fuck, I still can't believe I did that? I guess when the crap hits the threshing machine, it's kill or be killed," whispered Smedley.

"Boyo, that is a different view on it," whispered O'Rourke. "By the way Smedley, what was that gibberish the German spewed just then?"

Smedley whispered as he wiped the blood off of his trench knife. "He said, 'I'm going to kill you both, then I'm going to lift...' whispered Smedley. "I don't know what the rest of that was gonna be, but I just figgered I'd stick my knife in the back of his neck."

"Take a big pull of that English whiskey there Smedley, me boyo," whispered O'Rourke.

He hesitated for a moment, but then took the flask and took a pull. "That shit is strong," Smedley said in a whispery cough

"Now boyo, I've got a good burn on the cigar," O'Rourke said as he passed the cigar to Smedley.

"Sir, I used to smoke a pipe a long time ago," whispered Smedley.

"Yes, yes, that's all blarney. But with this, you're a virgin. Let it pass over your palate like your blessed mother's cooking. Let the smoke trickle past your lungs, then gently exhale as if you are blowing off old dandelions," encouraged O'Rourke. "Smedley, me boyo, you go ahead and take a deep drag," he said as he passed the smoldering cigar to Smedley.

Smedley took the burning stogie between his fingers and put it to his mouth, inhaling deeply.

"The exhaling is pure ecstasy, like being with your favorite woman of ill repute on Easter Sunday," whispered O'Rourke. "Here you go son. Pull anchor on this English whiskey. Forthright, you in, me boyo?"

"Roger that," whispered Forthright, taking a long drink from the flask and wiping his mouth with the back of his bloody hand. He looked at Smedley for a moment and said, "Deadly Smedley. The mighty Bugeater."

"Here Deadly Smedley, take another drag a big old puff of that Cuban cigar," whispered O'Rourke.

"I, I, think I'm going to be ill," whispered Smedley as he began to turn green.

"There, Smedley Darlin', go around the corner," whispered O'Rourke. "There's nothing to be 'shamed about son, I puked my guts many a time on bad English whiskey." He looked at Forthright and winked his one good eye. As they heard more cannon volley in the distance.

***

"Squadron leader. This is Gilhooly. How is my transmission? Over."

"You have good propagation, Sir," said Wild Bill.

"Col. Gilhooly, do you hear me?" Martin broadcasted.

"Roger," Gilhooly answered.

"Look to your right, Sir," said Martin from his radio phone.

"I have them," Gilhooly said. Col. Gilhooly could see the Bat formation as he turned his head sharply to the right. As a squad of Bristols flew by, he could see the formation breaking up.

Wild Bill saw them, too. To signal his men, he circled his right hand over his head. He signaled to his two right wingmen pointing to the East trenches. They each gave him thumbs-up and broke formation. His next action was to circle his left hand, to go wide left.

The pilots gave thumbs up, and they broke formation left. Wild Bill was left alone to face the oncoming hunter squadron.

"Martin," said Gilhooly.

"Yes, sir," said Martin into the radio phone.

"All the Dingbats are here," said the Col.

Martin answered, "Sir, you're telling me. My ex-wives are here."

Gilhooly curiously looked at his radio phone and hung up, shaking his head, saying, "Speaking of dingbats..."

***

"Crow," whispered Wilson. "The aeroplanes are about ready to tangle assholes."

Multiple flashes and bangs came from a hidden East trench line of the Germans, and half of the third trench of the Germans exploding into gunfire, mortars, machine gun fire slamming into the right flank at the end of the number two trench line.

"Enougha that fucking whisperin'," said Sullivan. "They finally come to play."

"Holy shit!" said Washington, "Did you hear that?" Over half the heads were nodding yes.

"Fuck, that's the sound of the tanks we were talking about earlier. They are back behind the trench," said Washington. Filtering through the trees, the men could see and smell black smoke and the clanking tracks of a large metal beast.

"Lieut. Shea?" said Wilson. "I need you to come back here."

"Why? What's agoin' on," said Shea.

"The traverse across from the bunker that Sgt. Jefferson and you caved in. The traverse is false," said Wilson as he led Shea down the ladder.

"Hush my mouth. Whata you mean, false?" asked Shea.

"The boys were trying to find a place to hunker down while the arty was going back and forth. Hannon leaned up against the traverse and found a hidden hatch. Inside, they found a trap door that goes down 15 feet to a room about 20'x15'. The boys cleared it. The Germans have about 10 earthen sleeping bunks down below. The roof is held up by three 6"x6" beams," reported Wilson.

"Decatur,"

"Yes, Mikey," replied Shea.

"They fucked up," said Wilson.

"Why? Whata them thar low-down varmints done?" inquired Shea.

"Look below the three beams. See those earthen sleeping bunks? The Huns set two artillery rounds in each one," said Wilson.

"Ain't they stupid? Likin' bein' in the middle of the swamp, huntin' cottonmouths wearing a gas mask and buck-ass necked," said Shea shaking his head. Shea and Wilson climbed the ladder back out of the hidden bunker.

"Blasted!" said Sullivan back in the trench. "Washington, why do you think the tanks aren't moving?"

"Because they have all the time in the world," said Washington. "I don't know when they'll move, but they will. They'll either go to the right side of the second trench or swing this way. They only move three to four miles an hour, but they can go over just about anything if they have a fascine. With the downed trees and craters from the artillery, along with the experience of the driver, we might get a few extra minutes to deal with these tanks," said Washington.

***

"Hawk," said Storms

"Yeah, Stormy, are you up? We're up. Do we have a good field of fire?" asked Sgt. Hawkins.

"It's as good as were gonna get," replied Storms, as they assessed the wooded area.

In the distance, they could hear artillery pounding away.

"Bolt, what did Capt. Psychologist say when you were up front?" said Sgt. Hawkins.

"All I gathered was that we were going to have a large party with exquisite chocolate Tally-Ho Sundaes," said Bolt.

"So we're in for a hell of a fight," Storms said as he reached out his hand. "You must be Cpl. Smalls, or should I call you Cpl. 37 mm," smiled Storms.

"Yes, Sgt., both are true," said Smalls meekly.

"So, how did that nickname come about?" stated Storms.

"Short arm inspection," retorted Sgt. Hawkins, interrupting the conversation in an uncivil tone.

"All us boys are about the same, 'til he shows up," Hawk said as he looked at Private Smalls. "The Doctor says 'drop your drahs,' and an ABR jumps out."

"What's an ABR?" asked Smalls.

"Alabama Black Racer," snipped Hawk.

"But I'm from Michigan," stated Smalls timidly.

"All right Pvt. Bitch, so you have a Michigan Black Racer. It sprang out and every officer drew his weapon, the French Doctor ran away screaming, and yelling 'tu beaucoup,' and all the other men went for their weapons," embellished Hawkins. "Then Capt. Psychologist says that was some crazy shit, then turns away laughin.'"

Hawkins paused and glared at Smalls. "We looked at that thang and our dicks shrank, Stormy," said Hawkins.

"Yeah, I feel for ya, brother," said Storms

"You see that stupid look on his face. That's the same look he had when it lurched out of his drahs," said Hawkins. "Just like mine and yours. That thang spits," Hawk said as he shook his head back and forth. "I know what we'll do, Smalls," said Hawk. "We'll go see Capt. Psychologist, and get his permission to take you on your first trench raid. Once we get up to the trench, you and Big Bertha slip in. You come up to the first Hun you see, take your 37 mm dick well in your hand, and you tap his helmet," explained Hawkins. "When he turns around, you can bitch slap him on his chin three or four times with your 37 mm Big Bertha," squawked Hawk.

"If I had to do that, I would," said Smalls, feeling bullied.

Then in a mocking way like a jealous sibling, Hawk said, "If I had to do that, wah, wah, wah."

"Oh, and Smalls, let me ask you a personal question," said Sgt. Storms.

"How big, right? All the boys agreed over 11 inches, and 1 pound," Hawkins answered Stormy's question. "Bigger than the weight, inches, and girth, of the 37 mm round," riposted Hawk. "Yeah, but I bet you one weekend pass, that he has small balls. That's right motherfucker. Smalls balls. Big dick, small balls," said Hawk.

"Are you married?" asked Storms.

"No," exclaimed Smalls. "I don't do too badly dating the female persuasion. I have four steady girlfriends."

"More like a herd of cows!" sniped Hawk.

"One more personal question. when you're about ready to jump the cooch," said Storms with the grin on his face, "Do you have to shoehorn the rest of that in?"

"Nope, not at all," punctuated Smalls, exposing himself in all his glory.

"I'll call the squad to help protect us," yelped Storms.

"I told you not to let that thing lurch out," shrieked Hawk.

Both men looked at Smalls who returned that deadpan look on his face.

***

"Calling Col. Gilhooly. Come in Col. Gilhooly. This is Wild Bill squelch...."

"I hear you Wild Bill."

"Col., squelch, we are now in attack squelch, squelch," said Wild Bill.

"Hey Willie of Jastas 72, go fuck yourself. I got your number pal. that's right baby right here," said Wild Bill to himself. He prepared himself to fight as two Medieval Knights—one Teutonic, the other one the American Doughboy—ready to joust. Both pilots pulled the handles of their deadly lances back as they readied their machine guns in the misty clouds on November 11, 1918, ready to clash over ideologies. Wild Bill cut loose his twin Lewis machine guns, missing to the right of the German's cockpit. The German pilot took evasive action, peeling hard to the right. With his wingmen tight in formation, Wild Bill followed suit, banking his aeroplane to the right.

"I got you fuckers. I'm taking you down, clown. Oh baby, I got your ass now," said Wild Bill. "That's right; a little to the left. Oh, yeah, center, right there sweetheart, right there," as Wild Bill ripped loose his twin Lewis machine guns, tearing up the lozenge camouflage and Iron Cross fuselage of the wingman, as sporadic hot shell casings hit Wild Bill.

"Col. Gilhooly, Sir," said Martin. "Are you hearing the transmission from the Wild Bill?" said Martin.

"Yes?" said Gilhooly.

"He's only transmitting, he can't hear us," said Martin.

"He has the floor show," grumbled Gilhooly.

Squelch. "Yeah, suck squelch, baby," Wild Bill yelled, while chirping away with his Lewis machine guns. Wild Bill bellowed at the German pilot, "Here, eat shit and die," as his tracers were wrecking into the wing of the Fokker D.VII. Wild Bill could see the German pilot's lips moving. He gave the counter salute of the squadron, "Come on slut, over to the right, that's it right, right, there baby, suck on this bitch," blurted Wild Bill as his machine guns tore into the motor. Oil spurted from the engine, causing billowing black smoke to engulf and blind the pilot.

"That's right fuck face, lick lead," blasted Wild Bill. The last burst from the guns took the German's head clean off, causing the plane to veer hard to the left, heading toward the earth and total destruction.

"Fuck yeah! Got me my first fried bun Hun!" yelped Wild Bill, as he watched his bird of prey go down in flames.

Wild Bill made a wide arc toward the trenches, as he pulled down the left and right Lewis guns, replacing the pan magazines.

***

"We downed one. Hey Crow," said Washington, adding, "The Germans are on the move."

"The tanks?" asked Sullivan.

"Yes," Washington replied.

Down low and at treetop level was the other part of enemy Jastas 72 squadron. Coming in one at a time, strafing the trench from east to west.

***

The German's spotted the Observation Balloon and made an arc to swing around from west to east.

Hawkins waited until they were almost in range. He repeated the rule to himself, lead for speed, lead for speed. "Fire," shouted Hawkins to the men around him. The 37 mms and the Hotchkiss machine gun opened up simultaneously.

"Motherfucker! I got your ass," said Sgt. Storms as he started to get the range on the right side of the Fokker aeroplane. The planes came in low between the armored cars and the observation balloon. The German Teutonic Knights were unaware that they were being fired on from armored cars. After two more adjusted rounds, Storms and Hawkins found the range and slammed into the aeroplane's motor. The fourth round minced the cockpit, instantly killing the pilot. The Huns' wingman saw what happened, and tried to increase the speed of his Fokker D.VII. But he was too late, three more well-placed rounds pulverized the fuselage behind the cockpit, peppering holes with Hotchkiss machine-gun fire. The Fokker split in two, as the dead pilot slid out of the cockpit backwards, doing cartwheels in midair.

"We got 'em," yelled Hawkins to Smalls.

"We got 'em," belted Storms to Bolt.

***

"Gus," said Sullivan

"Yes, Sir."

"So, what are we up against?" asked Sullivan.

"If it's a male tank, it will have two six-pound cannon; one in each sponson. They both have a 100° sweep of fire. There are three Lewis machine guns; one in the front, one in each of the two sponsons. The

Germans changed out the British machine guns for the MG08/15s as the tanks were moving. The female tank will probably have five machine guns, also the German MG08/15s once they are done," speculated Washington.

"Oh crap," said Doc, adding, "A tank just crossed the third trench, and it looks like they changed out one of their weapons."

"They did, how quaint?" said Washington.

"They must have built the tank bridge," said Sullivan.

"It's a flamethrower," said Doc, the tank came to a halt spewing flames 25 yards ahead.

"Crow."

"Yeah, Doc."

"What's our next move?" asked Doc.

"We keep to our plan. I'm going to take Lieut. Washington, John, Tom, the buck-toothed princess, and go get Smedley. Sgt. Lightfoot, in your estimation, how far do we have to navigate to our target?" asked Sullivan.

"There are two Sgt. Lightfoots. Which one are you talking to?" said Ugh.

"Talking to you, John," replied Sullivan.

"Then I would say as far as the Crow flies," said Lightfoot looking to the sky with a straight face.

"Funny, that's real funny, John, me boyo. I guess you're so funny you can carry the German Wex flamethrower," said Sullivan.

"Wait a minute. Give it to the kid, he needs the experience," said Ugh.

"No, I need a man of your experience," said Sullivan.

The air was pierced with the sound the motors of the Aeroplanes as the still mist surrounded them.

"Lieut. Sullivan,"

"Yeah, Thug."

"I'll go get Smedley and German jerk off," said Thug.

"Thank you, sir," said Sullivan.

"Tom," said Sullivan. "Tell Privates Jackson and Lofton to fall in with the rest of the boyos." Suddenly, German Fokker D.VII firing their Spandau MG08/15 kicked up large stringers of dirt, erupting around the top of the trench. Hot on their trail, shooting his tracers was Wild Bill. "Get down boys, here they come again," yelled Sullivan.

***

"Capt. Martin, Look to the east. One of the Heinie's guns just blew up for no apparent reason," said Gilhooly.

"Good," Martin said watching the smoke off in the distance.

***

"The tank is on the move, and it's getting much closer," said Doc. A large stream of flame belched from the right side six-pounder's barrel, scorching the side of the trench wall.

"Where have you two knuckleheads been?" snapped Sullivan as Wilson and Shea climbed out of the trapdoor.

"Down in a bunker," said Wilson.

"And what, by Saint Michael, were you doing down there?" asked Sullivan impatiently.

"I had an epiphany. I wired the Bangalore torpedoes and the sticks of dynamite to explode all the ordnance in that bunker. It's going to implode," said Wilson.

"Does implode mean fall in?" said Sullivan sarcastically.

"Why, yes it does, Great Swami," said Wilson.

"Then why in tarnation, didn't you just tell me that?" said Sullivan with a grin on his face. "So you're telling me you're ready to go?"

"We're good. We're going to try to lure the tank to drive over the bunker," said Wilson.

"How clever. A flamethrower running it out from the six pounders," mumbled Washington to himself.

"Capt. Washington. Look over there sir," said Jefferson. "They failed to put on a fascine. They don't even have their unditching beams on the tank," said Jefferson.

"Just like Lieut. Sullivan said. They built a little tank bridge over there," said Washington pointing to the northeast over a trenchline.

"Back up," ordered Sullivan. "I don't need any fried doughboys."

"Fuck!" yelled Shea. "We're needin' thata thar tank to come up next to the trench so we can get it over that traverse."

The sound of tracks clanking, metal hitting metal, came closer to the trench.

In a flash, Wilson jumped on the duckboard in the middle of the trench, yelling and jumping up and down. "I'm over here Dickless." As soon as the tank was within range, Wilson tossed his grenade hitting the tank and harmlessly exploding on the ground. Wilson quickly jumped out of the way of machine gun bullets sprayed his direction. A stream of flame followed.

"It worked, Sgt. First Class Dickless," shouted Shea as the tank pulled hard on the right track to get closer to the trench. More cannonade could be heard from the distance. The men could hear sporadic machine gun fire, rifle fire, and the thuds of mortars launching from the east where the Germans were, and landing near the American's side.

***

"Capt. Martin. Come in Martin."

"Roger, Col. Gilhooly. I hear you."

"Any luck?" asked Gilhooly.

"No sir, Wild Bill is still just transmitting.

"I love when Leprechauns fuck me in the arse early in the morn, before I've had me coffee," said the Col. under his breath as he watched the dogfight above, with the tracers sparking through the early clouds and mist on that November 11, morning, 1918.

Martin and Gilhooly could hear Wild Bill singing while he was trying to maneuver in behind one of the German planes, "Drain my barrel in old Christmas Carol. Deck my balls on good ole Holly, and her half-sister Dolly, for a little fo-lol-lol-lol-ly." Wild Bill yelped, "Finally, a fucking Fokker, you are filleted," as he cut loose with his twin Lewis machine guns. "Get over to the right, bitch. Now that's it baby, right there," as Wild Bill's machine guns cut through the camouflaged wings of the German Aeroplane.

***

"Sir, with all due respect, where the fuck are we going?" said Smedley.

"Deadly Smedley, do I smell a little alcohol, cigar smoke? The worm and world has turned for you, Professor?" Lieut. Washington asked as he looked at him with a smile.

A large stream of dragon fire spit up the trench, spreading out its reach. "Might want to stay away from the flame with that breath, Smedley," Washington said. "Shea and Wilson set an ambush for this tank that's heading our way. As soon as it is incapacitated, we go over the top."

"Excuse the fuck out of me, Sir," said Smedley, "But, who is going top and who is staying down?"

"It's not pretty. He was crawling on his stomach and it appeared that the round landed dead in his back, splitting him in two from the right shoulder down," reported Doc.

"Sgt. O'Keefe," Hannon said as he rose from the duckwalk.

"Yes. Hey Hannon, haven't seen you in a while. How's it goin?"

"I've never seen nothin' like that before," said Hannon pointing at Jackson's dismembered body.

"That's gonna burn in, son, but don't bury it," Doc consoled.

"Lieut. Shea," said Doc. "Come on over here. Jackson was crawling on the ground and the round hit him in the deltoids," said Doc as he pointed out the body parts naming them off. "Anterior deltoid, lateral deltoid, posterior deltoid, and it took out the left dorsal surface," said Doc. "Also, the rotator cuff, humerus, and scapula are completely gone."

"Woah, don't put no sugar in my grits," said Shea. "All I understood was toids, Doc. Tell me what y'all said, likin' an old bear shittin' in my house, son,"

Doc shook his head back and forth, and said, "For you hillbilly officer and gentlemen types who give preference to eating pickled pig's feet, mustard greens, bacon fat, and pecan pie, washing that down with a gallon of sweet tea."

"Yankee carpetbagger, that's pee-can, not pecahn," said Shea.

"Anyway, it hit him in the shoulder blades, splitting him in two, taking his arm with it," said Doc.

"I've had hemorrhoids. Got rid of them pretty quick due to having my asshole ate out by my favorite NCO. Can't say I ever had deltoids though. By the way, Shea, what was that thing they just fired at us?" asked Wilson.

"It's called a flamin' onion. It's a 37 mm Gatlin gun. Last time I was on leave, I ran into some British soldiers who have dealt with this flamin' onion. They have a German name for it, and I don't know how to pronounce it in German; but it means Light Spitter," said Shea.

"They make more of a mess when they're a spitter. I knew some gals from The Seven Sisters colleges back home, by the name of Swallow," said Wilson as he scratched his jaw.

***

"By Saint Michael," whispered Sullivan. "I can't believe that Needledick the Bug Fucker, made his hair-brained scheme work for all his blarney bullshit." Sullivan slid his Brodie helmet back, and scratched his head.

"Who," whispered Washington.

"Wilson," said Sullivan. "Wait, 'til the next time I see him."

The German-in-tow began lisping in a whiny whisper, "Mein Gott, was ist das für ein ranziger Geruch in diesem Bombentrichter?"

"Smedley. What did puss n' boots have to say?" whispered Washington.

"He said, 'My god, what is that rancid smell in this shell crater?'" whispered Smedley.

Fire increased from the German's east trench line to the right flank of the American's second trench line.

"Sir, I have to agree with peckerhead," whispered Smedley. "This place is ungodly."

"Damn it, Crow. You busted one off. Next time call for the mask," whispered Ugh.

"Crow" whispered Thug. "We have all told you to point that shit toward them; then the war would been over sooner."

"I have not known you boys long," whispered Washington. "But if you have been like this since 17, the Grim Reaper is gone to die in France of a most hideous death from some of the most righteous flatulence that one has ever smelled. You should be in our vehicles when one of the boys cuts loose," whispered Washington partially gagging.

"That was a blast from the past of bad wind in me. It was probably the bite of me Brodie and the rat," whispered Sullivan.

"Crow."

"Yes Lieut. Washington. I can't pull rank on you, but we need to get the hell out of here before we draw fire and we go up in flames with all that squeak gas trapped in this shell hole."

"I'm with Lieut. on this one," whispered Thug.

"Thanks Lightfoot. How did you get that MP 18.1 fancy weapon away from Mr. Shea?" asked Sullivan.

"Didn't want his bloomers around his ankles in the trench, being the first time, he would have used it. No way he had enough time working with it. Not like a good old shotgun," whispered Thug.

"Told him I'd like to give this thing a try. He said, 'be my guest.' So, I took it and the four drums, and thought it didn't look that hard to operate," said Thug, as he looked over the weapon.

***

"General O'Rourke, one of the Bats shook loose from his pursuer," Forthright reported. "Sir, he made a fancy move, now he is banking hard to the right. Looks like he's coming back at it again. He's made his correction and is coming in lower."

Tracers cut through the air and ripped through the back of the German aeroplane. The top wing split off in half and the plane went into a death dive with the pilot still in the cockpit. A burst of flames lit up the mist as the plane hit the farm pasture below on that chilly Monday morning, November 11, 1918.

"Holy shit. Batshit just made that piece of shit into a smaller piece of shit," said Forthright as a large cannon near the river blew into the air intermixed with wheel and carriage, German helmets, and half torsos in feldgrau uniforms.

"Alright me boyos, it's time to move," whispered Sullivan. "Ugh, how far do you think from here to that bunker."

"Well, a rough estimate from here to there is 355 feet. When you convert that into yards, that's 118 yards; but since we're in Europe, we have to go to meters for the conversion, which turns out to be 107.8992 meters from here to there, Crow. Of course, as the Crow flies," whispered Ugh with a deadpan look.

"By Saint Michael. That's a pretty precise measurement," Sullivan said as he turned to Thug, who was shaking his head back and forth and rolling his eyes.

"He can hear a snake piss," whispered Thug.

Ugh whispered, "You two are pia papi," as he twirled around his ear with his finger.

"Lieut. Sullivan, you and I just got complimented by my father. He says we're both mentally abnormal."

"It looks like it's just a hop, skip, and a jump," whispered Lieut. Washington.

Sullivan added in the old tongue, "*Mé stát seo fíoras abair aiféaltas siúd ta conas Roibeard Hill agus na sos de ceanncheathrún foireann Feoite bhi a preab, foléim, Agus léim.*"

"Old man, what are ya mumbling?" asked Ugh.

"I said I state this fact with regret. That is how Bob Hill and the rest of Headquarter staff perished was a hop, skip, and a jump," whispered Sullivan.

"Why, what happened?" asked Washington.

"Before you arrived, Lieut. Washington, we were talking about our losses. The facts were stated and those same words were used—a hop, skip, and a jump—next thing we know, we lost our Commander and Headquarter section, and I'm the new Commander," whispered Sullivan.

"I apologize, I did not know," whispered Washington.

"My good man, how were you to know? That being said, we are going by twos—myself and Lieut. Washington, Thug you take the arsehole with you," whispered Sullivan.

"What do you mean? I've carried my old man all day," whispered Thug, smirking.

"No, Lieut. Sullivan, I will drag fuckhead around," expressed Smedley.

"Good man, Smedley. Next, my two Darlin' sons, Ugh and Thug," whispered Sullivan as he looked at John and Tom.

"Thanks, Dad," whispered Thug.

"Alright boyos. Ugh and Thug, you go first, followed by Smedley and toothless wonder. Lieut. Washington and I will come out last," whispered Sullivan.

"Sgt. Lightfoot, how about you lead out this time. Age before beauty," said Thug to his father.

"Son, think about this. If I'm running with this flamethrower, and it gets shot, I'll go up in a ball of hellfire. Kid, you'll come out looking like a piece of overly done steak with your head on fire!" said

Ugh. "What would I tell your mother? You know how she loves your hair. So move out Sgt. Smartass."

The pair made their way out of the shell hole, trying to conceal their movements. The German right side of the trench came to life with machine-gun fire, catching Ugh and Thug a few yards from a shell crater. They scrambled to the ground, but, luckily to their fortune they were in a depression. As they crawled along on their bellies, the German 08/15 machine gun belched out a stream of white hot lead that raked the terra firma. The father and son felt the dirt hit their uniforms from head to foot, and just barely pelting the flamethrower.

"Are you ready kiddo?" yelled Ugh, adding, "They are gonna have to change their belt any second."

"I have to change my long johns," whispered Thug.

"Son, U kamakutu nu."

"I love you, too, Dad," replied Thug.

"As soon as he pauses, we move," stressed Ugh. Just then another Hun stood up, with the potato masher in his hand, and the machine-gun belt ran dry. Ugh grabs his son and they both dash for the shell crater.

"Noooo!" yelled Sullivan. The German's first grenade missed to the right as he raised his right arm ready to throw his second grenade. Suddenly, the German's chest, stomach, and back opened up like a crevasse and his inners spilled out onto the ground. From his shoulders up, his blonde hair tossed about his wide-open blue eyes, and lay five feet away from the rest of his body.

"You got the bastard. That was a nice shot Cpl.," yelled Private Pick, as the grenade rolled into the machine gun nest, detonating.

A fountain of metal and dirt spewed into the air, throwing the German on top of the nest with his lower right leg missing. He screeched, *"Sag meiner Frau und meinen Kindern, replied liebe sie,"* as he put the luger to his head. At the same moment, a 37mm opened up, piercing his chest with the precision of a surgeon, killing him instantly as his luger fell to the ground.

"Okay boyos, let's move. Hurry up and get in that crater." Sullivan leads his men to the crater and they jumped in to take cover. Ugh and Thug were in the crater. Sullivan said, "Let me look at the both of you. Are you two boyos hurt? What were you doing rolling around like Tweedledumb and Tweedledumber?" asked Sullivan as they crouched inside the shell crater.

"Lieut. Sullivan, the older Sgt. Lightfoot was informing me that the party of the first part was trying save me, the younger Sgt. Lightfoot. I was pointing out that I was saving his life, the older Sgt. Lightfoot, party of the second part," bullshitted Thug.

"Tsuni papi," mumbled Ugh.

"I'm not a bonehead," snickered Thug.

"Sergeants Dumbass Lightfoot! That's right, both of you look at me. You know, one of you has that blasted flamethrower on your back. Did you two knuckleheads think about that?" whispered Sullivan, looking from man to man, each staring back with puppy dog eyes. "I didn't think so. Lieut. Washington, where did that shot come from and who made that outstanding kill?"

"That would be Sgt. Deadeye Dick Williamson, Sir. He has made it his mission to turn that cannon into a sniper rifle. Somehow or another, Deadeye and his crew got their hands on a two-inch telescopic sight, Model 1906, and fitted it on the 37 mm. If there's a target of opportunity, Deadeye is going to have a kill shot," whispered a rather proud Lieut. Washington.

Sullivan leaned against the curve of the crater, and wondered, "Smedley, what did that Hun have to say before he met his maker?"

"He said, 'Tell my wife and children, I love them,'" whispered Smedley.

***

"Col. Gilhooly this is Martin over, can you see anything?"

"Only with me one good eye. I can hear the motors, but me one good eye see the tracers," said Gilhooly.

"Sir, did you say 'one good eye sees the tracers?'" joked Martin.

"No, you blithering idiot, it's not plural, I see the tracer with me one good eye," replied Gilhooly.

Suddenly, two Teutonic Germans Fokker D.VII aeroplanes came out of the mist. These large Warhorses were ready for battle. They started to spit out rounds at Gilhooly in the observation gondola. The Col. had a new dance card; he was doing an Irish jig in the gondola trying to avoid the rounds as they swooped by in an arc to the left.

Wild Bill, chirped over the radio, "There you are you fuckheads. I see your tracers!"

"Col. Gilhooly, do you hear me?" Martin hollered into his radio phone. "Are you okay, Sir?"

"Mr. Martin. I am so fucking euphoric! If you could please, get one of your men to tell the cooks that I'm gonna need a mug of scald. Then there's a wee bottle in me footlocker. I don't know how long I will be here," said Gilhooly.

The gunners had just set the round and powder bags on a 155 mm Howitzer carriage. In an enormous explosion, a German round found its mark precisely. The explosion sent wood and metal high into the air, punctuated by the shrill cries of men. Col. Gilhooly's head snapped to the right and down to see contorted torsos, arms, legs on fire, heads with their Brodies on flying through the air. Some of the gun crew had evaporated from view, leaving Col. Gilhooly feeling distraught that he could not come to the aid of his fellow soldiers.

***

"Gentlemen. Faller me! From this point forward, it's action of violence. So, let's move out smartly. In your case Mr. Wilson, just move out," said Shea.

"Lieut. Shea?"

"Yes, Wilson."

"Which one of us? There is Cpl. Willson, too, Sir."

"I think the right and left hog nuts just answered," said Shea, smirking.

CHAPTER 9

The American detachment started to move out of the trench. They could hear German ankle boots pounding the duckboard, heading right toward the Doughboys with the Germans suddenly quickening their pace. The Yankees and the Huns came face to face at the place where the dead German remained nailed on the doorway of the false traverse with large shards of wood.

Shea yelled, "Faller me!"

Jefferson joined Shea, followed by Wilson and Doc as they rounded the traverse. Everything went into slow-motion. On the duckboards, three mammoth Germanic warriors wearing ankle boots. This cold day, the German warriors wore the blouse of the Feldgrau uniform, with a large gray coat and a Stahlhelm helmet. The modern Germanic warrior in 1918 has razor-sharp entrenching tools, knobbed clubs, trench knives, rifles with bayonets, gas masks, bags of grenades, and the infamous Berserker attitude.

The battle began when a Heinie advanced on Shea with his ominous knobbed club raised high above his head, yelling, "Du stirbst, du verdammter Amerikane." The German repeated his threat in broken English, "You're going to die, you fucking American."

Thus began a clash as if they had stepped back into Gaul at the time of Caesar, 58BC, when warriors wore gamaschen and sandals, with wool trousers, animal skins, and knee-length tunics. They wore the awe-inspiring Suebian Knot atop their heads and slightly tilted to the right to appear taller and more menacing on the battlefield. A slaganz, or clubman, specifically chose a knobbed club and a shield for close combat. Other warriors were assigned specific weapons and tactics: spears, swords, or knives. All warriors carried a shield and the same Berserker attitude.

As the German fixed his gaze and swung his club directly at Shea's head, Shea raised his shotgun and fired two rounds at point blank range, blowing out the German's chest cavity, through the back of his coat and launched him five feet back.

Sgt. Jefferson, took on another hulking German in hand-to-hand combat. The two men exploded into each other as if they were in the great Rome Coliseum in the Gladiatorial games. But this time, on the duckboards of France, November 11, 1918. Sgt. Jefferson gained the advantage by getting his hands around the German's head and, in one fell swoop, snapped his neck. More Germans flowed into the trench and hit Jefferson square in the back, knocking him to his chest on the duckboard, as a Hun plunged a trench knife deep into Jefferson's shoulder, wedging between bones and muscle and remaining stuck in his flesh. Jefferson, quickly regained his footing and grabbed the Hun throwing him up against the trench wall, and swiftly hacking his entrenching tool deep into the right side of the Hun's neck. A geyser of blood soaked Jefferson as the Hun fell down, lifeless. The smell of excrement rising from his corpse.

Doc wrestled a wild-eyed Hun to the ground, yelling and cursing, "Die you fucking douchebag," as he thrusted his trench knife through the eye of the berserker, who released an ear-piercing scream as Doc pulled out his knife with the eyeball attached. Doc jabbed the knife with his eyeball still attached back into the eye socket a second time, forcing his blade deep into the man's brain until the screaming stopped. He reset the eyeball back in the socket and removed his blade.

Wilson yelled out, "Fuckheads, put up your Dukes. Here's mine," as he unloaded three rounds of his shotgun into the chest and ribs of two Huns. A third tried to grab the barrel, but Wilson was too quick, shoving it underneath his chin and pulling the trigger. A hole the size of an egg burst out the top of his helmet and as Wilson said, "Go fuck yourself douchebag, you just got hit by the Duke." Another Boche grabbed Wilson from behind. Wilson spun around, taking to the offense, with a hard butt stroke to the jawline of the precious private. The Hun hit the duckboard, then rolled up against the firestep. Wilson served him up the last two rounds to his chest and face, and yelled, "I'm, too young and pretty for this shit. Reloading."

Shea opened up with this Model 12 shotgun. Using slam fire in rapid succession, blood and brain matter hit the other engaged Americans and Germans, punctuating the violent clash of ideologies.

As Shea fell back, he yelled, "Shit fire! Loadin'! Keep amovin'!"

***

"Sgt. Worth."

"Yes Lieut. Kirby."

"How is our ammunition holding out?" asked Lieut. Kirby.

"We're holding our own sir, for now," yelling Sgt. Worth over the machine gun fire and mortars being fired at their location at the end of the second trench.

***

Pvt. Lofton was holding his own in the third trench until he grappled with a fierce German. Lofton made a fatal error by overextending himself. The German, seeing his opportunity, dragged his blade across Lofton's throat. Blood gushed onto the duckboard. The German laughed until Private South came up behind him, put his 45 to the back of his head and fired two shots. He watched brain matter hit the sandbags. "Laugh now, asshole."

Private Hannon yelled, "Watch out, Cpl. Wallace." A Germanic warrior raised his hobnail club to strike. Cpl. Wallace blocked the blow with his BAR, and quickly caught the German's jaw with the butt of his Browning, pushing the Hun back far enough to see Wallace squeeze a three-round burst in his chest.

"Fuck off, corpse," Wallace said as he spat on the German.

***

"Col. Gilhooly, how do you hear me?"

"Roger, Martin."

"Again, Sir, are you okay," said Martin with concern.

"Let's see, Captain. Me fucking gondola is shot-up, like the Swiss Guard shooting a gigolo trying to break in the Vatican nunnery. I can barely see out of me one good eye from the misty clouds, and I have a touch of the gout. Other than those, it's a grand morning. Top of the morn', me boyo. On top of that, I don't know where the fucking Germans are," clamored Gilhooly through his radio phone. "Remember, those Leprechauns I was telling you about?"

"Yes, Sir," said Martin.

"Now, they stuck a loaded shillelagh up me arse. And Martin, I'll bet ya one Sunday's Tithing, and I don't mean 10% of me own givin', I mean the whole congregation's offering," said Gilhooly.

In the distance, a tremendous ball of fire rose from the second trench, followed-up by earth-shattering sound of cannon shells hitting their mark.

***

"Meet your maker," Webb yelled as he let loose with his BAR to the stomach of an oncoming Hun.

The Hun remained standing and yelled, "*Mein Gott Ich bin tot*," as his lower intestine slid out onto the duckboard.

"Malfunction," yelled Cpl. Webb as he struggled to recharge his weapon.

Three Germans jumped 17-year-old Pvt. Foster, knocking him down and ripping off his helmet, and striking him with their entrenching tools and clubs. Cpl. Webb cleared his malfunction, and loaded a new magazine. Seeing that they'd pounded Foster's head into a grotto, Cpl. Webb started firing from the hip. He cut down two of the Germans with one burst. Pvt. Butler jumped on the back of the third Boche, pulling his helmet back, and plunging his knife into his throat. A large schism opened up as a massive fountain of pressurized blood spurted all over trench.

Shea, turned around, raised his shotgun and put two rounds of double-aught buck in the knees and legs of a couple of Germans, knocking them down on the duckboard. Sgt. Jefferson quickly jumped on one of the Germans, snapping his head back and piercing through his ear with his trench knife, killing him instantly. The volume of blood painted a grotesque abstract on the trench walls leaving a void where a German and American battled abound.

The melee between Germanic warriors and the Americans was getting more animated in the trenches. Sgt. Jefferson quickly grabbed his 1911, and before he aimed his two rounds at a German's head, he heard the Hun yell, "Fick dich ins Knie, du Arschloch!"

Jefferson quickly glanced around to see that the Germans outnumbered the American doughboys, and pulled the trigger snapping the German's head back as the round exited his head and into the German behind him. "Two fat hogs for the price a one," Jefferson screamed.

Shea yelled, "Keep fuckin movin, men!" A German caught Shea on the back of the shoulder with a spiked club. Doc, Jefferson, and Wilson observed what happened to their friend, and immediately dropped their engagements and went on the offense. The German reared back to land the killing blow on Shea.

Wilson's well-aimed shot removed the hand and weapon from the body of Shea's adversary. Moving the gun slightly, the next shot removed the German's face, killing him instantly.

"Shea are you okay," said Doc, as they helped him to his feet.

"Feels like a gator jumped up and bit me," replied Shea.

Germanic warriors materialized out of the mist. Shea yelled, "Fall back."

"Get the fuck out of Dodge City, Kansas," yelled Wilson.

Privates Tierney and Lincoln were engaged in their own hand-to-hand battles. As they rolled around on the duckboard cussing at their German counterparts, the German who was fighting Tierney made a fatal mistake. Tierney grabbed him from behind and slit his throat. A blanket of warm blood covered the German's chest. Tierney turned to help Lincoln, and was greeted by three Germans who knocked Tierney down and ripped off his Brodie. The Germans beat Tierney to death with clubs and entrenching tools, screaming, and yelling.

Lincoln promised, "I'm going to kill you, motherfuckers."

Out of the corner of Lincoln's eye, three figures in Brodies ran behind the Germans. They immediately sprang into action to avenge the death of Tierney. General O'Rourke put his 45 single-action

Peacemaker behind the right ear of a German. O'Rourke discharged his weapon, as German's left eye and skull fragments scattered the side of the trench wall. Forthright grabbed the other Hun, shoving his 1911 in the middle of his back and pulling the trigger rapidly twice, killing him on the spot.

***

Webb and Reagan, kept a steady stream of fire with their BAR's.

"Ammo," yelled Webb.

Reagan shouted, "Ammo now!"

Lincoln kept up the supply of ammunition, with a belt strapped around his waist carrying the extra rounds. Lincoln crouched down beside the men, "Here's your ammo, men."

"The Germans are pulling back," yelled Doc to his unit.

"Good let's get reconstituted, and take astock a what we got," said Shea to his men as they fell back further in the trench.

Smart, Forthright, Wilson, and Doc yelled in unison, "Outgoing grenades," as they pulled the pen and heaved their grenades over the trench.

Three, two, one. The explosions catching the Germanic warriors flat-footed. Body parts flew up and over the top of the trench. High-pitched shrills of men being torn apart, yelling "die Mutter!"

"You're dead, mutter fuckers. Compliments from the fighting 69th," yelled Wilson.

"Lieut. Shea," said Lincoln solemnly. "Tierney's dead."

Shea nodded silently.

Cpl. Wallace rounded the corner to meet up with the men.

"Cpl. Wallace, where the fuck have you been," said Shea, in a pissed-off tone.

"Lieut. Shea," said O'Rourke.

"Yes, General," Shea answered.

"He might've saved your arse, boyo," said O'Rourke.

"Oh? And how is that, sir?" said Shea.

"Cpl. Wallace you go ahead and tell him," said the General.

"Lieut. Shea the BAR jammed. I tried to charge my weapon. So, I pulled back around where the tank fell in, I knelt down to clear my weapon, and I heard moans and groans, so I peeked down into the crater. The German tank crew and about 15 others were starting to tumble out of the tank. They packed them in tight. So, I hurried up and got my weapon cleared. I made a beeline to get the First Sgt and General O'Rourke. So, we dropped three grenades in and then I raked the area," explained Cpl. Wallace.

"We've been taking care of a passel of hostiles," said General O'Rourke.

"After this, we'll get our reports made out. I'll make sure this is ahighlighted like a momma hog with a brand new litter of piglets. That should aget you promoted to sergeant," said Shea.

"Thank you, sir," said Cpl. Wallace.

***

"The Boche will be licking their wounds for a few minutes," said Sgt. Jefferson in his low, commanding voice.

"Sgt. Jefferson, turn around here. It appears that you have been selected for a complimentary souvenir knife, with no purchase necessary. Compliments from Heinie the German. Con-cop-ulations," said Shea, as Doc extracted the trench knife from Sgt. Jefferson's right shoulder blade.

Doc said, "Take off your trenchcoat, Son, and let me have a look at that."

***

"Crow," said Ugh.

"Yes," replied Sullivan in a whisper.

"I feel it in my bones. Premonition, Intuition, Divination, and Prognostication," whispered Ugh. "See Crow. You're not the only Poosa, which means crazy, sonofabitch who knows big words around here," whispered Ugh with a shit-eatin' grin.

"So, tell me Sgt. Lightfoot, John, one each," whispered Sullivan. "What, by Saint Michael, are you talking about?"

"Crow, I don't think that General and his trollop are in that tank," whispered Washington. "Ugh, look how slow they're going. They're great at making shit, but they lack common sense."

"It's like fighting a forest fire with a bucket of water, like some people do," whispered Ugh.

"So, what you are saying, Tom?" whispered Sullivan.

"When we get done here, we split up. Me and yake petu, will take on the tank, and all you others check that concrete bunker," whispered Ugh.

"Thomas?" whispered Sullivan.

"Yes, Lieut. Sullivan, I'll take crying daughter with me," chuckled Ugh.

"Well, if you're going to put your two cents in, make sure they make sense and that makes sense," whispered Sullivan. "With that kind of forethought and planning, plus your determination, in about six or seven years, you'll get that extra stripe, Sgt. Lightfoot."

***

"Col. Gilhooly. Do you hear me?"

"Yes, Martin. Roger that."

"Can you see anything, Sir?"

"Again son, only with me one good eye," said Gilhooly.

"Sir, the men are worried about powder bags getting damp," said Martin.

"Mr. Martin," asked Gilhooly.

"Yes Col.," replied Martin.

"If me whale-arse cousin was over here, he could take care that problem," said Gilhooly. Following with his old Irish tongue, puball agus scáthbhrat.

"Sir," said Martin, looking at his radio phone with eyebrows raised.

"What I said young man was, tent and awning. In his youth, my fat-arse cousin had to have his clothes made at Dennis's Tent and Awning. If we had his uniform, it could cover all the powder bags of your battery and this Observation Balloon. As an added bonus, we'd have enough tent and awning to do a three-ring circus, and we would all be dry," added Gilhooly. "On top of all that malarkey, if me fat-arse cousin, was to stand in this gondola, the gondola, support cables, and this Observation Balloon would throw out a high-pitched shrill in agony as it plunged to the earth landing, somewhere in China," said Gilhooly. "That shrill could be just as loud as the 1883 eruption of Krakatoa 1900 miles away."

"In Europe, they would not let him stay at a hostel," continued Gilhooly. "So, the plain fat fact was that they were afraid the foundation would crack and it would fall over, and his hideous looks would scare away other customers. He has layers of fat that he doesn't know exist, those layers of fat are around his head and neck area. Then my fat-headed cousin likes highlights of the fast life. Faster women and the fastest drinking—or is it the other way around? He has bought that gullet lock, stock, and barrel belly that leads right down to his fat-arse islands. You should try to feed him 300 pounds of fish at once—he is the original Great White Whale. You have heard of Jonah and the Whale? Well, me numbskull cousin, he swallowed the other whale and spat out Jonah. That man will never let you get a word in edge wise," said Gilhooly, panting.

After a moment of silence, the radio crackled, "Capt. Martin?"

"Yes, Col. Gilhooly?"

"Thank God, son, you never had to spend days with me cousin," said Gilhooly.

"Why is that sir?" asked Martin, waiting in anticipation.

"His breath, his body odor, lice—he even had them as a boy. His rancid feet. Just like bein' next to the seafood market at La Nueva Viga, Mexico City, or a good whorehouse," replied Gilhooly.

"Martin," said Gilhooly.

"Yes Col.?"

"Try to keep up a good rate fire, me boyo."

"Yes, sir," said Martin.

Col. Gilhooly put his spotting scope up to his good eye. He turned his head scanning a wide arc to the left, spotting two oncoming German Aeroplanes.

"Squelch, ov squelch er squelch, here squelch there. Over here, over there… there you are, you peckerhead, over there."

At the same time, Wild Bill spotted the Teutonic Knight, his adversary, coming out of the light, misty clouds.

"Get over bitch. That's it, right there," said Wild Bill, as he let loose a five-second burst. Then, click…click. "Fuck! Out of ammo," howled Wild Bill, as he banked hard to the right. "Fuck me, this is a sonofabitch, flying with your knees while changing pans out," said Wild Bill as he locked and loaded his Lewis machine guns.

"Col. Gilhooly, are you reading Wild Bill," asked Martin.

"Yes, Martin. He still can't hear us. I know what's going on because I heard his last transmission," said Gilhooly.

"Another thing sir. I would love to know where the rest of the Bat squadron is," said Martin.

***

"Sgt. Hawkins," said Smalls as he observed the sky.

"Yeah Small balls, big dick," quipped Sgt. Hawkins.

"Yeah, that's me. Look just a ways behind our guy. A Boche plane. I don't think Wild Bill sees him," said Smalls.

"Here he comes," hallooed Hawk. "Here he comes, fire!"

The Fokker came in behind Wild Bill, less than a hundred yards, Spandau machines gun blazing away. The first burst went through the lower right wing, tearing a quarter of the canvas off. Wild Bill made an evasive pitch to the left. Unknown to the Germans, 37 mm shells were being fired from the ground, just missing the undercarriage of the aeroplane.

"Sgt. Hawk, elevate a little bit more and lead him," said Smalls.

"Small ball's big dick, I got this handled," said Sgt. Hawkins arrogantly, as the Teutonic Knight made his arc and returned to his position behind Wild Bill. Hawk made his correction, and the first and second round tore into the engine block of the Fokker, sputtering to an abrupt halt, igniting in a large ball of flame. The third and fourth rounds followed immediately and hit right behind the cockpit. Flames engulfed the pilot, and the plane plunged into a death spiral. Wild Bill had been keeping his eye on the one German in front of him, and turned just in time to see the other Fokker burst into apocalyptic flames and descend to his death.

Wild Bill quickly fixed his attention to get another kill. "Don't try to speed away asshole! Holy shit, is that you, Willie? I see your squadron commander's flag, limp dick," said Wild Bill, as he let loose with this first burst, which hit the plane, but did no real damage.

"You motherfucker, stay still," yammered Wild Bill. He fired again as he crawled closer to Willie, who made an abrupt left turn.

"Oh, no ya don't. Willie, don't try to pull the old chandelle move on me, fuckhead," laughed Wild Bill. "I'm staying with you, Willie baby," clamored Wild Bill as his scarf fluttered in the wind, chomping his cigar.

***

"Martin, fuck the coffee, just get me that bottle up here. Put it in the bucket, me boyo," said Gilhooly.

"Why sir?" said Martin.

"Look to your right," said Gilhooly.

Martin looked to the right to see Willie trailed by Wild Bill. Wild Bill, was heard blurting over the radio, "Over here, over there, this yank is everywhere. Willie, you German dandy, here eat some of Uncle Sam's candy and nuts." Suddenly Wild Bill let loose his twin Lewis machine guns. Tracers were taking bits and pieces off the Fokker's canvas tail, and a sequence of bullets riddled the right horizontal stabilizer. Willie turned around holding a Lugar in his hand, and shot 3 to 4 times. The Hun hit the throttle like a man on his last mission, which made Wild Bill adjust his fire and flight, losing precious seconds.

Wild Bill yelled, "Slow down and save petrol, douche bag."

"Col. Sir. Willie is getting awfully close, sir," said Martin, this time with a little more urgency.

"I hear you, son," said Gilhooly, raising his spotting scope.

"Sir, we don't have enough time to cable you down." In a keen, clear voice, "Sir, I think it would be wise to parachute off the gondola now. Right now, Sir," said Martin.

"You don't worry about me, Son. Aloysius Finn Gilhooly, Esq. has never failed a mission," Gilhooly stated in a cold, calculated tone. He dropped the radio telephone on the gondola floor. "By Saint Michael, it's going to be a grand day," mumbled the Col. as he followed the flashes of Spandau machine gun tracers, and watched as ordnance slapped and clapped holes in the gondola. The torrid firing from Willie, the Teutonic Knight's Aeroplane stopped abruptly. Gilhooly observed that the pilot had jammed his machine gun.

"Jump! He's about 200 yards away," yelled Martin in his radio telephone, with no one on the other end to receive his transmission. Gilhooly nonchalantly picked up a weapon that was sitting in the corner of the gondola. Calmly unsheathing the weapon, and placing the empty sheath over his left shoulder. He could make out the Knight's facial features of anger and insanity, about to ram the gondola. Leaning hard forward out of the gondola toward the aeroplane, the Col. lifted his weapon, cocked the hammer back, aimed, discharged his weapon and yelled "Beirt madras comhrac thar a cnámh!" The gun recoiled, throwing Gilhooly into the badly damaged gondola wall, splitting it wide open. Gilhooly fell out of the gondola and quickly deployed his chute.

At almost the same moment, Wild Bill chirped, "I got your dumbass motherfucker!" He was about to unleash his twin Lewis when Willy's head exploded.

Wild Bill yelled, "Nooo, he's fucking mine." Fragments of skull, gray matter, and blood splattered on Wild Bill who was not protected from this stew. Willie, the headless Teutonic Knight and his great aerial steed collided and then pulverized what was left of the gondola. Immediately, the headless pilot and his crippled bird of prey fell hard to the right and descended, dragging the gondola in tow. As the aeroplane and gondola fell away, the Caquot observation balloon exploded into a massive, hot cloud of fire and sulfur.

Wild Bill banked sharp to the left narrowly avoiding the plane and the engulfed balloon cascading down to earth. He looked down through the drizzle and light fog to see the Colonel floating in his parachute, descending slowly to the ground. The Col. hit feet first, then his arse second, like a 200-pound sack of American Irish potato, head last.

Martin grabbed his bag and ran 20 yards across the damp, mushy ground, with the brown grass whipping at his legs and grabbing at his coat. "Colonel, are you okay?" he yelled as he approached.

"Yes, yes. I'm fine, boyo," replied Col. Gilhooly, lying flat on his back surrounded by a tangle of risers, strings and chute. "I've fallen harder off me horse in battle. If you don't mind boyo, could you pull the leaded shillelagh, out of me arse? Oh, and did you happen to bring that bottle, me good man?"

"Why yes, I did," replied Martin, pulling a bottle out of his bag and handing it to the Colonel.

"By Saint Michael," looking to heaven, "That's the last time I put me arse in a bloody observation balloon," said Gilhooly pitching back a drink.

"How many missions does that make for you in a balloon, Sir?" said Martin.

"That was me first and me last time, as it was with that Suntasach parachute jump," replied Gilhooly, adding, "That means remarkable, 'cause I came over from the cavalry." He took a pull from his bottle and swiped the back of his hand across his lips. Gilhooly swished the whiskey in his mouth and spit out a bloody tooth. A red stream of drool ran down his chin, and he continued, "Martin, there's another thing about me fathead cousin, too," said Gilhooly, catching Martin unaware. "He walks like a pigeon, but has two cow hooves for feet. Here you go, son, take a swipe of this," he said, handing Martin the bottle. Martin wiped the lip of the bottle and took a swig.

"So, every month on payday, he asked me—his cousin—to file down his two hind hooves, re-shoe him when needed, and run a curry comb through his head and tail. I tell him, 'Go fuck yourself, go see the blacksmith.' What a cheap bastard," said Gilhooly, shaking his head.

"I would tell him to open a bottle of beer between those fat arse island cheeks, and he says to me, he says, "I'll do it, by God." He did it. Then hands me my bottle. And furthermore, he is Fiarshúileach," said Gilhooly.

"Sir, didn't quite catch that last statement," said Martin.

"That's in the old tongue, me boyo. Me cousin was cross-eyed in his youth. And to look at him now," said Gilhooly. "Sé gabhs a láidir coimpléasc amharcag é."

"Sir," said Martin. staring at the ground.

"What I said, son, was, 'It takes a strong constitution to look at him,'" said Gilhooly, adding, "As a little Darlin' child, I was subjugated to little cross-eyed Clancy. So many hours in a day. And so many a sleepless nights. Plus being around him will make you lose cognitive academia." Gilhooly paused as he took a drink. He pulled out a pipe and pouch, and dug the pipe into the pouch. He pulled it out and pushed his thumb in the bowl. He struck the match and quickly lifted his hand to conceal the light, and set it against the tobacco.

He took a long draw from his pipe. "Martin, this is good Cuban pipe tobacco. You'll find none sweeter in the world." He waved his hand in front of his face to bring the escaping smoke into his face, like he did in his youth while fighting in the Indian wars.

Martin rolled his eyes, "Yes Sir."

"The brains on the O'Rourke side. It's like dealing with a Pis Pap brain," said Gilhooly as a wide grin spread across his face.

"Sir, didn't quite understand what you said," said Martin. as he flicked away a lice from his shoulder. "Col. Gilhooly, sir. With all due respect, did you just say you had piss brains?"

"No, you buffoon. In the old Irish tongue, pis, is the vegetable pea, and pap means mash," said Gilhooly. "So, their brains are pea mash. Also, he was a molly-coddled and slightly-colicky child, even to this day."

Martin looked at him with wide eyes. "Sir, there in the gondola. What kind of weapon was it that took the pilot's head off like that?"

"Me boyo, it's a Holland and Holland side by side. I have a friend who is an armorer. He took six inches off the barrel. That little darlin' fires a 600 nitro, express-rifle cartridge and carries a 900 grain, 58 g projectile," explained Gilhooly. "All the lead is melted down and antinomy is fused in, then he reloads 'em," said Gilhooly.

"I've never heard of that weapon," said Martin.

"You wouldn't, lest you live in Africa. This is basically an elephant gun, for when you're going through thick brush," said Gilhooly.

"So, Col., did you yell something before you pulled the trigger?" asked Martin.

"Hell yes. I said, 'Beirt madras comhrac thar a cnámh!' Means two dogs fightin' over a bone," said Gilhooly.

"That was a hell of a shot," said Martin.

Gilhooly laughed and nodded his head, "Yeah, but not as good as Billy Dixon's shot of the century with a 50-90 Sharps, distance of more than 1500 yards. Knocked a noble Comanche off his steed at the second Battle of Adobe Walls. If my cousin, the General, saw that parachute jump, he would never let me hear the end of it, young Mr. Martin.

"Did I ever tell you the story about when we were in East Africa? We got assigned to watch the German East Africa Company. That is all I can tell you about that or I have to execute you on the spot," said Gilhooly with a straight face. "What I can tell you is that every four weeks we would get fresh instructions on our supply run. But this one time we got arrested by the German East Africa Company. The Germans accused us of poaching elephant tusks out of German East Africa. According to the Germans, the elephants would take one look at Cousin Clusterfuck and die, Plus, there were so few of us we couldn't steal the ivory. But that didn't stop them of accusing us of stealing ivory. No sir. Me and Nancy Clancy Clusterfuck O'Rourke, Esq. we looked at each other and told them we didn't. Then we invited them to stick it up their arses. It was some shady Russian Bolsheviks and German secret police working for the German East Africa Company," said Gilhooly.

"So, we had to leave the country. I will bet you two cans of beef and three biscuits soaked in water for a day that my boneheaded cousin, will say something like sé salaithe a chuid blúmars."

"That translates to what, Sir?" said Martin.

"He soiled his bloomers," Gilhooly laughed as he took another drink and relit his pipe.

CHAPTER 10

In the distance, a new round of cannon explosions could be heard by both sides as the new sun peeked up from the eastern horizon.

"I'll bet ya one month's pay that me cousin probably soiled his bloomers. And on top of that, he probably landed like 290 pounds of American Irish shit," O'Rourke whispered. "Did you feel the earth shake when he hit? He made an instant trench line."

***

"We have to change part of the plan. Holy shit," whispered Thug in a surprised tone.

"Sgt. Williamson," whispered Thug as he pulled his tomahawk out and ran his thumb along the edge. He placed it back in his belt.

"Son, what are you doing here," interrupted Lieut. Washington.

"I had a gut feeling that I'd be more useful up here with the Lewis gun, Sir. Cpl. Ford is more than capable of handling 37 mm and the rest of the crew. I sent them back, Sir," whispered Williamson.

"Where'd you get the Lewis gun and ammo?" asked Washington.

"About six months ago, Sir, playing poker with drunken British soldiers, I modified this little beauty. I brought five pans of ammo, 47 rounds each," replied Williamson in a hushed tone.

"I'll leave it at that," whispered Washington.

"Sgt. Williamson," Thug asked. "My father, the other Sgt. Lightfoot, will be more than happy and gracious to take one of those leather ammunition cases off your back and put it on his."

"Why, what is he carrying?" whispered Williamson.

"I'm carrying the flamethrower, and by the way junior," whispered Ugh.

"Junior? I'm in trouble," mumbled Thug.

"Son, when we're out of this mess, I'm writing your mother, Old Hag," whispered Ugh.

"The Big Chief is gonna scalp me alive," mumbled Thug, surprised.

"Keep your blarney down," nipped Sullivan. "Young man, I can take all the help right now." He whispered.

***

In the new morning mist, five rounds from the flaming onion unleashed toward the trenches. Two rounds landed inside the trench harmlessly, the other three fell upon no man's land.

"Is that those fucking blooming onions?" whispered Wilson.

"Do gators lay eggs?" Shea whispered as he covered his head. "The Heinies is agettin' ready to come our away. Forthright, old man, who we got left fer pickins?"

"Wallace, Webb, and Reagan on BAR. Lincoln, Hannon, Smart, South, and Butler on support. Then we got ourselves you, Decatur, the General, Sgt. Jefferson, Sgt. Wilson, Doc, and yours truly," whispered Forthright.

"Well ain't that just a kick in the goobers," whispered Shea.

"Mr. Wilson," said Shea quietly and he turned toward Sgt. Wilson. "I want you to sneak further down the trench."

"Now it's getting interesting," whispered Wilson.

Shea whispered, "I want you to get their attention. When them thar old boys turn around, they will see your Medusa head and will turn to stone instantly. Thata way, we can cut down them thar odds," Shea's pearly whites glowing through his bloody, muddy, mud face, finishing with a thumbs up as he gave Wilson a nod yes.

"Shea, old man," whispered Wilson sarcastically. "I'm in the Bat squadron. Here's their salute." He raised his middle finger with a vigorous salute to Shea.

***

"Ugh, me boyo, get up into the machine gun nest and take a wee peek," whispered Sullivan.

Sullivan and the men heard the thump of another five rounds from the flaming onion. They saw the rounds nearing Shea and his command.

"We have to take that thing out. They are getting a little too close to Shea and the other men," whispered Washington.

"That's no blarney. I fully agree," said Sullivan.

"There are more than we thought; that Lewis machine gun will be a big help," reported Ugh.

"Lieut. Washington and I will take out the mortar. Ugh and Thug, take this gentleman with you. I didn't quiet catch your name son," whispered Sullivan to the soldier.

"Sgt. Williamson, Sir."

Sullivan directed, "When the Germans round that corner, you and these two knuckleheads jump in from the back and make their life very uncomfortable," as he ran his finger across his throat.

"Smedley, get your shotgun ready. If this poppin' fresh arsehole smiles at you, stick it up his arse with extreme prejudice," whispered

Sullivan. Smedley gave a silent nod yes, as he shoved the shotgun underneath the German prisoner's neck.

"What about that tank?" whispered Washington, pointing at the tank as it turned around and headed the opposite way.

"Let it go," whispered Ugh.

"All right boyos, we're gonna forget goin' after that tank if it's heading away," Sullivan replied quietly. "Ugh is right on this one. The General and his trollop are not in that tank," whispered Sullivan.

"Lieut. Sullivan?"

"Yes, Sgt. Lightfoot."

"Remember the Philippines? That was the last time you told me I was right about something," whispered Ugh. "I reckon that was about 1900."

"Crow?"

"Yes, Thug?" Sullivan asked

"They've all rounded the corner," Thug reported.

"Good luck boyos, were going to need it," whispered Sullivan. Sullivan and Washington were the first to move out in the mist, crawling along large open craters left when artillery pockmarked the landscape. Sullivan and Washington split off from the others to find the flaming onion mortar. Ugh, Thug, and Deadeye Dick started to crawl out, keeping a very low profile on the ground to the trench.

"All righty, y'all, this is it. Is everybody reloaded?" asked Shea. The crew all replied with thumbs up. "Then foller me," he said waving his hand high in the air. The men quickened pace behind Shea. They could hear the pounding of the German boots on the duckboard, and the oncoming Germans could hear the American doughboys approaching as well. Again, a great clash of ideologies.

Doc and Smart were in the lead, followed by Lincoln and Pvt. Hannon in 2 x 2 formation. Next came Wallace and South, Webb and Butler, Shea and Wilson, Jefferson and Forthright, followed by the General. Doc and Smart were first to spot the Germans as they rounded the traverse.

Shea yelled, "Move!" Doc and Smart jumped onto the firestep and slammed their bodies against the trench wall to get out of the line of fire. Lincoln and Hannon went to the left in the same fashion. Before the Germans realized what was about to happen, Cpl. Wallace and Webb opened up with a spray of red-hot lead from their BARs, followed by Shea and Wilson slam-firing their shotguns into the main body of the German formation. A German engaged Smart, and as they grappled, the German swung Smart around just as Shea let loose with his shotgun. The round penetrated Smart's back, exited through his chest, and right into the German. The two fell to the ground.

Shea exclaimed, "Shitfire! God forgive me."

Over the wails of pain and pounding of hot metal plunging into soft flesh, Wilson yelled, "Meet Duke Shotgun, the meanest motherfucker in the trench." The blistering fire was inflicting heavy damage. As they watched in slow motion as chests, rib cages, arms and legs, and craniums were torn apart. The morning of November 11, 1918, a red hue painted the walls, and a scarlet mist rose from the trench like embers from a fire.

Pvts. Lincoln, Hannon, and Butler yelled in unison, "Outgoing grenades!" as their arms moved in perfect arcs, releasing the small but lethal killing and maiming instruments. Their main objective was to disrupt the back half of the men in the German trench line.

The Browning automatic rifles fired slow and steady, striking large voids through fragile bodies.

Shea and Wilson yelled, "Fuck me! Reloadin'!"

Wilson laughed crazily, "I'm startin' to sound just aliken y'all, Hog Jowl Shea."

Wallace and Webb followed, "Reloading!"

At that time, the General and Forthright yelled, "Outgoing grenades!"

The carnage was immediate. Blood and body parts painting a tapestry on the trench walls. Unexpectedly, the blood-soaked Germans did not break and run to the rear. They gained their strength and advanced. Shea saw the berserker instinct blazing in the Germans' eyes. Their ominous presence made it evident that there was a 2 to 1 advantage for the Germans.

Privates Hannon was the first man hit. A large and muscular sauerkraut picked Hannon up by the straps of his round-about, and threw him onto the firestep like a sack of grain. The German pulled his trench knife, quickly impaling it into Hannon's shoulder. Hannon fought the German off, trying to wrestle away the knife. A second German approached, raising his entrenching tool and swinging.

Wilson ran up to Hannon and put his shotgun to the base of the first German's neck, pulling the trigger and nearly severing the head of the attacker. The head of the dearly departed flopped against the middle of his chest and he fell hard to the ground. Wilson immediately swung the barrel of his shotgun and expelled another round into the face of the other German, sending him three feet back and into a faceless death. Wilson turned around and saw that it was too late for Hannon; an entrenching tool was planted deep into his neck creating a large crevasse.

***

Bringing up the rear of the formation, the General and Forthright engaged in hand-to-hand combat with three Huns. The first Hun struck at the General with the blade of his entrenching tool, which ricocheted off O'Rourke's brodie. The German had overextended himself and had lost his balance. O'Rourke took the opportunity to put his peacemaker to the German's head and pulled the trigger. Another German knocked O'Rourke onto the duckboards. Sgt. Jefferson reacted as he watched the Hun lift his trench knife, going in for the killing blow. To the amazement of the Hun, Sgt. Jefferson seemed to morph from the All-American Doughboy to the Uifhednar Berserker with glowing scarlet eyes like the Werewolf Warrior from old Germania. Jefferson grabbed the large gray overcoat and lifted the Hun about 4 inches, then scuppered his teeth deep into the Hun's neck. The Heinie let out a screech of agony as a geyser of blood sprayed all over Jefferson's face, into his mouth, covering his teeth and weeping into his eyes.

Shea yelled, "Behind you!" Jefferson quickly turned around with the Hun still in hand as a human shield. The third and last German drilled his spiked club into the back of his comrade.

A shotgun blast broke the air. Grown men began calling for their mothers in both languages. Then BAR fire, and cussing, crying, wailing, and dying on both sides. Two more Germans shuffled onto the duckboard, stopping cold with astonishment on their face. Private South aimed his BAR; the burst put both of the Germans down. Sgt. Jefferson saw what South had done, and gave him a big thumbs up.

Then out of the air, Shea noticed potato mashers heading their way. He yelled, "Get down!" The Americans and some of the Germans took heed and hit the duckboards. Shea was unaware that a Stielhandgranate, a German stick grenade, had landed at the feet of Private South. They ripped South's upper half of his chest and head away his from his body, intermixing with two German soldiers, and igniting some of the BAR ammo, sending shrapnel and bullets into the three Germans, killing them instantly.

Shea yelled, and Wilson followed in the refrain, "Fuck you! Reloadin'!"

"Outgoing grenade," Shea shouted, then hit with slam fire on three Germans, tearing large gaps in their heads and faces.

Cpl. Wallace had been holding his own, using the BAR as a single-shot, picking German's off, one at a time.

Private Butler yelled, "Outgoing grenade," and flung his ordnance in an arc toward the end of the German trench. Suddenly, two Germans tackled Butler to the ground. He kicked one off, and then his right index finger found its mark, taking the German's right eye completely out of its socket. The other German thrust his trench knife into the chest of Butler, who in turn screeched, "Fuck you, I don't want to die this way," as blood gurgled out of his mouth with his last labored breath. Sgt. Wilson turned around to realize what happened and immediately went to work, as now the Germans were coming for Wilson. They did not see Duke, his shotgun, held low at his hip.

The Germans were yelling, "Die, Amerikaner toten!" Wilson's first shot at the German at point-blank range, hit him in the midsection, lifting him up and blowing him back three feet.

Wilson yelled back. "Kiss my ass!" Then one of the Germans was about to blindside Sgt. Jefferson. Wilson's second shot took out the legs of that Hun, then Wilson immediately put the barrel of his shotgun to the Hun's chest and pulled the trigger. He yelled, "Good morning asshole, it's November 11, 1918."

Reagan pulled his 1911 and planted a bullet in the forehead of an oncoming German, and was knocked to the ground by another Hun. He planted his gun deep in the ribs and fired. Reagan pushed the dead man off of him just as three large German soldiers ambushed him, one on each arm as the third slashed his throat wide open with surgical precision, laughing maniacally the whole time.

***

"All right boyos, are we clear?" whispered Sullivan.

They nodded yes, Sullivan and Washington moved up first, taking a left to clear the trench. Thug crawled up and into the machine gun nest and peeked over the sandbags to see two Germans looking away and crouching on guard. Thug motioned to Ugh and Williamson to come up to the machine gun nest. Thug signaled Ugh and Williamson with two fingers. Ugh slowly pulled off his flamethrower, and withdrew his tomahawk from his belt. Thug did the same.

As the clash of warriors could be heard in the near distance, all three men stood up. Ugh threw his tomahawk, landing square into the German's shoulder blade. The other sentry looked up, caught off guard without his helmet. At that same time, Thug let loose, finding his mark right in the middle of the German's forehead and dropping him instantly. The wounded Hun tried to remove the tomahawk, and Williamson let fly with his switchblade, hitting the German in the throat. Williamson jumped on him, taking his blade out of the German's throat, finishing the job. He wiped the blood from his blade on the shoulder of the German. Thug took his tomahawk out of the forehead of the other German and did the same.

***

The men heard another five rounds from the flaming onion.

"There it is," said Sullivan, in a low voice.

"How do you want to tackle this," asked Washington.

"Me eyes see three, four, five, and there is the sixth guard, and an NCO, that's seven," whispered Sullivan.

"For a second, I thought you were gonna have to take your boots off," whispered Washington.

"Me toes are hidden pretty well in this brush. Well young man, I guess that's four for me and three for you," replied Sullivan.

"The two of us boyos have a trench knife, a 45, and a couple grenades between us. Those black-hearted devils have their entrenching tools, trench knives, stick grenades, rifles with bayonets, possibly a 08/15 machine gun, stuck up one of their arses, and that Gatling cannon," whispered Sullivan.

Washington replied with a smile and said, "That makes me sweet and sappy all over."

"I will tell you what, Mr. Washington," Sullivan said and they got on their knees and crawled to the Germans.

"You see the German Sgt.? I'm going to become a searganach." He crawled past Washington a few yards up to the German NCO, who had walked right past Sullivan, not seeing him because of the downed trees and artillery craters. The NCO turned his back, giving Sullivan the chance to sneak up behind with his knife drawn. In one swift motion, Sullivan covered the Hun's mouth, wrapped his left leg around the Hun's right ankle, toppling him and pushing his head down, slitting his throat.

Washington crawled up to Sullivan and said, "Nice kill. And pray tell sir, what did you say earlier?" whispered Washington.

"I said Killjoy, by Saint Michael," replied Sullivan in a low voice.

"How about we ask them to surrender," whispered Washington.

"They'll only surrender if me pull me shirt up, and me trousers down. I'll become a belly dancer from America," whispered Sullivan.

"Crow," whispered Washington.

"Yes, Gus," Sullivan answered.

"They wouldn't surrender. They would puke and die, but that would be one way to get the job done and end the war earlier," said Washington.

"I'll take the three on the left," signaled Sullivan.

"I guess I have the three on the right," Washington nodded, as they shook hands and went their separate ways.

Sullivan was the first one to come up on his quarry. As he was on his belly looking over a dead log, a German rose up and turned to his comrades.

He asked them, "Welcher von euch Arschlöchern, scheiße seinen Bauch raus?"

All of his comrades replied, "Nein."

Sullivan laughed and mumbled under his breath to himself, "There is a good solid silent one, for ye boys, from me boys, and compliments from the fighting 69th."

Washington moved silently 15 yards and waited like the King of the Harlem Hell Fighters. Up in a flash, Sullivan moved in with a trench knife in left hand, 45 pistol in right hand. Three Germans turned around with great revelation as Sullivan jumped on them at once. Sullivan quickly got the better of one, slamming his trench knife up to the hilt into the throat of the German. One of the Germans slammed into Sullivan from the right, knocking him down along with his victim and slapping the pistol out of his hand. By this time Washington had crawled around to the German, who was on sentry duty.

The sound of Sullivan's scuffle made the German turn his head that way. Washington sprung up like a man possessed, surprising the other two Huns. Thinking quickly, Washington kicked the outside of the first German's knee, making the German fall to the ground grabbing the bone protruding from his knee. The other German looked down at his friend, then frantically up at Washington, as a deadly flash slammed into the middle of his forehead, dropping him immediately. As the young soldier fumbled for his pistol with the bottom of his leg twisted backwards, Washington quickly turned his pistol, shooting twice, and dispatching the young German. The sentry turned his head back around and charged at Washington with fixed bayonet.

He stopped and shot, the round hitting Washington's left shoulder, making a clean exit. The German lunged at Washington with his rifle and bayonet. Washington stuck out his left foot, making the German trip and fall, thus putting his newly acquired 45 on top of the Feldmütze field cap of the German and discharged his weapon twice, yelling, "These Krauts sure like to dance the Waltz with the lead balls."

Meanwhile, Sullivan was having quite a consternation with his two Germans. Washington stood up and heard the commotion going on with the Germans. Sullivan raised his foot and kicked one of the Germans with all of his might, yelling, "Get off me arsehole!" The other German had plunged his Nahkampfmesser trench knife deep into Sullivan's shoulder, twisting it and growling like a berserker. The Hun was going in for the executing blow, when Washington shot him twice, blasting him off of Sullivan.

Sullivan and the other German rose up and faced each other. At that moment, the German realized he had Sullivan's knife embedded in this side. Sullivan had a knife deep in his shoulder. The two enemies looked at each other like two stuck Gladiators. Sullivan could see that his opponent was a veteran of the trenches. Scars marred his blackened face, his eyes were sunken and beady. Sullivan spoke directly to the German in a very callous loud Gaelic tongue, "Marbh fear iniss ar bith eireaball."

Sullivan took the German's knife out of his shoulder, and the Hun followed suit. Both men lunged at each other in a mad dash, eradication in their eyes. Unknown to the German until it was too late for him, Washington grabbed his belt and pulled him close putting his 1911 behind his right ear pulling the trigger, double-tabbing his foe.

"Son, whatcha doin'? I had this under control!" exclaimed Sullivan.

"I think saving your life," whispered Washington.

"You owe me; he was my kill," Sullivan said.

"How?" asked Washington spotting the blood oozing and making Sullivan's trenchcoat wet. "Let me see that shoulder."

"Someday, me fair young Lieutenant, I will call in a favor," whispered Sullivan, with a straight, stern face. "Looks like you fared no better."

"Just a clean wound on me," whispered Washington.

"Let me look at it, boyo. It does look like a clean-shot, Nancy. Here, take your finger and plug that dike, and engage them with your other hand," whispered Sullivan, as he snickered.

"You have kind of a deep wound yourself. Pack it with this snot rag. By the way, Crow, what did you tell me before I killed him," asked Washington.

"You mean Marbh fear iniss ar bith eireaball? Why, that means dead man tells no tale," said Sullivan as he spit blood and put his finger on the side of his nose and farmer-blew blood on the dead Germans.

"Here's me hand for saving me life," whispered Sullivan, extending his hand to Washington.

"The feeling is mutual, me boyo," whispered Washington, smiling at his friend.

Suddenly, Sullivan and Washington could hear boots coming their way.

"There they are," whispered Washington.

"Is this thing loaded?" said Sullivan, reaching for the Gatling cannon.

"No idea, Sir," whispered Washington.

"Help me turn this confounded thing toward them," whispered Sullivan as they jostled the aim toward the oncoming Germans. "Maybe we can scare them to death. I'll get on the handle, and crank like a windmill."

Then Sullivan saw the Germans and started cranking like mad. The first 37 mm projectile hit the leading Hun in his chest, immediately splitting his chest wide open. The other four rounds exploded into the other Huns on impact. Their bodies were rended into small fragments of flesh and bone.

"I hear more coming. Let's hunker down here," whispered Sullivan.

"Gus?"

"Yes Crow?"

"I just thought of this. I made a tactical error. You and I are hunkered down here, I'm the commander, and you're the executive officer," whispered Sullivan. "If we both get killed, the chain of command..."

Washington put up his hand to cut him off. "If that is the case, Shea would take right over. So, I call that learned lessons," whispered Washington.

"I know what I'll do, by Saint Michael. I'll put the Executive officer with the First Sergeant for more learnt lessons. With the First Sergeant's boot stuck up his arse so far, he will be able to taste coffee and boot polish!" whispered Sullivan. "Now, I'm startin' to think like a dumb arse officer. Makin' mistakes," smiling slyly as he shook his head back and forth.

***

"Capt. Martin? What's the status?"

"Colonel, it's been a spell and I ain't seen or heard our pilots."

***

The battle in the trenches was getting desperate, and the bloody Huns kept pouring in. Shea immediately went to work knocking down the odds with his shotgun.

"Wallace, on me," yelled Shea. The two opened up in the middle. A fresh batch of six Huns who did not see the boys, stepped out from the traverse, opening up on the Huns. Arms, forearms, hands, and parts of heads were being mangled off between the BAR and shotgun ripping up the bodies of the Huns. The BAR was doing twice the duty. Rounds would perforate through the men, tearing up the man directly behind him.

Shea yelled "Reloadin'!"

Immediately Wallace stepped in and started right back up yelled, "Reloading," as he tried to insert a new magazine. Three Huns jumped on him knocking him to the ground. With his BAR falling to the duckboard, Sgt. Jefferson immediately picked up one of the Huns with all his strength, lifting him up over his head like Atlas holding up the world. He threw him onto the advancing Huns, knocking them down. Sgt. Jefferson turned around to see the German stomp his boot into Wallace's chest to give himself leverage to pull his hobnail club out of his skull, like a lumberjack trying to retrieve his ax from a piece of cordwood. He was met by Wilson's Duke Shotgun, which excavated a large cavity in his chest.

Cpl. Webb was keeping up a steady stream of fire when the BAR suddenly jammed. As he proceeded to clear his weapon, three Huns jumped on him peeling off his Brodie helmet and caving his head in with the hobnail club. Forthright was engaged with two Germans; they threw him against the firestep and trench wall. General O'Rourke, who had just dispatched his own enemies took matters into his own hands, with extreme prejudice. O'Rourke grabbed his tomahawk from behind his back, and before the two Germans could react, O'Rourke slammed Forthright and the two Germans, knocking them off their feet. One of the Germans fell to the ground. As he scrambled to get to his feet, O'Rourke went berserker with his tomahawk, giving back some of the same savage medicine. The first blow embedded deep in the right side of the German's neck, O'Rourke yanked hard to remove the tomahawk as blood gushed out of the gaping wound. O'Rourke reached high over his head and wielded the second blow, hitting the right collarbone, breaking the bone. O'Rourke pulled the tomahawk up and with force, exploding the deathblow into the back of his neck as blood pulsated out in rhythm with each heartbeat.

O'Rourke turned around like a Tasmanian Devil to see Forthright and the German rolling around on the ground. The German's trench knife was swatted away by Forthright, and landed on the firestep. As Forthright jostled with the Hun, he locked down the German's wrist to the firestep as he squirmed to reach his knife. General O'Rourke lifted his bloody tomahawk and locked eyes with his adversary, who shouted a guttural, "Oh, verdammt!"

"Ja!" O'Rourke bellowed and then summoned all his brute power, bringing down the tomahawk and striking the fingers of the German, hacking off all but the thumb. Forthright saw his opportunity to draw his 45, jammed it underneath the chin of the German, and pulled the trigger.

***

"There they are," whispered Ugh.

Then Thug, Deadeye Dick, and Ugh rounded the traverse, coming up just behind the Germans. Ugh hit the igniter of the flamethrower. Thug opened up with the MP 18.1, and Deadeye Dick started up the Lewis machine gun. The bullets were penetrating very quickly into one German and going right through to the next. They were on the wrong end of a pincer move. The MP 18.1 and Lewis machine gun fire struck a bag of German potato-masher grenades. The sounds of battle were all around. Multiple explosions sent shrapnel through the meat of the Germans, filling the air with the shrills and the high pitches of death. Parts of legs, arms, and internal organs of Germanic warriors burst apart making a bloody German goulash on the duckboards.

***

Doc lifted his trench knife, clasping the front of the Hun's helmet, vigorously thrusting his head backwards and plunging his trench knife to the hilt into his right eye.

The surviving German scrambled to get to his feet. Four more large Germans rushed into the arena, seizing Jefferson. The soldiers grappled for their lives. Shea aimed his shotgun and exterminated each German at point-blank range.

"Here comes the Calvary," Wilson yelled as he shot a gigantic warrior in the face, blowing out the back of his head.

Shea turned his attention the remaining German wielding his hobnail club. Jefferson snatched the club and bludgeoned the German with his own club. Shea shoved his 1911 to the base of his skull and squeezed the trigger. The German went limp on top of Jefferson, pinning him to the duckboard. Jefferson rolled him off and got to his feet.

***

At the rear of the trench, Forthright brawled with two young Huns. With his one good eye, O'Rourke saw Forthright's struggle, and pulled his trench knife. Gen. O'Rourke slit the throat of the young German, making a clean exit through his left side. "Me Bucko, how do you like that for your very first shave?"

A German stood, pistol pulled and pointed at Forthright's head. At the same time, Forthright pulled his 1911 and pointed it at the German. Both warriors pulled their triggers at the same time, hitting their targets. Forthright's bullets entered the chest of the young German, killing him instantly. The young German hit his target too. Forthright was knocked to the ground. He reached for his shoulder where his flesh seared like a branded bull, feeling his warm blood oozing from the wound.

O'Rourke reached down to help Forthright to his feet and yelled, "Sé tá sinn bhí géarshiúlach."

"What the hell does that mean?" asked Forthright.

"It is time we were moving—time to remove our arses," replied the General.

Across the trench, Private Lincoln hastily dispatched an enemy soldier by digging his thumbs deep into the eyes and feeling the warm gelatin of his enemy's brain between his fingers. He clutched the eyeballs that had landed in his fist and yanked them from the young man's eye sockets as the German screamed "MUTTER."

Three Huns approached and witnessed their buddy being mercilessly slaughtered. Lincoln tried to stand but stumbled to the blood-soaked ground. The Huns savagely beat him in the head and shoulders with spiked clubs. Forthright and O'Rourke came to his aid and shot all three dead, but it was too late for Lincoln.

***

Ugh had worked his way up from the rear with his flamethrower ready. He hit the igniter, spewing out a river of flame making the Germans into human torches. Thug aimed his MP 18.1 and sliced through them like a scythe.

Shea and the rest of boys observed the Germans' plight, so they opened up with the weapons and ammo they had left. Jefferson, Shea, Doc, and Forthright yelled, "Outgoing grenades!" The Germans could see that they are being squeezed and tried to get down on the ground to find cover.

Shea yelled, "Incomin' gerr-nade" as it hit the duckboards and rolled off. Shea immediately jumped on it, followed by Sgt. Jefferson.

With quick hands, Sgt. Jefferson located the potato masher and pulled it from underneath Shea, tossing it over the top where it exploded harmlessly.

CHAPTER 11

"Heaven musta taste like alligator shit," said Shea. "On accounta I'm afeelin' like shit."

"Lieut. Shea," said Sgt. Jefferson with a low commanding voice. "I have to agree with one of your statements sir, but I differ with you on the other."

"Which one is which, Sgt. Jefferson," asked Shea.

"I agree sir, that you do look like shit. And I differ with you sir, I don't feel like shit," said Sgt. Jefferson.

They could still hear groans and moans from the dying Germans and injured Americans. All firing had ceased, and the smell of blood, feces, and burning flesh permeated the air. "All I gotta say John Henry, you're all sunshine on a cloudy day." Shea extended his hand and gave Jefferson a manly hug, "You big somesabitch, thanks for saving my Georgia peaches. Just think, Sgt. Jeff, if our units had done started out together, this here war woulda been cleaned up by 1917.

Shea turned to Ugh, Thug, and Deadeye. "It took you damn Yankee boys long enough," said Shea.

"You know me, alligator fucker, Sir, I like to make a grand entrance," said Thug. The men all shook hands, smacked each other on the back, and hugged.

"And you are?" asked Shea.

"Cpl. Deadeye Dick Williamson, Sir," replied Deadeye.

"Well hush my mouth. Your Lewis machine gun came in handy. I can see why you're called Deadeye," said Shea.

"Thank you, Sir," replied Deadeye.

"No, Corporal thank you," as Shea and Deadeye shook hands.

"Men, gather all the weapons, ammunition, an anythin' else useful we can find," said Shea. "Doc, I made a quick head count . We got yourself, the General, Forthright, Jefferson, Wilson, and yours truly. I count six of us. How many of us went into that trench?" asked Shea.

"19 of us, Sir," replied Doc.

"Fuck me!" mumbled Shea.

Shea stood and adjusted his equipment, and bent over to pick up an abandoned Nahkampfmesser and slid it into his belt without wiping the dripping blood from the blade. "Alrighty fellers, let's move out and find us Lieut. Sullivan an' Lieut. Washington, and head to that concrete bunker," said Shea, adding. "When we see Doc, make sure y'all get your wounds looked at."

Shea called to Ugh, "Come here, Ugh, I'll help y'all take that flamethrower offa yer back. You did an righteous job," Shea said as he handed the device to Junior."

"Oh no," said Thug, as he waved it off.

"And why not?" replied Shea.

"Because I don't get to vote," declared young Mr. Lightfoot.

"Why hells bells boy, I voted you to carry the flamethrower, then I seconded that thar motion," asserted Shea.

"What a lousy system," mumbled Sgt. Lightfoot.

"You are so right, Thug," said Shea.

"Whata we got left for ammunition?" asked Shea.

"Four shotguns, tubed up, and two reloads on the sweepers," reported Wilson. "As far as the BAR. Six clips apiece, Sir."

"And how are we doin' with our 45 ammo," asked Shea.

One at a time, the men reported, "Good to go, Sir."

"Let's move out smartly; except you Wilson, you just move out," said Shea.

***

"There now, all patched up," said Sullivan as he lifted the fabric away from the through and through perforation in Washington's shoulder. Washington winced, and Sullivan, "You sound like a wee baby."

Washington said, "Yeah, you get a shoulder full of hot lead and see how you feel. Much different than the cold butter knife wound you got."

"How much ammunition do you have left?" asked Sullivan.

"Six clips left and two hand grenades, a knife, and a bad attitude," replied Washington.

"That'll have to do; by Saint Michael, that warms me cockles," said Sullivan as he shuttered.

Sullivan and Washington stood up and gathered their equipment and their thoughts. They sought cover and concealment while they moved toward their objective. They used brush and fallen trees as cover, and could still hear the distant chatter of machine gun fire, artillery explosions, mortar fire from the East trench where the Germans were held up. Aeroplanes flew overhead, coming in at treetop level to strafe the trench. Sullivan scanned the area with his binoculars, looking for any enemies on guard.

"There's two arseholes, Mr. Washington!" whispered Sullivan as he pointed "Between the two big trees."

"I see a couple sentries," said Washington with a snicker on his face.

"That's them," replied Sullivan.

"Shh. What is that clinking sound?" whispered Sullivan as he pointed into the air.

"Which way did it come from?" asked Washington. Both men turned around and looked. Washington was greeted with a rock in the chest.

"See that, punk?" whispered Ugh to Thug, "I told you I would hit one and both would turn around."

"Glad you boyos could join us. Where are the rest of the boys," whispered Sullivan.

"Right around the corner Lieut. Sullivan," answered Ugh.

"Minus Doc, he went to check out the second trench to find our wounded," whispered Ugh.

"Alright boyos," whispered Sullivan. "We found the concrete bunker."

***

"Col. Gilhooly, can you walk ok?" asked Martin.

"I think I'll be fine son. Still no word on the Bat squadron," replied Gilhooly. "Ceoch. Young man, that means it's misty."

"Yes, I concur, Sir. Do you hear an engine?" said Martin.

"I do," replied Gilhooly.

Squelch "you" squelch "motherfuckers," said Wild Bill over the radio.

"Sir, I'm picking up Wild Bill," replied Martin.

"Gimme that handset, boyo," said Gilhooly.

Martin handed the handset to Gilhooly and flipped the switch. Martin looked up from the radiophone just in time to see three

German aeroplanes coming out of the fog, flying low and strafing the ground and scoring a hit on one of the French 75s, which blew up, taking the extra artillery surrounding the area with it. The ground heaved into apex of blood, shrapnel, body parts, and mud.

"There you are, you motherfuckers," blurted out Wild Bill on the radiophone. "I got something for your asses."

The three German planes abscond from Gilhooly and Martin. Unknown to the German pilots, Wild Bill hit the accelerator and approached within 25 yards behind the left wingman.

"Right there, baby, I got you," Wild Bill blurted as he let loose with his twin Lewis machine guns. A torrent of tracers streamed right up the back of the fuselage, tearing gaping holes out of the canvas. The final burst took half of the pilot's head off, while his bird of prey took a hard left and started death spiraling toward the earth. Wild Bill screeched as he watch the smoke rise from the terra firma below. "Oh yeah, baby, how do you like that, bitch? God, that feels great."

Wild Bill cut a glance over to the remaining German aeroplanes. He sliced a hard right, catching the German unaware that obliteration was careening from his left side. Wild Bill was 10 yards away, and opened up his machine guns. The first burst slammed into the motor first and worked its way down the fuselage. Smoke and fire billowed from the Teutonic Knights Aeroplane, and Wild Bill saw that the German's left arm ablaze. The next burst of lead tore into the German's cockpit, sending canvas, wood, and the pilot's grey matter into the air. Tracer sliced the tail off the aeroplane, sealing its fate. The plane plummeted to the ground, squealing and sputtering its last propeller whirl, embedding its nose into the earth, exploding on impact.

"That's right, fuckhead. I should have put marshmallows on my propellers," exclaimed Wild Bill, laughing like a mad scientist as he flew directly through the smoke and debris on his way to his next foe.

***

"Shea," whispered Sullivan. "Do you have everybody?"

"Yes Sir, them thar still livin'," whispered Shea.

"Look between the two trees over there," whispered Sullivan, pointing as he handed the binoculars to Shea.

"I see 'em," replied Shea in a low voice.

"And where's Smedley and the toothless wonder at," whispered Sullivan.

"Right here, Sir," Smedley answered as he walked up, with the injured prisoner in tow.

"Wilson, where ya at, boyo?" whispered Sullivan, looking around the area.

"I'm here, Sir," answered Wilson.

"Boyo, take the boche, give Smedley your BAR and clips. Smedley we're moving you up into a spot where you can cover us as support. By the way, Corporal Smedley, I want to congratulate you on your mission of getting toothless up here," whispered Sullivan, shaking Smedley's hand.

"Thank you, and Roger that, sir," whispered Smedley eagerly.

"Mr. Smedley," said Wilson. "You're moving up to the big-time son. Make me proud."

"Sullivan, you better come here and take a look," whispered Washington. "Look left of the bunker, 200 yards out."

"By Saint Michael, let me guess, the tank is coming back," replied Sullivan.

"Well shit, I'm gonna have a tank stuck up me arse. Washington, Jefferson, Forthright, you stay here with toothless. Thug, you're on the flamethrower," ordered Sullivan."

"No shit, Lieut. Sherlock," said Thug.

"Ugh, Shea, Wilson, Williamson, and meself will support ya," explained Sullivan. "Gentlemen, you know what we have to do. Let's move out. Ugh, lead out and make a wide arc left of the shell craters." The men slowly moved out from the wooded trench area and to the more open areas of the field,¬ navigating large craters left by the artillery.

"Boyos, let's make a dash to the bunker," barked Sullivan. The men zig-zagged across the field from shell hole to shell hole. Suddenly, the German-commandeered British tank machine guns opened up, forcing the men to get down inside the craters for cover.

"Them is movin' thata tank thisa way," exclaimed Shea.

Wilson yelled, "You just got that, Lieut. Obvious?"

Out of the clear blue sky, 37 mm shells start raining and pounding the tank.

***

"You hit him, Hawk," said Smalls.

"That's right, bitch, keep loading," yelled Hawkins.

"Stormy, shoot the shit out of the tracks," said Downs.

Two armored cars, one driven by Ford and another driven by Pick, appeared suddenly over the hill; they made a wide left arc out of the view of the German tank, hitting it on the right side of the tank as the cars raced toward Sullivan, Washington, and the men.

The two cars poured in fire as they approached the tank. "Hold your fire," yelled Sullivan.

A Hun machine gun from the tank fired on the armored car to no avail, as the rounds bounced off the welded steel panels. Suddenly, a 37 mm shell found its target on the right track, disabling the tank in the middle of the field. The two armored vehicles swung a U-turn to the left and start heading behind the detachment.

"All right me boyo's, we're going to prance and dance up to the side of the tank," Sullivan explained to Thug and the others.

"I suppose I have to run with this bitch? This gotta weigh more than my first girlfriend, " mumbled Thug,

"You can dance with it if you want," said Sullivan, adding, "What would you like to do, Sgt.; have me carry you and your fair damsel out there like a date at the Noncommissioned Officer Spring Dance at Fort Riley?" chagrined Sullivan.

"No boss, but I will lead, so let's go," said Thug.

Shell crater to shell crater, the men moved slowly up to the right side of the tank. Machine gun lead was coming from the concrete bunker in the middle of the third trench line. Strands of dirt pinged up in the air as three machine guns peppered at the men.

"All right boyos, the German's have to change belts out. NOW! Let's go," yelled Sullivan, as the six men moved into a shell hole closer to the tank. Thug sent a stream of fire onto the tank.

Washington yelled, "Sgt. Lightfoot, aim at the ports of the machine guns. Try to get it inside their tank and get them hot and smoky. Force those fuckers out."

The German machine guns pounded continuously at the men in the shell holes.

"Them thar is bitchin' an yellin' inside the tank," indicated Shea.

"Ich kann nicht atmen. Der Rauch und das Kohlenmonoxid bringen mich um."

Suddenly the hatch opened up and eight Germans roll off, staggering. They were immediately met by 37 mm shells and Hotchkiss machine-guns, tearing apart flesh and bone. Smoke bellowed from the tank and two additional 37 mm shells slammed the side of the tank. Sgt. Lightfoot followed with a stream of fire, engulfing the Germans into bluish yellow flames.

***

"You hit the motherfucker," said Corporal Smalls from an armored car.

"I'm a lucky fuck. I got in just afore he did," yelled Hawkins.

"I'm sorry to disagree with you, with all due respect Sgt.," said Smalls. "You hit the door."

"Bullshit!" exclaimed Hawk.

"Kind of like the aeroplanes and short-arm inspections, Sgt. Hawkins," said Smalls, adding, "As they say, a day late and 27 mm short!"

CHAPTER 12

Bursting out of the clouds came Wild Bill, yelling, "I got you, motherfucker." Wild Bill cut across the bunker of the third trench, silencing the machine gun nest with three surgical bursts.

The last Jaeger Hun opened up from the air on the craters below. The men painted themselves to the sides of the shell hole to avoid the fire. Wild Bill pulled back on the throttle, circling around the last tank. He spotted the Hun, and gave chase.

***

"Wild Bill's back on the air," said Martin, as they listened for Wild Bill's aeroplane motor and fire, trying to find him on the radiophone.

"Col. Gilhooly, Col. Gilhooly, do you hear me?" declared Wild Bill. "You owe four cases of whiskey to me and the boys. The good shit. My four boys knocked down a mixed bag of 18 German Fighters and Bomber Aeroplanes. Them assholes tried to come through the back door. I got one more Hun prick to find, so I will be flying around for a bit longer," exclaimed Wild Bill.

"Fuck, all I can say is cathbhuach thar bás agus an diabhal," said Gilhooly.

"You can say that again… But exactly what did you say?" asked Martin.

"It means victorious over death and the devil," smiled Gilhooly, as he took a bottle from his trench coat and took a big long pull on his whiskey. He handed the bottle to Capt. Martin.

***

Through the mist, Wild Bill fixed his eyes on the last German foe. The Fokker D.VII turned to the left, and the pilot's eyes opened to saucer size. Wild Bill waved his hand as if to say, "Go home," The German pilot reciprocated with a salute to Wild Bill, and Wild Bill responded in kind. Wild Bill pulled a hard right arc toward the tank.

***

"All right boyos, let's make it back to the trench. First Sgt. Forthright," said Sullivan. "Do we have everybody now?"

"Yes, Lieut. Sullivan," answered Forthright.

"Washington, are all your men accounted for?" said Sullivan.

"Yes Sir," replied Washington.

"Boyos, we're going to take that confounded concrete bunker," replied Sullivan.

The flat ground became eerily quiet, and the air stood static and light with fog. The men moved in and out of the trenches and shell holes, with only the sounds of their boots in the squishing mud, their heart rate, and their thoughts. As they crept up and around the bunker, they could see that the French General's vehicle had been camouflaged. Near the remaining trees and brush Sullivan spotted the heads of two sentries.

Sullivan used hand signals to instruct Washington to move around the backside of the bunker. Washington gave Sullivan a thumbs up and pointed at Jefferson, Shea, and Thug and then indicated to them to follow him around the backside of the bunker.

Sullivan, Forthright, Wilson, Ugh, General O'Rourke, Smedley, and the German prisoner. Wilson dropped to the ground in a low crawl, keeping his eyes on the Stahlhelm of the German sentry. With his prey in sight, Wilson circled behind the sentry, past the machine gun nest which Wild Bill had obliterated along with its occupants, some of whom were still groaning in agony and dying.

Wilson sprung to his feet and tackled the nearest sentry, slicing his throat from ear to ear. The sentry's der Genosse immediately turned and reached for his weapon; but before he could react, Wilson plunged his trench knife deep into neck at the collarbone rendering him lifeless. Neither sentry knew what hit them; and the men quickly dragged the bodies out of sight.

Sullivan and Washington stood outside the door of the bunker and gestured to Smedley to assist in interpreting the German and French voices yelling inside the heavy metal bunker door.

"Laddy, what is the Froggy General saying?" asked Sullivan.

"Sir, it sounds like the French General also can speak German," whispered Smedley.

"Okay Smedley, tell them fellers we have the bunker surrounded," said Sullivan sternly. "Also, tell them to have their hands up, no patty fingers, no blarney or bullshit," he continued, as the men drew their 45s.

***

"*Ich habe gesagt, 'Achtung, Achtung, das sind die amerikanischen Auslandseinsatztruppen. Wir haben den Bunker umzingelt. Kommen Sie mit erhobenen Händen raus und machen Sie keine Dummheiten,*" said Smedley in perfect German.

"What did you ask them, boyo?" inquired Sullivan.

"Yes Lieut. Sullivan, asked the French General in German what she said?" asked Sullivan. then Smedley asked in German.

"General Renard, könnten Sie das bitte ins Deutsche übersetzen, damit ich es meinen Kommandanten sagen kann."

"I said, 'General Renard, could you please translate this into German so that I can relay it to my commanders.'"

"General, Sie können mich erschießen, weil ich die Pläne der 18.1-Maschinenpistole gestohlen und versucht habe, sie an General Renard weiterzugeben. Ich werde mich jedoch nur trösten, dass Sie Ihren Waterloo kennengelernt haben uns, oder noch besser, ich sollte sagen, sie haben dich und deine Männer, denn du tröstest dich sehr, wenn du weißt, dass deine Männer mich brutal bis zu meinem Blut vernarbt haben. Aber es ist das Blut, das ich frei für Frankreich geben würde. Viva la Frankreich," said the French General.

"After all that," pronounced Sullivan, "What in the blue blazes did he say?"

"Lieut. Sullivan. The Gen. said this, 'General, you can shoot me for stealing the plans, of the 18.1 machine pistol and trying to pass them to General Renard. Although, I will take sheer solace, that you have met your Waterloo. By the appearance of these gentlemen who have us, or should I say they have you and your men, as you take great comfort in knowing that your men have brutally sodomized me until I bleed. But it is the blood that I would give freely for France. Viva la France.'"

"That is when he shot her," replied Smedley.

"Thank you Smedley for your interpretation," said Sullivan.

"We got 'em by the short hairs, Tom and John Lightfoot," said Sullivan happily.

"Sir, I said 'attention, attention! This is the American Expeditionary Force. We have the bunker surrounded. Come out with your hands up, and no patty fingers, no blarney or bullshit," reported Smedley proudly.

A German voice replied from the bunker, "*Ich bin General von Rottschwinghammer von der kaiserlichen deutschen Armee. Ich gehe davon aus, dass Sie mit mir die Bedienungen Ihrer Kapitulation besprechen möchten?*" the boisterous voice shouted, followed by a loud guffaw upon the request.

"Smedley, old boy," said Shea gesturing to the voices within the bunker, "Let me guess. That athere old hog doesn't want to come out, knowin' he's agoin to get one in the back of his ear." Shea loaded a new clip in his 45 and slid back the slide to chamber a new round.

"No sir," he said, "My name is General von Rottschwinghammer of the Imperial German Army. Do you wish to talk conditions of your surrender?" Smedley reported with a half-smile on his face.

Sullivan said in old Irish tongue, "*Prás Liathróid.* Smedley, me boyo, I said brass balls. I will show them brass balls." Sullivan goes up to the door of the bunker and whacked it three good times.

"Cpl. Smedley"

"Yes Lieut. Sullivan." answered back Smedley.

"Tell Bonaparte that we have him Trumped, and one more time to come out."

"*Achtung, Achtung, habe ich gesagt! Das ist Ihre letzte Warnung, kommen Sie mit erhobenen Händen heraus. Und machen Sie keine Dummheiten!*"

"What did you tell them." said Sullivan inquisitively

"I said attention, attention this is your last warning. Come out with your hands up. And no funny business," replied Smedley.

"Smedley."

"Yes Lieut. Sullivan."

"Tell them we are not going to shoot them." said Sullivan.

"*Gen. Ich wurde mir von meinen vorgesetzten dass sie nicht erschossen werden wenn sie aus der tür,*" interpreted Smedley.

Then the door of the bunker slowly opened. The first person out was a dainty female with long, flowing, raven black hair, piercing black ice eyes. She was exquisitely dressed, but had a gun forced to her head, held by the German General. The woman and the German General exited the bunker, followed by the French General and four German aides who held their Luger pistols to the French General's head, with two German guards bringing up the rear.

"*Général, vous pouvez me tirer dessus pour avoir volé les plans du Pistolet-mitrailleur 18.1 et tenté de les transmettre au général Renard. Bien que, je tiens à vous consoler que vous avez rencontré votre Waterloo. Par l'apparence de ces messieurs qui ont nous, ou mieux encore, je dois dire qu'ils ont vous et vos hommes, car vous vous sentez bien en sachant que vos hommes m'ont brutalement sodomisée jusqu'à ce que je saigne. Mais c'est le sang, que je donnerais gratuitement pour la France. Viva la France,*" the woman said forcefully, with gusto. The German General squeezed the trigger and shot her in the head.

Washington pulled 1911 and proceeded to shoot a German aid in the head. The General dropped his weapon on the ground. And raised his hands over his head. The French General picked up the weapon and walked up behind the German General. Then started to pistol whip the General, forcing him down on his knees. Then stripping him of his overcoat and placing it over the lifeless body.

"Cpl. "Smedley"

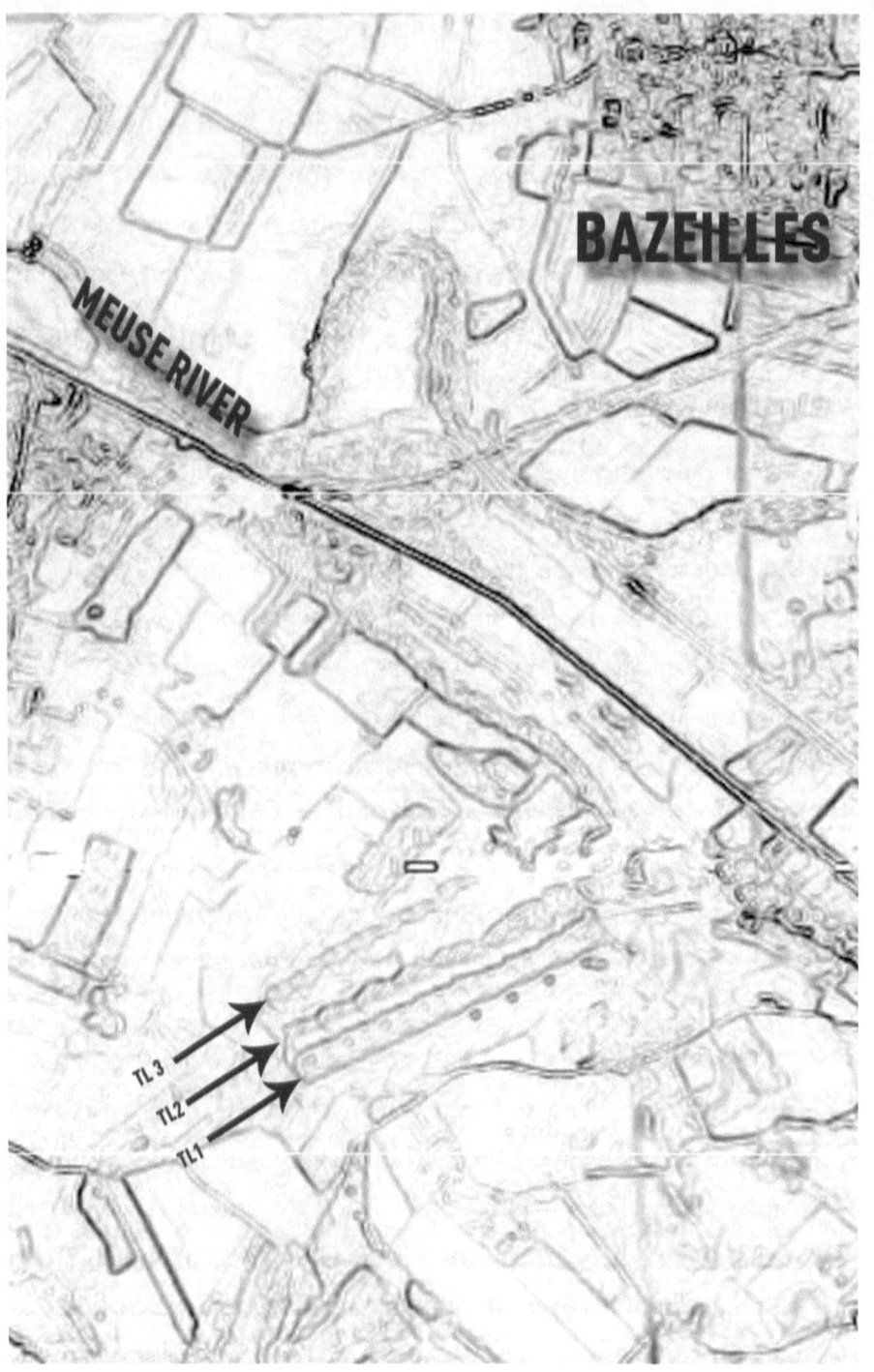

"Go sniff around the machine gun nest and see who's alive." said Sullivan. adding. "And gather up the left side machine gun crew. And go help Doc."

"Yes Sir." as both replied yes as they left for the middle trench.

"Cpl. Smedley." said Washington.

"Yes Lieut. Washington." said Smedley.

"Ask the French General why the German General shot the woman," asked Washington.

"Meine Lieut. möchte ihren Namen zu kennen, und warum Deutsche Allgemeine, Schuß, der Frau," asked Smedley.

"Capt. Washington. I asked him, 'My Capt. wants to know her name and why, the woman was shot.'"

"*Ihr Name ist Josephine Zoe, die Weiße Dame, La Dame Blanche des französischen Nachrichtendienstes. Sie hatte geplant, die MP 18.1 dem General zu stehlen und sie auf unsere Seite zu schmuggeln, von wo aus wir fliehen würden. Aber wie Sie sehen, wurden wir gefangengenommen. Dann haben sie uns hierher gebracht, solange bis sie Verstärkung haben. Sie haben im Bunker gesagt, egal wie das hier ausginge, würden sie sie erschießen, weil sie eine Spionin ist,*" said the French General.

Shea said, "Smedlee, you Nebraska rattlesnake boy. I would love to feed you chitlins, cornpone, and mustard greens with a big piece of pe-can pie and a shot of grandpas moonshine just to whistle that down, just to know what old Gen. Froggy French legs ribbited," said Shea.

"Sir, this was his translation" said Smedley.

"The woman who was shot her name is Josephine Zoe, The White Lady La Dame Blanche of the French intelligence. She had stolen plans of the MP 18.1 from the General and she was going to smuggle it to our lines with her, and we would make our escape. But as you can see, we're taken prisoner, so they brought us here until they could bring up reinforcements, they said in the bunker no matter which why this went, they would shot her for being a spy,"

Sullivan sounded off, "Shea, Wilson, and Forthright, check prisoners and the bunker."

"Gen. Darlin' could be a good fellow and keep an eye, on his eye teeth." said Sullivan.

"I would be delighted, me boyo, to keep an evil eye on him." said O'Rourke. as he took a big long drink of Bush Mills.

"Lieut. Washington," asked Sullivan... "What happened back there with the German officer."

"I decided to go to the executioner this time," said Washington, as he took off his glasses to clean them.

"Cpl. Smedley."

"Yes Lieut. Sullivan."

"Find out what these three other German officers, names are and the enlisted?" indicated Sullivan.

"*Wie heißen Sie und welchen Rang haben Sie,*" asked Smedley.

"*Hauptmann Thomas von Richter.*"

"*Oberstleutnant Franz Oppenmeyer.*"

"*Oberst Max von Schlepheim.*"

"*Gefreiter Reinhard Scholz.*"

"*Gefreiter Dieter Ludendorff.*"

"Capt. Sullivan, this is what I asked them. 'What is your name and rank?' This one is Captain Thomas von Richter. These guys are Lieutenant Colonel Franz Oppenmeyer, Colonel Max von Schlepheim, Lance Corporal Reinhard Scholz, Lance Corporal Dieter Ludendorff."

"What's yonder in them thar grenade bags?" said Shea, as he grabbed two bags.

"And I have the other one," said Lieut. Washington.

"Lieut. Washington and Lieut. Shea please bring your bags with you." said Sullivan in an uneasy tone

"Holy Mother Mary Magdalene?" divulged Sullivan.

"Is that I think it is," said Gen. O'Rourke as he uncorked his bottle, took a quick pull, and then handed it to Shea.

"Hells bells that smells," said She "I thought I was goin to find somethin to eat, not a litter of Scalps," as he looked in the satchel.

"Smedley"

"Yes Gen. O'Rourke."

"Ask the Hun what is the meaning of this," demanded O'Rourke.

"Sgt. Wilson"

"Yes Lieut. Sullivan."

"Give me a count of what's in those satchels." said Sullivan.

"Mr. Smedley," said Gen. O'Rourke. "Tell him who I am and ask him what is the meaning of the satchel full of scalps. And tell them I want answers now and not to give any gibberish. If not, I will slap the shit out of his head," said O'Rourke in a stern tone.

"General O'Rourke, lassen Sie mich sagen, ich bin nicht sehr erfreut, Sie kennenzuleren, aber unter den gegebenen Umständen, also von einem General zum anderen, möchte ich Ihnen als Symbol meiner Kapitulation meinen Jagddolch anbieten," said Smedley.

"Young Mr. Smedley, I know you are a lost child. So, what bullshit did he just spew?" asked O'Rourke.

"Sir, I said, 'This is General Clancy O'Rourke Esq., AFE. The General demands to know why you're in possession of human scalps—and no gibberish talk. If you don't answer right, he is going to slap the shit out of your head," replied Smedley.

The German General said quietly, *"General O'Rourke, lassen Sie mich sagen, ich bin nicht sehr erfreut, Sie kennenzuleren, aber unter den gegebenen Umständen, also von einem General zum anderen, möchte ich Ihnen als Symbol meiner Kapitulation meinen Jagddolch anbieten."*

"This is his translation, Sir, 'Gen. O'Rourke. Let me say I'm not pleased to meet you, but under the circumstances, from one Gen. to another, I would like to offer you my hunting dagger as acceptance of my surrender," said Smedley.

"Cpl. Smedley."

"Yes Gen. O'Rourke."

"Tell the General this. 'For your gracious offer of surrender, I propose we have a toast." O'Rourke eyeballed his new trophy.

Smedley translated, *"Aufgrund Ihrer freundlichen Geste der Kapitulation, schlage ich einen Toast vor."* Gen. O'Rourke pulled out his bottle of Bush Mills and uncorked it and handed the bottle to Shea and said, "Hold this a minute boyo, by all means have a pull." He reached into his coat trench pocket and pulls out a bottle of Ristols and handed it to the German General. "There you go, General. Cough that down." He gave the General a stern look with his one eye.

The General responded, *"Gen. O'Rourke, Sie mir gerade überreichen, könnte vielleicht ein Geisteskranker trinken, wenn er sich nicht zuerst übergeben müßte. Menschen waschen ihre Genitalien und ihre Füße mit diesem Zeug. Sie geben Ihrem Leutnant eine Flasche Bush Mills und sie geben einem gleichrangigen General der kaiserlichen deutschen Armee dieses Zeug. Aber die deutschen Generäle aus der kaiserlichen Armee, die Kriegsgefangenen sind, können nicht wählerisch sein."*

"Cpl. Smedley," said Sullivan. "You know the drill."

"Yes, Sir. He said, "General O'Rourke, what you just handed me, a cretin might drink, if they do not throw up first. People wash their genitals and their feet with this. You handed your Lieut. a bottle of Bush Mills, then you hand a fellow General from the Imperial German Army that. Then again, German Generals from the Imperial Army, who are prisoners of war can't be choosy." He took a drink of the Ristols with a slight smile.

The German General looked at Gen. O'Rourke, and politely said, *"General O'Rourke, ich habe Sie nur eine kurze Zeit gekannt und Sie sehen aus wie ein ergrauter Veteran von vielen Kriegen und Einsätzen, aber wenn ich Sie in Ihrer Jugend gekannt hätte, würde ich sagen, Sie haben damals geschielt. Also, heben wir unsere Flaschen Hammelpisse in Salut auf Ihr damals schielendes Auge."*

Smedley translated, "Gen. O'Rourke, I've only known you a short period of time, and you look like a grizzled veteran of many wars and campaigns, but if I was to know you in your youth, I would say that you were cross-eyed at one time, so let's raise our bottles in salute to your once crossed eyes with this bottle of mutton piss."

"Cpl. Smedley, give the General some niceties and tell him this. 'Dear Gen. Gen. O'Rourke wants to know who did this treachery, AND why now. Is there a relationship or correlation between the scalps and the MP 18.1?" He gave the General the evil eye.

Smedley reported, *"Der sehr verehrter Herr General O'Rourke möchte wissen, wer diesen Verrat begangen hat und warum gerade jetzt. Und gibt es eine Verbindung zwischen dieser scalps und der MP 18.1?"*

"Mein Name ist Generaloberst Gottfried von Rottschwinghammer. Ich verurteile oder dulde nicht die Handlungen von Männern in der Hitze des Gefechts, wo Trophäen wie dieses Jagdmesser erbeutet werden. Ich habe mich mit einem Mann um meine Ehre duelliert und ihm das Leben und sein Jagdmesser genommen. Nehmen wir an, Sie haben sein linkes Ohr genommen oder seine Haare entfernt. Sie nehmen etwas anderes als Wunden, um zu zeigen, dass Sie im Nahkampf waren. Ich bin nicht hier, um amerikanische Skalps zu nehmen. Meine Befehle lauteten, diese kleine französische Hure daran zu hindern, die Pläne für die MP 18.1 zu bekommen, und über den Meuse River zurückzukommen. Also, um Ihre Frage zu beantworten, es gibt keine Beziehung zwischen mir und denen, die Sie finden möchten," said the German General coldly.

Smedley said, "My name is Generaloberst Gottfried von Rottschwinghammer. I do not condemn nor condone the actions of men in the heat of battle where trophies are taken, like that hunting knife. I dueled a man over my honor, and I took his life and his hunting knife. Let's say you took his left ear or removed his hair. You're taking something other than wounds to show that you've been in hand-to-hand combat. I'm not here to take American scalps. My orders were to stop that little French whore from getting the plans for the MP 18.1 and to get back across the Meuse River. So, to answer your question, there is no relationship between myself and those whom you wish to find."

"What the fuck is his name?" asked Wilson, smiling at Smedley.

"All I got General Got Rot," said Wilson as he drew his 45 and shot between the legs of Von Richter.

"Smedley," said Wilson. "You tell him the next one is in the nut sack," cracked Wilson.

Smedley said to Hauptmann von Richter, "*Der nächste Schuss, der abgefeuert wird, trifft deine Eier.*"

Ludendorff yelled frantically "Nein, nein. Fragen Sie Prinz Stefan. Er kennt alle Antworten."

"So, what did he say Smedley, me boyo," inquired Sullivan.

"He said, 'No, no, ask Prince Stephan he knows all the answers,'" said Smedley.

"And who the hell is Prince Stephanie?" asked Sullivan.

Ludendorff and Scholz pointed out Prince Stephan.

"Well, lookie here. Our new-found friends are introducing the venerable Prince Stephan as that piece of shit over there, with his two front teeth kicked in," chuckled Wilson.

"This should be interesting," said Lieut. Washington to Lieut. Shea.

"You got that right, Sir."

"Smedley, old man, ask this poppin' fresh arsehole who he really is. Then ask him why he's dressed like a common soldier," said Sullivan.

Smedley spoke to the Prince, "Sind Sie Michael Katz oder Prinz Stephan? Meine Leutnant möchte es wissen."

The Prince replied, with blood dripping from his chin, "*Ich bin Prinz Stephan Michael Katz. Ich bin als einfacher Soldat verkleidet, um mich unerkannt durch die Gräben zu bewegen.*"

"Lieut. Sullivan," said Smedley. "He says he's Prince Stefan Michael Katz. He is dressed as a regular soldier in order to move around the trenches more easily," said Smedley.

"Damn boys, looks like the Hun is apissin' through a screen door when he talks," said Shea.

Prince Stephan sprayed, "*Wie Sie sehen können, sind die Beweise überwältigend. Während der Angriffe auf unserer Schützengräben, haben die amerikanischen Neger und die scheusslichen Indianer mit ihren Schrotflinten fürchterlichen Gräueltaten an unseren Soldaten verübt .... Sogar Ihre eigene Regierung hat Rundschreiben über die geheime Informationen der schwarzen amerikanischen Truppen an das französische Volk und das Militär ausgegeben, damit sie Sie behandeln würden, wie den lezten Dreck, der Sie sind.*" The German looked at each American surrounding him, and spit through the hole in his teeth, peppering Smedley's face with blood and spit. He continued slowly, "*Sie Amerikaner sind Egoisten, Vergewaltiger, blutrünstig und unzivilisiert. Weder unsere deutschen Militär noch das deutsche Volk würde diese Art von Greueltaten begehen. Ihre Wilden und Neger sind verdorben, abscheulich und schändlich und haben solche schrecklichen Taten der Menschheit seit fast zwei Jahrhunderten zugeführt. Das war in Ihrem Land üblich. Jetzt geschehen diese Taten hier auf den Schlagfeldern von Frankreich. Es wird eine Wiedergutmachung geben müssen, Kriegsverbrechen werden bezahlt werden und wir haben alle nötigen Beweise hier direkt vor uns,*" said the Prince.

"Sir, his translation was. 'As you can see the evidence is overwhelming. Your American Niggers and the horrible American savage Indians have been instigating and performing these atrocities, along with using your American shotguns on our soldiers during the trench raids. Even your own government was giving out circulars about the secret information concerning Black American troops to the French people and its military, so they would treat Black Americans like the filth and rubbish that they are.'"

Smedley paused for a moment and then continued his report of what the German said, moving in close and getting eye to eye with the German, speaking deliberately, "He also said, 'You Americans are egotistical, rapists, bloodthirsty, and uncivilized. Our German military empire or the Germanic people would not do these types of atrocities. Your savages and niggers are depraved, loathsome and the nefarious and have done such hideous acts to mankind for almost two centuries. That was commonplace in your country. Now you bring it here to the fields of France. There will be war reparations, war crimes to pay for, and we have all our evidence right here."

"*Sé cosúlaigh chun éist é féin fadchainteach,*" said O'Rourke. "In the old tongue, that means, 'He likes to hear himself talk.'"

"I would like to haul off and bust him right in the kisser." said Smedley in a hard tone. Gen. O'Rourke adding to Smedley.

"Have a drink son."

"Gen. O'Rourke"

"Yes son, what do you think sir." suggested Sullivan?

"*Prionsa chun ceann cócaire chun niteoir buidéal chun bochtán,*" said O'Rourke. adding. "From the Prince, to Head Cook, to Bottle Washer, to Pauper."

"Na madra tá gaisce a chuid fiacla." said Sullivan.

"Boyos, I just told him the dog is showing his teeth."

"Go ahead Smedley and tell him," said Sullivan as he looked at the Prince with a scornful eye. "Prince, to Head Cook, to Bottle Washer, to Pauper." translated Smedley.

Again, the Prince, spittled, "*Nennen Sie mich, was Sie wollen. Unter einem großen Führer wird Deutschland, das große germanische Reich, sich eines Tages über ganz Europa ausbreiten. Ich würde mein Leben darauf setzen.*"

"Smedley."

"Yes Sir. his translation was. 'Call me what you want, Germany, the great Germanic country will one day migrate again, covering all of Europe with a great leader. I would bet my life on it.'"

"Mr. Wilson, what was the count on that," said Sullivan.

"150 scalps were in those three satchels." said Wilson.

Then a crack like a lightning bolt from a special handloaded 325 grains of propellant, in a copper jacket for the 45 Colt, with 28 grains of tin, antimony, and lead to make the head of the bullet. A special cast and dies that will concave the bullet head in ¼-inch, with 2 crosscut channels 1/8-inch down. A standard Colt single-action Peacemaker with a seven and half inch barrel, cut down to 4 inches with the injector rod removed. The bullet pierced the Prince square between the eyes as it blew the back of his head out. Skull fragments pelted the Brodie helmets of Washington and Wilson.

Generaloberst Gottfried Von Rottschwinghammer turned around to Gen. O'Rourke as he put his bottle of Ristols down and said, "That is what I call a Loterie Royale, or it could be a Lotto di Genova. The pistol's action is a little tight and slightly pulls to the right, but has excellent stopping power. Compared to German craftsmanship, this rudimentary, at best. That is the 16th man that I've killed in a pistol duel. Although that was not much of a duel, those unfortunate scalps were not his to take. The real warrior would have taken his trophy with him at that time." He added, "I do apologize, from one Gen. to another, taking your pistol from your belt. I'll sit out the rest of the war in some for Godforsaken POW camp. Thank God. The only comfort I will have is this bottle of warm Pipistrelle Bat Piss," said Gen. Got Rot.

"Gen. O'Rourke are you married?" said Gen. Got Rot, as Gen. O'Rourke looked at the German General counterpart holding his warm pistol.

O'Rourke's mouth wide open in utter silence with his one eye opened to saucer size, cleared his throat, and muttered, "No, thank God."

"My wife, she's a bitch constant bitch, bitch, bitch. Like a reoccurring nightmare. It makes my headache, my second youngest one, she says come live with me Papa, wherever I end up," said Got Rot.

"Thank God for this War and a POW camp. I'd like to dress her as a Storm Trooper, in full gear, carrying a Mauser, Lugar, a Wex Flamethrower, a 08 machine-gun, with 3000 rounds of ammunition strapped to her back. On top of all that, the bitch bag will have a grenade bag, cosmetic bag, for old hag bag, the two bags underneath her eyes, a douche bag, I'd like to put her into two trash bags, a feed bag, bread bag, two mortar rounds, two mines, two rolls of barbed-wire, a stretcher, split that between the 08/15 Machine gun sled, with that Minenwerfer, pulling a Four Horse Artillery team, and the rest on her back, and tell her to attack a machine gun nest, that's in no man's land, covered in mustard gas with her gas mask off," he muttered, and continued, "I have read L. Frank Baum, Wizard of Oz take the wicked witch of the East and her sister. The wicked witch of the West. They pale in comparison to my wife. They are Vatican nuns," said Gen. Got Rot, shaking his head.

"Gen. O'Rourke, what he said about Germany migrating, I have not a clue about that. But when it comes to the leaders of this country, probably the next one we get will be the biggest raging asshole. How do you say in America, crazy as a pet raccoon," said Gen. Got Rot, adding, "We always get the loons. Me and my wife tried one last time to reconcile our marriage, so as of last year, I have a one-year-old daughter."

"Gen. Boyo, after all the artifacts have been looked at. Here take a big pull Bush Mills, this will clear your throat. A man with that much wind, blarney, and Bullshit as much me, will have a huge thirst," said Gen O'Rourke, adding, "You should see how me hippopotamus looking cousin, Col. Aloysius Finn Gilhooly, Esq. drinks" said O'Rourke. "He flatulates while he eats and drinks like he's in the Blue Nile, then it comes out like the Brown Nile. Quite disgusting that side of the family. They just don't know how to hold their liquor and food, and they never let you get a word in edgewise. That Observation Balloon, on the outside was doing its job for the Army. Poor Bastard. But on the inside, it was screaming bloody murder for him to get off," he said as he handed the bottle of Bush Mills back to his counterpart General.

"Here's a very large question. What you wanta to do with them thar varmints, Lieut. Sullivan?" queried Shea.

"Lieut. Washington," said Sullivan… "Can your men escort the French General, and take the dearly departed little princess, the German General, his aides, and get them back to the second trench?"

"Gen. O'Rourke. Would you like to go to the rear Sir." said Sullivan.

"Give me a few minutes son, to think about it," said O'Rourke. as the General. Sat down and pulled his bottle out. Taking a long drag of his whiskey.

"No, I'm, going to stay." said O'Rourke,

"Lieut. Washington."

"Yes, Sgt. Storms."

"There's a vehicle coming this way from the South, sir. Looks to be American," said Storms.

"I bet it's the seven sisters come to help," said Wilson.

"With fresh supplies, new uniforms, and a gallon of water to wash up," added Wilson.

"And then right back to the front," said Forthright.

"By Saint Michael, boyos, did you ever think maybe the war is over?" said Sullivan.

An engine materialized out of the clouds, low to the ground. It was Wild Bill, who tossed a small object over the side of the Aeroplane. As it made its way to the ground Forthright, was the first to pick it up and open it.

"This is a woman's large kerchief," said Forthright. "There's a message written in blood? It says, Who shot me in the ass? Not funny. Wild Bill."

The men looked up at Wild Bill's aeroplane. They saw a beautiful woman, with long flowing raven-black hair, waving her hand back and forth. They heard her, with crystal clarity, say over the roar of the engine of the Bristol in a beautiful French accent, "Au revoir assholes, au revoir."

The men could see the rest of the Bat squadron forming up, now with their passengers giving the Bat squadron salute, heading for new and more dangerous adventures.

"I have seen a lot of things in my day. I filed many a report. But that one is not going in. What happened here stays here," said O'Rourke.

"Tell me, buckos, who did it?" asked Sullivan.

"It weren't us, we was in the trench," said Shea.

"Dog smells his own hole and soul first," said Sullivan.

"Lieut. Washington, your men in the trucks were running the 37 mm and they also, know the difference between German and American Aeroplanes," said Sullivan.

"Cpl. Williamson, you were on the Lewis machine gun was with us, until he jumped into the trench," said Washington.

"Doc was in the trench with us with Forthright and the General," said Shea.

"So that leaves Smedley, holy Mary Magdalene by Saint Michael, Mr. Smedley," said Lieut. Sullivan.

"I cannot tell a lie. I'd never shot at an Aeroplane. I'd heard something about leading the Aeroplane," explained Smedley. "So, I popped off a few pans," said Smedley, with a remorseful look on his face.

"Deadly Smedley. Next time led by example you overeducated Bugeater," quipped Forthright.

"Deadly Smedley, you cornchucker, you get an A+ for effort and trying to shorten the war, but you get a D+ for recognition of aircraft," said Wilson.

"Lieut. Washington, a soldier has gotten out of the truck with a bottle in his hand and is heading this way. Looks like he's yelling something," said Sgt. Storms.

"Boys," yelled an extremely large soldier.

"The war's over in Europe," said the soldier.

"And I'm aimin to get gooded and drunk. Where's that the little teetotaler Smedley, he kin drive me back to the rear," said the soldier in a heavy southern accent.

"Cpl. Smedley."

"Yes, Lieut. Sullivan."

"NO," said Gen. O'Rourke.

"That will now be Sgt. Smedley. You and all the others here that fought here," said O'Rourke. "I have given you all battlefield promotions, along with some of the United States Army's highest medals," he said with his chest puffed out.

"Now Sgt. Smedley, who is this soldier," inquired O'Rourke.

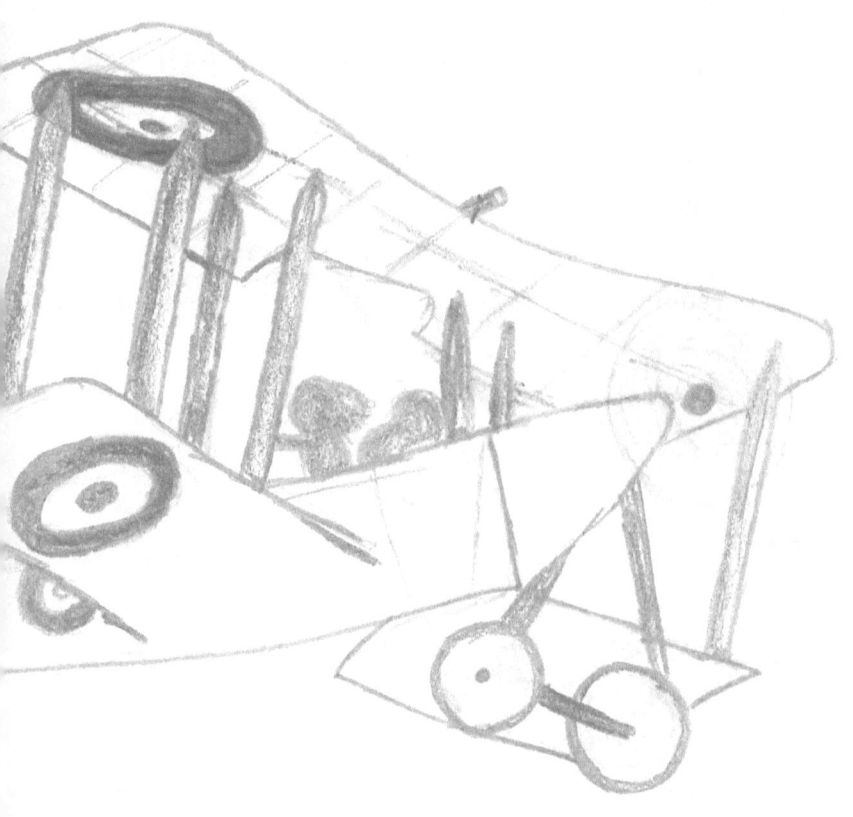

"Sir, this is First Sgt. Smith Smith Jones, my company First Sgt.," said Smedley.

"So, you're First Sgt. Smith Jones," said O'Rourke, as he looked at him with his one good eye.

"Sgt. Jefferson."

"Yes Lieut. Washington," responded Jefferson.

"Go gather up the men, find a little wooded area have them go over the vehicles, do a weapons check, and get a count of everything. Once you get them going, you come back here immediately," said Lieut. Washington.

"Yes, Lieut. Washington," responded Sgt. Jefferson.

Washington adding. "Remember security, security, security at all times."

"Yes Lieut.," said Jefferson.

"First Sgt. Smith Jones, do you have any orders from Headquarters Command?" asked O'Rourke.

"Why, yes I do General," said Smith, in a condescending southern tone.

"Let me see what me one good eye can read," said the General, as he patted deep, into his breast pocket and pulled out a monocle attached to a rosary and said, "Glory be."

"Well gentlemen, here's what it says. It says we have signed an armistice between Germany and the allies. This went into effect at 11 am, Paris time. And, me boyos, what time is it?" asked the General.

"Sir... crap! I have a bullet in my watch," said Forthright, as he looked at his pocket watch.

O'Rourke continued, "Posthaste removal of all Hun soldiers, from Belgium and France in the next 14 days. It also says here that all Allied and German prisoners are to be released."

"I know what we can do with them. Let's do what Sam likes to do," said Wilson.

"And what might that be, bucko?" asked the General.

"Hang them up by their ankles. Then beat the crap out of them like a piñata full of shit," said Wilson.

"Or have old Stan cut on them, 1000 shaving nicks," said Shea.

"And who were those two gentlemen?" inquired the General.

"They're part of the company, Sir. Them thar is the sniper team. They was awounded just about three days ago. Them ole boys, they can shoot a skeeter off a hummin'bird's nose," said Shea.

"We wanted to send them old boys, candy and flowers. We ended up sendin' them a Hun canteen full of licorice lice droppings. They said when they're all done with them thar army careers they want to open up some type of an fancy American-Mexican-Japanese eatery," said Shea, adding, "Them ole boys, call it fan-cee cuisine."

"Well, what do we do with them now?" said Forthright.

"Lieut. Shea, please come here for one moment. I want you to grab all your gear and these prisoners take them to the middle trench with Ugh and Thug. See Doc about your wound. I'm sure this First Sgt. won't mind if we use his truck to get these prisoners back," said Sullivan.

"So off with the boyos," said O'Rourke.

"Say, are you related to..." said Smith Jones, suddenly interrupted by Gen. O'Rourke.

"Lieut. Decatur take Sgt. Smedley with you," said Gen. O'Rourke in a cold-blooded tone to First Sgt. Smith Jones. "Be a good lad. Go do your mission."

"Yes, sir," said Shea, as he gathered his gear and started walking back toward the second trench.

"Boys, let's drink a toast to the war bein' over, and to the U-ni-ted States of America, and the great glorious confederacy," bellowed Smith Jones.

"Boyo, I can live with half of that," said O'Rourke.

"Here you go, Gen'ral. This is pert-near gen-u-ine moonshine, right from home in them thar hills. It's perty potent stuff," said Smith Jones as he handed the jug to the General.

"Yes, that will clear a nostril or two. But not as good as God-given Bush Mills," said the General, adding, "I've tasted better horse piss out of the shell crater at Gettysburg," smiled O'Rourke.

"No, don't hand it to him," said Smith Jones, as he looked at Washington. "Here Lieut. You have a drink. I didn't quite catch your name,"

"It's Lieut. or Sir," said Sullivan in a hard Irish tone.

"Lieut. Rastus, you can use your piss cup," said Smith Jones in a toxic tone.

"That's right kindly of you, First Sgt. Smith Jones," said Washington as he pulled his tin cup out, and blew the dust out of it and wiped it out with his hand.

"Here Lieut. you take the next drink," said Smith Jones with a slight scowl on his face.

"No, boyo, you go ahead and give Lieut. Washington a drink. Where I come from, the Cmdr. goes last," said Sullivan as Smith Jones started to chuckle.

"Sé tá ní mórán níos mó ná mé," said O'Rourke, looking up at Smith Jones.

Sullivan started to laugh.

"What's so funny?" said Smith Jones.

"The General and I were just commenting on your professionalism," said Sullivan with despise eyes.

"Here give me the jug." Sullivan tilted his head back and flung the jug over his shoulder to pour a drink directly into his open mouth.

"Yes, yes, that could possibly beat up your liver," said Sullivan.

"I guess in America e'ry man has himself a choice," said Smith Jones.

"Really?" shot back Lieut. Washington, as he put his canteen cup out to get a drink.

"What I meant to say, is every white American has a choice. Here you are, boy. You cleaned your cup out," said Smith Jones as he poured the moonshine into Washington's cup. The two men shared a death stare for what was seconds, but seemed like an eternity.

"I heard in the rear them old boys talkin' 'bout cuttin' scalps off the Germans, but I have one better," said Smith Jones.

"I know these old boys they alivin' in Decatur county Georgia by the name of Shea. That's why I asked earlier if he was related, but as the sayin' goes, I got cut off," said Smith Jones, adding, "The slicin' Shea's; they hate niggers, but not as much as I do," said Smith Jones. He and Washington locked eye to eye at each other with animosity, and Smith Jones took a long pull from the jug, putting it down wiping his mouth with the sleeve, never breaking eye contact.

"And what do you do there," asked Gen. O'Rourke.

"I'm a Grady County, Deputy Sheriff. Daddy's the sheriff, my mom's brother is the judge of the county, my older brother is the prosecutin' attorney, and I have an older first cousin is the county defense attorney," said Smith Jones. "And here's to the grand glorious Confederacy and all that she stands for," he said as he took a drink.

"Here boys who wants another pull?" said Smith Jones.

"No," said Gen. O'Rourke. "I've had enough. Plus, I have my own."

"No, I don't want another pull neither. I'm living on the Gen.'s good graces," said Sullivan as he looked at the General with a smile.

"I'll have a little more," said Lieut. Washington forcefully, as he stuck his tin cup toward Smith Jones.

"Did I hear you say please, Nagger Boy?" said Smith Jones, intoxicated.

"Pardon me. I didn't mean to be so churlish, and First Sgt. Smith Jones," said Washington.

"You don't get much sun, do you First Sgt. Smith Jones," said Washington.

"Why?" replied Smith Jones.

"Because you look a little pasty in the face. After the war you might want to go to the doctor and get that looked at," Washington said as the two men looked at each other square in the eye.

"So, tell me a little bit more about these Shea boyos," said Sullivan.

"Yes, most the time they drive around from county to county, takin care of problems for the locals," said Smith Jones.

"So, they are paid to kill," said Washington.

"You said that, Lieut. Sambo."

"Not me," slurred Smith Jones.

"Smith Jones, you spout off one more time," said O'Rourke, adding, "You're not going to like the end result."

"Are you threatenin' me," said Smith Jones.

"You said that, not me," said O'Rourke. "And by the way, Washington and Sullivan are now Captains," as he handed his bottle of Bush Mills to Sullivan.

"So, I have to call him Capt. Cotton. That's about the best place for you. In the cotton fields, Capt. Cotton," said Smith Jones.

"That is Capt. Washington," said O'Rourke shooting a stern look.

"But I too am a little interested about these Shea boys," inquired O'Rourke.

"So why do they call them the slicing Shea's?" said Washington.

"You ever seen a hog get butchered? They shoot it behind the ear, slit thar throat, hang 'em upside down, guttin' him, letting him bleed on out. And then barbecue. Then they throw anythin' remainin' into Lake Seminole to feed the gators," said Smith Jones as he took another drink of moonshine.

"Now, the most fucked up one, I ever heard of, and most funny… but, like I said, just hear say," said Smith Jones. "Somethang about their littlest brother. His old lady was some half nagger bitch, then I heard somethin about her brother comin up missing. Decatur County gave Daddy a missin person report," said Smith Jones. "And a course, we looked real hard, but we couldn't find him," said Smith Jones, as he smiled. "It's probably a lie any way. Those worthless naggers—them thar lazy monkeys love to run," said Smith Jones.

"Now Capt. Cotton, if you ever declared to come down to lower Georgia, I'm sure we'll show you a real warm Georgia peachy good time," said Smith Jones.

"First Sgt. Smith Jones," said Gen. O'Rourke. "Did you send this communication?" he asked, showing him the paper.

"Why, yes I did, and I do it again," said Smith Jones, with a look of disdain.

"And you don't think there should be consequences?" asked O'Rourke.

"I don't see nothin' wrong with it," as Smith Jones pushed back another drink.

"Lieut. Washington, I'm back, Sir. The men are all squared away," said Sgt. Jefferson.

"Jesus fuckin Christ. Look atchu, fixin' ta be a big black nagger buck," said Smith Jones.

"Sgt. Jefferson let me introduce you to First Sgt. Smith Jones," Washington said, as Jefferson and Smith Jones met eyes.

"Don't 'spect me to shake his go-rilla hand. I don't want that shit comin' off on me," said Smith Jones.

"This is the last time that I'm going to tell you to knock it off," as O'Rourke looking at him with one eye.

"Y'all can go fuck this," said Smith Jones. "I'm goin out there and take me a big Ole Miss piss," said Smith Jones as he went over the top.

"Gen. O'Rourke."

"Yes, Capt. Washington, earlier what did you say to him."

"What? You mean *Sé tá ní mórán níos mó ná mé?* That means he is not much bigger than I," said O'Rourke.

"I was getting a crick in my neck looking up at that gentleman," said Washington.

"I think let's throw him in a bunker and chunk a grenade after Mr. Asshole, and we'll say that he went goofy," said Wilson.

"He would probably eat it, and then blow bad wind and shrapnel and kill us all," said Sullivan.

"Capt. Washington," said Wilson. "Is there a fancier term for the word goofy?" he said as he cracked a smile at Washington.

"Why, yes there is," said Washington. "Before I formally diagnose Mr. Narcissus, I would like to propose a toast. 'To God, to the United States of America for all the good they stand for, and to the War being over, and to fighting together instead of each other, against one common enemy, and to honor last, all our fallen heroes," said Washington. Then men raised their bottles or cups, and wiped tears away.

Smedley piped in, "I told you, that he was a large asshole!"

"Smedley, get going like I said, boyo" said Gen. O'Rourke.

"Here we go. It's not that he's goofy," said Washington. "It's more along the lines of a fucking imbecile, and obviously racist. He's the village idiot, Deputy Sheriff of the town. Gentlemen."

Washington paused, looked at the men, and said, "You must remember race is taught outside and inside the HOME… or it is not. And it is up to the individual to break the cycle.

"Gen. O'Rourke," said. Washington. "Sir, I'm going to try to paint him into a corner."

"And how, pray tell, are you going to do that?" asked O'Rourke.

"Sir, just follow my lead, Sir," said Washington.

"What I miss, Nagger boy," said Smith Jones in a highly inebriated state.

"You are a great big strapping lad," said Gen. O'Rourke tightening his fist into a ball.

"Yeah, I'm bigger, and Capt. Coon, you are a nagger. I am better," said Smith Jones as Washington cut across toward him.

"You're also a bed wetter," quipped Washington cantankerously.

"What did you just say, to me Capt. Aunt Jemima boy?" said Smith Jones.

"I didn't stutter, peckerhead I said you're a bed wetter," reiterated Washington, looking at him.

"Look at your uniform its wet in the crotch and half down your leg," said Washington.

"I slipped and fell, Capt. Uncle Tom," Smith Jones said, seething as he sat on the firestep.

"You will go through a battery of tests from the military. The Gen. and I will make the recommendations, along with our reports and you're in luck. There's a mental facility at Central State Hospital. It's in Milledgeville, your home state Georgia. And maybe the government might help you financially," said Washington.

"I've heard a that place," said Smith Jones. "It's for idiots and dummies and monkey face fuckers like you, Capt. Coon," said an infuriated Smith Jones.

"You must be the purest of Paleontologists. To you I might look somewhat like a monkey, but to me your IQ is lower than the muscle and mental Go-rilla you portray. You're an imbecile, and you have the IQ of an amoeba," said Washington.

Smith Jones looked at Washington, dumbfounded, not saying a word.

"My, for a big boy you look little unbalanced, unhinged like you want to hit somebody," said Washington.

"If we was back in the USofA and on Georgia proper, Grady County, you, me, and the slicing Sheas would slice you up like a Fourth of July picnic pig, Sambo," said Smith Jones. "Next time they burn a cross, your head might be stuck on it… if not your black ass. Even a piece of white trash talks to me like that 'sgonna get the same," said Smith Jones.

Suddenly, two 45 caliber slides sounded.

"You talk out your arse one more time, I'm going to put a bullet in your leg," said Sullivan.

"Fuck that. I'm not going to shoot him in the fucking leg, Sir. There's something missing between his ears and I plan on parking a 45 slug there to fill that void," said Wilson.

"What I'm trying to do, First Sgt. Smith Jones, is save your career and rank," said Washington. "I can write up a report. The General will sign off on it. I'll say that you have this problem that obviously both your mother and father most likely have the same problem. Urinating themselves…"

Smith Jones interrupted, "What's urinatin' mean?"

"It means pissing yourself. It means your poor parents slept in a wet bed. Something about heredity and bladder. You can't help it that you piss yourself—that you wet the bed all the time. I bet Doc would know the proper medical term for it," said Washington.

Smith Jones began to tighten up, with his fists and jaw clenched and his face reddening as Washington diagnosed the issues.

"It won't be so bad laying around in that hot George sun, swatting mosquitoes and flies away from your dirty diaper sheet, there's always a plus side. The only friends you'll make will drool on you," said Washington, adding… "I figure about 8 to 10 years at Central State Hospital. You'll master basket weaving, pottery, you'll master playing wooden hoops."

"I ain't got a problem, 'cept you and your kind," said Smith Jones as he sat on the firestep listening intently. He continued, "Fancy talkin nagger, just cause you think you went to school up north. You don't know how life runs down there. If it wasn't for us they would be a starvin'. Plus, we overly educated them the right way. They just don't know how good they got," said Smith Jones, adding. "They're lazy pieces of shit. They're the stupidest people in the United States," said Smith Jones.

The barrel of a 45 pistol pressed hard against Smith Jones's temple as his eyes widened. Sgt. Wilson held his 1911 in his left hand and put his right index finger on Smith Jones's lips and told him. "Shhh," Wilson said, then close to Smith Jones's ear, he whispered, "That is an Officer speaking and you are to hold all questions, until after the briefing. Thank you." Wilson pulled his pistol back and turned around. He slowly sat down on the opposite side of Smith Jones.

"Or there's the General's way. Sir, I will turn this over to you," said Washington.

"First Sgt. Smith Jones, did you write this letter?" Gen. O'Rourke asked as he produced the letter.

"Why, yes, I did. An' everythin' I said in that letter is the gos-pel truth," said Smith Jones.

"Well in that case, boyo, if you don't want to sign off on the plan Capt. Washington proposed, I'll come up with an appropriate military punishment," said O'Rourke.

"I'm 'spose ta sign something he made up sayin' I piss my pants? That is a bald-faced lie," said Smith Jones.

"Or there's my way. You have heard of Field Promotions?" said O'Rourke.

"Why, yes I have. I'm going to get one to Major, so, I can put Captain Coon in his place," said Smith Jones, contemptuously.

"No son," said O'Rourke. "You're getting a field demotion, going from First Sgt. to Buck Private," he said as he pulled General Got-Rot's knife out.

"General, you have an alligator mouth," said Smith Jones.

"Now standstill son. I'm taking these stripes off your blouse," said O'Rourke.

"You do not want to touch me, General. First of all, I'm 7'0" and a little over 400 pounds," said Smith Jones.

"I did not know they stacked shit that high!" said Wilson, adding,

Then Smith Jones snapped his head to Wilson who was looking back with his 45 pointed at Smith Jones.

Smith Jones said, "Y'all come on down, too, Yankee boy," as he panned the area. "There's plenty of room in Lake Seminole for y'all," Smith Jones said as he turned his head back around just as Gen. O'Rourke caught him clean with the right cross below the ear.

"If I could say in the old tongue," said O'Rourke, "That I would, Mé beidh buille tú dubh agus gorm," as Smith Jones went from sitting to going down to his knees, swaying very gently in a circular motion.

"I hear something crack," said Washington,

"What was that sound I heard," said Sullivan.

"I think this sack of shit has a glass jaw," chuckled Wilson.

"Holy whiz shit," said Sullivan. "Looks like a small hunk of jawbone sticking out just like Sampson with a jawbone of an ass. His left ear is bleeding, too," said Sullivan.

"General O'Rourke," Forthright piped in.

"Yes, Mr. Forthright."

"What did you hit him with? And also, what did you say to him?" asked Forthright.

"I gave him a little love tap with me open hand. Who would have known, that he was a Miss Nancy Edwina that wore a diamond tiara?" said O'Rourke, surprised.

"I told him I would beat him black and blue," said O'Rourke.

"Sir, I don't doubt the word of officers, just some of their actions. But I saw something in your hand. Would you care to elaborate?" said Forthright.

"It was old Julia," said O'Rourke.

"Who is old Julia?" said Forthright.

"Julia the Jawbreaker, Brass Knuckles," as he scratched his cheek, looked around like a thief, and brought out his brass knuckles from his pocket. He twirled the object with his right index finger and a smile crossed his face.

"General, me Darlin'. That is your grand plan?" yelped Sullivan.

"I'm thinking," said O'Rourke. "Capt. Washington, you will put your plans on hold. The lovely Darlin' is out for a few lullaby minutes."

"Sir, Gen. O'Rourke," responded Washington…. "I think, Sir, that I was painting him into a corner like I had suggested. I just needed a few more minutes."

"Now, as me one eye sees it, he attacked me. Sgt. Jefferson stepped in and saved the day and me arse, too. And as in any court you must produce evidence—me evidence will be me pretty face," said O'Rourke.

Sullivan, scratched his head and said, "I'm not quite following you Darlin' Sir."

"You're not a General yet, me boyo. Just watch the old dog go to work," said O'Rourke. "As you can see by his glass jaw, that he has marks on his face. So, Sgt. Jefferson, let me see your hands. Looks like you have hands of Marion the Librarian—all soft and pretty," O'Rourke continued with the smile on his face. "I need you to beat me pretty face on me left side. Don't hold back your punches. Don't be a Marion the Librarian, with those soft hands of yours," he summarized as Sgt. Jefferson looked on, wide-eyed.

"What did you do in civilian life," asked O'Rourke.

"I was a boxer," replied Jefferson.

"I'm blind in one eye and can see out of the other. So don't hit me right side eye so I can still see out of it. Hold on, wait just one minute, Marion, look at Smith Jones's hands. They're too clean. We're going to change that," O'Rourke said as he pulled out his peacemaker. O'Rourke held the gun by its barrel and stretched out the right hand of Smith Jones on the firestep. He lifted his arm and struck Smith Jones hard on his knuckles with the butt of the gun. Then he proceeded to do the same to the left hand. O'Rourke asked the men, "You think he's had enough or do we need to break a knuckle or two?" All agreed it was fine.

"So now me face and his knuckles have to match up." said O'Rourke.

"Sgt. Jefferson, do your duty for God and Country," as he closed his one good eye. Starting to laugh. Putting his hand over his eye and says in the old tongue, "Tá mé iompú a dall súil." said O'Rourke, then, "What that means in English is I'm turning a blind eye," anticipating a thump from Sgt. Jefferson. O'Rourke opened his one eye and looked at Sgt. Jefferson, who had a puzzled look on his face.

"It's okay, John Henry, do this for me," said O'Rourke.

"Alright Sir, you best close that one good eye," said Jefferson in his low commanding voice. The next instant, Gen. O'Rourke was slammed up against the trench wall, but was still standing.

"Damn, General, I gave you a good shot. Are you okay?" Said Jefferson.

"I see your arm got a wee bit weary putting the books away at the library, Miss Marian. After that, shall we go picnicking?" goaded O'Rourke.

"Okay Gen. O'Rourke," said Jefferson in his low tone.

"Get your pretty General face out there," said Jefferson. The second blow landed directly on his left jawline, reeling him back, and this time making his head snap to one side.

"Wait a minute, wait a minute," said O'Rourke, as blood came out of his mouth.

"Let me check me mouth a minute," as he dug into his mouth, saying, "I got you little bastard." He pulled a tooth out of his mouth and held it up to display, and said, "That pearl of a sonofabitch!"

"Now I can say in the old tongue *A súil le haghaidh a súil-a fiacail le haghaidh a fiacail*, which means gentlemen," said O'Rourke. "An eye for an eye, a tooth for a tooth, by Saint Michael, that tooth had been plaguing me for two weeks now." O'Rourke pulled out his bottle of Bush Mills and handed it to Sgt. Jefferson.

"Here drink some liquid courage. And also Mr. Jefferson, you're not done with me yet," said O'Rourke.

"I'm not?" said a surprised Jefferson as he handed O'Rourke back the bottle. Then O'Rourke put the bottle in his trench coat and pulled out a bottle of Ristol's, opening it up and taking a big drink and swishing his mouth around. He spit it back out on the ground, and said, "I don't want to waste God's elixir on me pearly whites. You need to beat in and around me left eye."

He smiled a bloody smile at Jefferson and winked. "Remember I'm blind in me one eye. If you hit me in me good eye, I cannot see," exclaimed O'Rourke.

"So, I can make me reports, let's get this mess squared away," O'Rourke said as he looked into the distance. "Before we get started boyos…I need to do this…." The General blasted dead wind. "Now that's out of me, do your worst son," said O'Rourke, laughing.

Suddenly, O'Rourke's body slammed against the trench wall.

"Saint Michael," said Sullivan. "You have a pretty good melon growing on your eye, Sir."

"A couple more, and that's it, you're a boxer?" said O'Rourke. Again, the General is slammed backwards, but this time Sullivan and Wilson are there to catch him as Forthright just watches.

"You can now quit playing patty fingers. I'm not a *dubh súileach* Susanna, so hit me." said O'Rourke.

"What did he say." said Jefferson.

"He's not a black-eyed Susan," said Sullivan.

"Last time, Sgt. Jefferson," said O'Rourke. "You boys ready in the back?"

"Yes Sir."

"Swing away." Sgt. Jefferson's right cross looked like it was coming in slow motion hitting him. On the left side of his patched eye, immediately breaking the skin. All three of the boys were launched against the trench wall. Blood ran from O'Rourke's cheek in a steady stream.

"Oh, shit, Sir. Here, I got a rag to help stop the bleeding," said Jefferson.

"Mr. Jefferson, you did an outstanding job, Sir," said Gen. O'Rourke, spitting blood out of his mouth, and adding, "I ask you to do this for a reason, son."

He reached out to shake Jefferson's hand, and said, "Is me face still pretty?" O'Rourke took a big pull of his Bush Mills whiskey and immediately handed over to Sgt. Jefferson.

"It looks like a new improved you, Sir. Although Sir, you do look like a black-eyed Susan now," said Sullivan, as he took a drink and chuckling.

"Well, first of all, we need to wake up sperm whale," said O'Rourke.

"Wake up Private moron!" said Wilson, as he kicked Smith Jones's, boot.

"What, what's, happin' to me," said Smith Jones, in a foggy state of mind.

"Do you remember anything?" said Capt. Washington.

"The General attacked me, and he hit me. Y'all witness to it," said Smith Jones with a slurred, slowed speech, painful grimace.

"Who hit you?" said Washington.

"That one-eyed fat General did," said Smith Jones holding his jaw.

"No, he didn't. You attacked the General," said Washington.

"Fuck you, nagger boy," said Smith Jones with hard grimace on his face of pain. He wiped blood away from his mouth.

"No, I think for once in your life," said Washington, "Someone said fuck you back," looking right in the eyes of Smith Jones. "If it wasn't for Sgt. Jefferson you might have killed the General," Washington said slowly.

"You mean to tell me that big ugly go-rilla hit me," said Smith Jones.

"Yes, but not before you injured the General," said Washington.

"You had been drinking that moonshine. They say that stuff will make you blind," said Washington. "And all these years drinking that stuff, I can see why you're so blind down south. How about a little drink of your moonshine? It'll help that broken jaw of yours," Washington said as he tried to give Smith Jones a drink.

Smith Jones knocked the jug away, his face writhing in pain, holding his mouth, slurring out, "Get away from me, Capt. Coon."

"We're going to play little game," said Washington. "It's called reverse psychology—a reverse role-playing game. I know big man, you're just aching to hear this. Aren't you big boy? I thought you might enjoy a little humor in there too," said Capt. Washington.

"Capt. Washington sir, Pvt. Smith Jones is straining and stretching his neck, just to see how this ends," Wilson assessed as he looked right at Smith Jones.

"What are you looking at, you Yankee piece of shit," spittled out Smith Jones in pain.

"Nothing, absolutely nothing, that's what I'm looking at," said Wilson.

"Or dead man walking," said Sullivan. Smith Jones slowly turned his head to look at Sullivan.

"Now that we've got all the pleasantries out of the way let me tell you a little something about myself. My civilian life, I'm a psychologist. I have rather a nice practice. It was funny, just yesterday this conversation was brought up once already. I was talking to these gentlemen of what life is like as an American of African heritage," said Washington. "Now here we are. With your jaw, as one might say, fucked up. Normally, I would not talk this way, but being in this violent environment and watching men die and giving orders for men to die, will change a man," said Washington. "That unfortunately is the nature of war. So, let's discuss the changing environment, or in your case or the south's case, of a non-changing environment," said Washington.

Washington stood and unbuckled his cartridge belt. "Like I said to these gentlemen, my family came from Grady County Georgia, but I was born in New York City," said Washington. "So that makes me just a good old American, but of African descent, Along with all other nationalities, that makes the melting pot of our Country. So, when you're ladled out, you should be Red, White, and Blue, with a hint of green. But there is also a Culture Pot: Respect, Food, Dance, Dress, and Language. But we must always remember, WE are Americans, first and foremost. No race, creed, color or country, should ever precede the word American," said Washington. "My family left the South because of peckerwoods like you, and someday there needs to be a great social and economic migration."

"The white-man's culture down South has stripped Americans of African descent of the most basic life. I mean everything. The South has literally and figuratively beaten Americans of African descent on all four cheeks. The grand and glorious South can't let it go. In a hundred years, will it be the better or worse?" posed Washington, adding, "For the sake of society and God, I hope it is better. Men and women—hopefully both working together—can get so much more accomplished. As Capt. Sullivan said, 'A man's actions, deeds, and his words will dictate a man's or a woman's worth.'"

"So, like I said earlier, we're going to do a little reverse role-playing," Washington said. "For this part, I'll be the Master and you will be the ignorant slave cracker bitch from America."

"Let's reverse Africa for America. So, in real life the slaves went to America, but in this scenario, you're going from America to Africa. See how I repeated it to you a couple times?" asked Washington. "That's so your dinosaur brain can process it. Let's start out with you walking around in Georgia. There's no horses, no automobiles, there's no running water. For example, in 1780 there were 300 tribes of the white man. You have free reign over this country for thousands of years."

"All of the sudden slave traders come to your shores they are killing, raping, and taking slaves—your family and friends," punctuated Washington. "Maybe they're lucky you might have escaped but for the sake of argument we'll say that you and your family get caught. You're going to sail all the way from America to Africa. Here again I gave more instruction, so your feeble little mind would process it. You're heading to Africa! You're crammed in that boat with no fresh air. The people down below are chained up. Piled upon each other like cord-wood. The sharks follow the line of dead. They're throwing the dead bodies overboard to the sharks. But you knew that already, didn't you? You pull into a port, and the slave traders will haul you off to the slave block auction, naked and chained."

"All the richest or the ones who want to own more property will be there. They are going to come and eyeball you. You're all naked like you are an animal. In a cageless zoo. They check your teeth. They make you walk, bend over, check your limbs, pinch you, looking for any injuries," said Washington. "Right now, Private Pasty Moron, your jaw and teeth and your morals aren't very aligned are they?" Washington said as he pushed down a quick drink. "Now, there's a real good chance this is where your families can get split up, or they keep the family together."

"They take one look at you. You'll go for an easy 1,600 bucks. Then they call you big pasty porcelain boy. You're going right out to the fields of cotton or rice, or out clear a swamp. I hear it drains a cracker after five years. Damn," said Washington. as he took his spectacles off and cleaned them. He slowly put them back on, "I bet you could at least pull 200 pounds of cotton a day, if not more. If you had big strapping sons, they'd fetch a good price, too. They'd be right out there beside you. Your womenfolk, depending on what they looked like, would go to the big house. But looking at you, I bet your wife could pull two wagons full of cotton with a strap around her head and a bit in her mouth," said Washington.

Smith Jones cut right through Washington with his eyes.

Washington continued, "Then from that point it's the taskmaster's lash. You look at them overseers sideways and they will take their whip and peel your skin off your back. You understand that Whitey? Sun-up to sundown. Bad food, no education, no right to get up and go as you please. Y'all white trash will be picking cotton like you're swimming upstream."

"The next thing you know, there's a high-pitched scream. You watch a man, a woman, or a child get drug off into the jungle by a lion, tiger.... Later, you find a child half eaten or hung from a tree," explained Washington. If you see a white man swinging between the trees, he's trying to find that lion that just killed your neighbor's child. His name is Tarzan, he's a good guy," said Washington.

Smith Jones gave him a look of death.

Washington closed in on Smith Jones, slowly moving in to breathe hot, liquored words into Smith Jones's ear, "Your wife, your daughters... will be basically raped by the owner or he might fall in love with her," said Washington. "What a torrid love affair that would be. The White plantation owner in love with one of his slaves and they have a child. But she's already has a man. The anti-miscegenation laws would go right out the window and crack the very foundation," said Washington as he smiled. "I bet you would like that."

"Fuck you, Tar-baby," spit Smith Jones slowly and deliberately with much pain showing on his face.

"By now, you've been whipped pretty good. Some of the friends that came with you or new friends that you made here, have been shot trying to escape... Or caught and hung like they do in Georgia. They get cooked and cut up like barbecue, and fed to the dogs and the gators in Lake Seminole. That's what Pvt. Pasty and the Shea boys would do," said Washington.

"That's exactly right eight ball," stated Smith Jones.

"Everything is a lazy African day for the South, living in tall cotton. But there is no Mr. Lincoln to write the Emancipation Proclamation, saying that all the White crackers, Peckerwoods, and Peckerheads are free from slavery from this point on. There is no war, no one comes to free you," said Washington.

"You take your story," said Smith Jones holding his jaw, and said, "Shove it up your Black ass."

"Now, now the best part is yet to come. One day they come to you and say 'You're free, hallelujah!' Now you can go anywhere you want to go. Do anything you want to do. Be anything you want to be, Mr. Smith Jones. You know and I know that's a bald-faced lie," said Washington.

"But we put laws on the books, saying no money in your pocket. You go to jail, then you work off your sentence. This is a contract to pay the landowner and/or sheriff's departments by cleaning up roads, swamps, ditches, on private land," said Washington. "You got the eight-box literacy law for voting. They are going to try to squash the 15th Amendment through the use of poll taxes. It is designed to disenfranchise certain voters. If you're lucky enough, you have around two bucks to pay for the right to vote. How pathetic that sounds: paying for the privilege to vote. That's right, Mr. Simpleton," he declared, "Voting is a privilege that you cannot arbitrarily take away."

"Since 11 states pretty much have the same practices, here's the real ball buster. Even the poor White trash don't get to vote until they say y'all have grandfathered rights," said Washington.

"That's right, even as we speak, in the trenches of France American Natives still do not have the right to vote," explained Washington shaking his head back and forth with a look of disgust on his face. "The Natives of America are wards of the government."

"So, the Civil War laid waste to the South," remarked Washington. "And then came Reconstruction. In turn, it made quite a few senators and congressmen misappropriate funds through the use of thievery, deception, kickbacks, stealing of taxpayers' money. Along with being racist, session, after session, after session. So more and more could buy a seat with all their special interest groups. It's like you're inbred, always sending the same type of crook. So this is what your family has to look forward to every day. Looking for work or food and probably just a hut and blanket to cover yourself. Then out of the night riding up on where you live here come some anonymous black-pillowcase-wearing racists with holes cut out so all you could see is their eyes."

"Looking for Yankee carpetbaggers, like yourself Smith Jones. If you are camping in the woods somewhere, and we ride up and find some 15-year-old male… Find a nice hanging tree and lynch and burn his dumb White ass…" said Washington, adding. "You might even catch a glimpse of Tarzan swinging amongst the trees. They rape the women because they won't report it. As you can see that's our new American way of life. To the Americans of African descent up to this point and beyond, this was just a little verbal taste from me, and I just can't wait for the reception back home," he said sarcastically.

"You know, knucklehead, at the very beginning of the slave trade, those footprints were ushered in by shadowy figures for the sole reason of greed. Sugar to molasses to rum to slaves. That is the cause, in the United States, why we have the consternation today and tomorrow and into the future, unless things change. You can never let it go. The old way. God pity your soul, son," said Washington. "If the South wants to ever rise again, you better do a lot of soul-searching." Washington gave Smith Jones a hard glazed look.

"So, the first thing I would do is make sure you love God, Jesus Christ, and the Holy Ghost. Take that large leap of faith in your attitude," said Washington to Smith Jones.

"Capt. Sullivan do have anything to add." said Washington.

"No Sir, I think you've covered it all, so much better than I ever could," said Sullivan, adding, "But there is the matter of the General."

"Mr. Sullivan?"

"Yes, General?

"Hold me bottle of elixir," said O'Rourke.

"Very well, Sir," replied Sullivan!

"Gentlemen, could you please help Private Smith Jones to his feet?" ordered Gen. O'Rourke.

"Yes, Sir," said both Forthright and Wilson.

"Private Smith Jones. You stand before me a broken man, you attacked a General officer, and I'll reference meself as witnesses. I've jotted down notes," as he patted his left breast pocket. O'Rourke pulled out a monocle attached to a rosary and placed it over his one good eye, cleared his throat, and took a quick drink of Bush Mills. He said, "For your actions on November 11, 1918. As a senior Noncommissioned Officer attacked said officer, again referencing meself as witnesses, until the intervention of newly promoted First Sgt. John Henry Jefferson, thus saving the Generals life, etc. etc.," said O'Rourke, adding, "There will be written statements in more detail." O'Rourke looked all around as all the heads nodded yes

"But I didn't do nothin," slurred out Smith Jones.

"Neither did they," said Washington. "So, Gen. O'Rourke, what kind of punishment will Smith Jones get in a military court?"

"When all this mess has settled, the trial will be swift, but the execution will be swifter," as Smith Jones whirled his head toward O'Rourke with wide eyes and blood coming from his mouth and a grievous grimace across his face. He said, "This is a kangaroo court. You can't do this," slurred Smith Jones.

"That's right boyo, we're in France, not Australia. You see, son, it's a special board of three Generals. The unique thing about them, Arizona 1881, New Mexico 1882, and China 1900," said O'Rourke.

"I saved their bacon one time or another in past campaigns and wars. So as they say, I'm calling in a marker. Jumpin' Geehosofat, I just had an epiphany! I will make you go out like a hero. The next MG 08 machine gun that we come upon, you stand in front of that. I'll put a belt of ammo in you and we'll say that you jumped in front of us and saved our lives, and I'll write the report as such," said O'Rourke. "Before the hanging you might want to have that jaw fixed. The Army will pay for that. Then the Army will get you a crack defense lawyer. I know just the man; his name is Col. Aloysius Finn Gilhooly, Esq."

"Gen. O'Rourke, may have a word with you in private sir?" said Sullivan in a whisper.

"Is that your same cousin that was in the Observation Balloon?" asked Sullivan.

"Why yes, son, it is," whispered O'Rourke.

"So, you're telling me he's also gone to law school," whispered Sullivan.

"Young man," said O'Rourke with a smile through the bruises on his face. "I didn't say anything about law school. Yes, he's a lawyer.

A shit-house lawyer. He's defended about dozen shit heads. I mean guilty men… I mean innocent men. By Saint Michael, he might get lucky because it is his 13th case. Then again, I doubt it."

"But I'll bet you a penny for a good potato that when he flopped his fat arse out that gondola yesterday, not only did the parachute beg for a quick death, but the land would have ruptured like the magma chamber of the great volcano at Krakatoa." O'Rourke smirked and patted his trench coat, and said, "Where's me pipe?"

"So, Capt. Sullivan, does that answer all your questions?" inquired the General.

"That certainly does, Sir," said Sullivan.

"So, Mr. Smith Jones, you know the gravity of what you've done?" said Sullivan.

"Wait 'til I get home. My pa," slurred Smith Jones. "His best friend is the senator from Georgia."

"But you'll be in a pine box not saying much," said Wilson.

Smith Jones eyes widened as he slowly shook his head back and forth.

"Gen. O'Rourke."

"Yes Capt. Sullivan."

"I think it's time we leave," said Sullivan.

"That is the best thing I've heard all day," replied O'Rourke. "Sgt. Wilson and First Sgt. Jefferson."

Yes, Sir," both replied.

"I'm putting Private Smith Jones in your charge. We're all heading back up to the second trench. Gather up all your equipment, make sure all your magazines are full, weapons ready to go, so let's strap it up and tighten up our shot group. Follow me," stated Sullivan.

All replied, "Yes, Sir."

***

"Doc, long time no see," said Wilson.

"Three things, old buddy. Number one, you look like shit. Number two, how come you're sitting off in a little side trench? Third, what you are writing?" asked an inquisitive Wilson.

"To answer your first question," said Doc, as he raised his thumb, "You need to look in the mirror. To answer your second question as he raised his index finger, I'm sitting here because of the poetry of butchery, confusion of infusion, and things at the end of this trench that aren't right I can't put in perspective," said Doc. "And to answer your third question," raising his middle finger and dropping the other two, "I'm rewriting the names of our dead."

"How many?" said Wilson.

"Every mother's son at the end of the trench is dead," said Doc, lamenting.

"Mikey?"

"Yeah, Doc?"

"I know you and Sgt. Jefferson have a very strong constitution. But this one gentleman, you're going to need a double shot of Bromo-seltzer, then a good snort. Understood boys?" asked Doc.

"Doc, if you're going to be here for a little while, could you please look over our prisoner?" said Wilson.

"Why is he a prisoner?" asked Doc.

Wilson explained, "This is Private Smith Smith Jones, Smedley's old First Sgt."

"Well, I'll be a fat baby in a shitty diaper," said Doc, adding, You sit down right beside me, big boy. I'll take a look at him. By the way, what the fuck happened to his jaw?"

"He fell going potty," said Wilson, with a large smile on his face.

"How are you doing. Sgt. Jefferson?" said Doc.

"A lot better than he's feeling," said Sgt. Jefferson nodding to Smith Jones.

With all his strength, Smith Jones muttered, "This is all wrong, I didn't do nothin. I'm agonna die on the hangin tree," sputtered out Smith Jones with blood squirting out of his mouth.

"I'll make sure you're good and dead," said Doc. "When they pull your body down from that hanging tree, I'll check your pulse."

"Thanks buddy," said Wilson as he and First Sgt. Jefferson took a left and started to walk up the middle trench. As they went a little farther, they met Shea, Ugh, and Thug.

"Where is Lieut. Sullivan and the General?" said Shea.

"Gen. gave some field promotions to Capt. Sullivan and Capt. Washington," said Wilson.

"Well flying Duck turds. That's better than a big ol' sloppy kiss from a 14 foot gator," said Shea.

"Lieut. Shea. They're not too far behind," said Jefferson.

"You won't like what you see in there," said Thug.

"How are me boyos doing?" asked Sullivan.

"Physically, I'm finer than a frog hair split four ways, other than the gator bite on my back. Mentally, what I saw on the end of the trench is a whole different story," said Shea.

"I reckon we have to call you Capt. Sullivan now. The first time you're fixin put those railroad tracks on, you'll put them thar on all catawampus," chuckled Shea. "I bet you're afixin to get all gussied up, uppity up, and highfalutin as Capt. Donald L. Sullivan, Esqwired, right to the brig for celebratin' too much on your pro-motion. Why us poor Second lieutenants, will lift the barge and tote that pale and be last to eat. In less than 12 hours you went from a Sergeant First Class ass, to dare I say, Captain dumbass," he said laughing.

"My impeccable good looks, grand personality, and my Herculean effort that's what sustained us through our time of need," said Sullivan with his chest puffed up smiling broadly.

"Your alligator mouth is full of alligator shit to match that tadpole ass of yours," said Shea.

"Why are you jacking your jaw? You made First Lieut.," said Sullivan.

"Thanks to the General," explained Sullivan.

"Well hush my mouth full of hushpuppies and grits. An' fry me up a pound of fat back and pour that hot grease and fat back right on top of those hushpuppies and grits! That is awful precious of that old General to do that for little ol' me, like drinkin' my first mint julep," said Shea in his Southern charm.

"Decatur, what are the losses," asked Sullivan.

"Hideous," declared Shea. "Doc would be the better man to talk to you about that. You aren't agonna like what you see," he said, looking down at the ground.

"That is the second time I've heard that in last ten minutes," said Sullivan.

"Smedley," said Wilson.

"Long time no spy," said Wilson. adding. "You look kinda peaked."

"First Sgt. Forthright?"

"Yes, Capt. Sullivan."

"Please take roll call," said Sullivan.

"Yes, Sir."

"Gen. O'Rourke?"

"Here, Son."

"Capt. Sullivan?"

"Here."

"First Sgt Jefferson?"

"Here."

"Capt. Washington?"

"Here."

"Lieut. Shea?"

"Here."

"Master Sgt. Wilson?"

"Present."

"But are you here mentally?" said Forthright.

"Better than that BB rollin' around in your head, Cowboy," said Wilson with a smile on his face.

"Master Sgt. John Lightfoot?"

"Here Top."

"Sergeant First Class Tom Lightfoot?"

"Here Top."

"Sergeant First Class James O'Keefe?"

"Here."

"Staff Sgt. Storms?"

"Here."

"Sgt. O'Brien?"

"Here."

"I'm glad to see you boys around," said Forthright.

"That makes two of us, Top cowboy," said O'Brien.

"Staff Sgt. Hawkins?"

"Here."

"Staff Sgt. Williamson?"

"Here."

"Sgt. Smedley?"

"Here."

"Sgt. Ford?"

"Here."

"Cpl. Gathers?"

"Here."

"Sgt. Moffat?"

"Here."

"Cpl. Pick?"

"Here."

"Cpl. Graham?"

"Here."

"Cpl. Bolt?"

"Here."

"Cpl. Case?"

"Here."

"Cpl. Wagner?"

"Here."

"Cpl. Willson?"

"Here."

"Cpl. Smalls?"

"Here."

"Cpl. Thomas?"

"Here."

"Cpl. Downs?"

"Here."

"Capt. Sullivan?"

"Yes, First Sgt."

"All present and/or accounted for, Sir," said Forthright as they returned salutes.

"Sgt. O'Brien?"

"Yes, Capt. Sullivan."

"How much action did you boyos see?" said Sullivan.

"All I can say, Sir, I saw holes go through the Aeroplane," said O'Brien.

"Ours or theirs? I too was glad to see you boyos around," said Sullivan.

"Capt. Sullivan?"

"Yes, First Sgt."

"Other personnel, the French General, the German General and the three aids, the two guards, and the demised lady, and the toothless princess, what you want to do with them?" said Forthright.

"They will go back to Headquarters with us," said Sullivan.

"Crow, what's the deal Private mush mouth," said Shea.

"It's a long story and maybe someday, Decatur, I will tell you all about it," said Sullivan.

"As you wish," said Shea.

"Doc, how about our dead?" said Sullivan.

"The Hotchkiss machine gun crew of Cpl. Lewis, Privates Smith and Mahoney. They are all KIA. The Stokes mortar crew of Sgt. Fields, Privates Newman, Slattery, and Alan also are KIA." stated Doc. "Webb, Wallace, Jackson, South, Tierney, Lincoln, Hannon, Reagan, Butler, Smart, Lofton, Quinn, and Foster all are KIA." he said shaking his head back and forth.

"Rest in Peace, men," Sullivan said making the sign of the cross.

Doc continued, "Platoon leader Lieut. Kirby and Staff Sgt. Worth are both dead. Also, Crow, regarding the roster of 35 men, Sgt. Worth never got back to me with it," said Doc.

"James do not put the guilt on yourself, you were both busy. Sometimes those unfortunate things happen in the throes of war," said Sullivan.

"Crow, you have not stepped into end of the trenches," said Doc.

"What are you talking about?" stated Sullivan.

"I'll tell you what he's talkin about. While the rest of us was assaultin the tanks and the bunker, the Germans made a bayonet charge in a coordinated attack. The left side of the third trench and that thar far eastern trench line, they poured down on the end of this here trench," said Shea.

"We had been in the trench all this time with their own fightin. You need to pop your head up and take a gander out yonder in the paw paw patch," exclaimed Shea.

"Mary Magdalene," professed Sullivan, standing up on the firestep to look at the carnage out in no man's land. "Someone did an outstanding job out there."

"Me and the boys sur-mised that it was that old hound dog Wild Bill, helpin' them out as best he could," said Shea.

"He did his work today, saving our bacon," said Sullivan.

"Capt. Sullivan?"

"Yes, Doc."

"Other than Lieut. Kirby and Staff Sgt. Worth and our people, those men will be buried in an unknown grave of 35 marked November 11, 1918," said Doc, as he turned and walked away rubbing the corner of his eye.

"And one other thing, old Dickless dog," said Shea. "That thar artillery hit that middle trench. There's some shit I ain't never seen," he said as he looked to Sullivan.

"Doc, get up here with me. Let's see what we got," stated Sullivan as he entered the end of the second trench. "By God, all the Saints and Mary Magdalene, I'm going to be sick." Sullivan doubled over and began to vomit a deluge of whiskey and bile.

"Here, drink this," said Gen. O'Rourke. "Bad case of the heaves, a good jolt of whiskey will deaden the taste."

"I've witnessed a number of things before, but nothing like this," revealed O'Rourke. "But you never get used to it."

"I can't believe this," stated Sullivan. "Different body parts intermixed with guts between German and American."

"Oh my God," said Wilson as he heaved violently among the slaughtered.

"The last thing. How can I describe this," Doc paused to think, "It's Lieut. Kirby and Staff Sergeant Worth."

"Where are they?" asked Sullivan.

"Right over here," Doc added. "We covered them up."

"Pull away that blanket so I can take a look," said Sullivan. "Saint Michael, what happened?"

"As you can see, Lieut. Kirby standing there on the firestep, or what's left of him. What I think happened is that Sgt. Worth was handing ammunition up to Lieut. Kirby. An artillery or mortar round went through the back of Lieut. Kirby, which blew out his chest cavity and disemboweled him," said Doc, wincing.

"Then as the round continued, it sheered Sgt. Worth from the waist down," said Doc. "Then it must've hit some more ammo on the ground behind him. The explosion catapulted Sgt. Worth's head into the chest and stomach cavity of Lieut. Kirby. Then the two of them were impaled on to that small log. Come around here you can see Sgt. Worth's face through Kirby's back."

Sullivan took another drink and say, "Holy Mother of God." Sullivan passed the bottle to Doc.

Doc replied, "Crow, he did not know what hit him, just by the expression of his eyes looking up. Plus you can see the bagel-sized knot on his forehead. Lieut. Kirby knew immediately. You can see he has a look of shock. One of the strangest things I've ever seen. One in one billion shot."

"Then there's more on this side, there was a lot of hand-to-hand combat in the mortar pit," said Doc. "Those are mainly our boys sir."

"Looks like the Stokes mortar crew of Fields, Newman, Slattery, and Allen got their shots in," said Sullivan.

"Four of our boys to about 30 of theirs," said Sullivan with a look of pride on his face.

"I see our Hotchkiss machine gun crew of Lewis, Smith, and Mahoney got their licks in too," said Sullivan as he surveyed the trench and stepped on the fire step to see the machine gun carnage.

"Capt. Sullivan."

"Yes, John."

"Sir, you had mentioned in passing that you wanted a satchel to carry your extra bottles of elixir," said John Lightfoot.

"Why, yes I did, Sir," said Sullivan.

"Well here you go. I found this up by the machine gun nest," said Lightfoot.

"Was anybody alive up there?" said Sullivan.

"Yes, Sir," said Thug.

"We left them that way, too." said Ugh. "We patched them up as best we could. Funny thing, though, one of their old boys came running at me. At the last minute, he threw his machine gun at me, so I stuck my trench knife in him. But I just managed to skitter the left side of his ribs. I got him down and opened up his trench coat, I gave him a pretty good cut. So, I stopped the bleeding, then I patched him up and set him up against the firestep still breathing. At least I did not give him a haircut. Then I scoped out that satchel. It's made of gen-u-whine leather," he emphasized, smiling broadly.

"Why thank you kindly." said Sullivan.

CHAPTER 16

"Doc, did you get to look over Private Smith Jones," O'Rourke asked, nodding toward Smith Jones."

"Yes, Sir I did," said Doc.

"Will he be able to testify on his own behalf at his hanging… excuse me, what I meant to say was when he goes to military tribunal for his court martial?" said O'Rourke.

"No, Sir. I seriously doubt it. Pvt. Smith Jones's jaw is severely crushed. His Condylar, Ramus, and Angle have broken away from the body of his jaw," said Doc, adding, "The Angle part has an open compound fracture. His left ear's been bleeding. Just think if he didn't have any teeth, we'd be talking about an Edentulous Mandible break. I know it's not Battle sign—or I should say he did not get it in combat. About fixing that Brontosaurus jaw; I'd be most surprised if they don't wire his mouth shut," said Doc.

"Doc, you got me at mandible jaw break, I have seen a Mandolin mandible jaw break before," said Wilson, as he rubbed his jawline. "Some drunk Cpl. from Alpha Company, didn't like the other drunk Cpl. from Headquarters Company playing the mandolin, so he took it away from him and caught him square on his left mandible."

"I know a bit about Brontosaur-asses," said Wilson. "Do you mean a Brontosaurus Excelsis, a Brontosaurus Yahnahpin, or a Brontosaurus Parvas? Those big guys measure 70 foot long, weigh in at over 15 tons, from late Jurassic Era. Some of the best and oldest Dinosaur fossils ever found at the Morris Formation."

"That sounds like you're describing me darling cousin, Aloysius," said O'Rourke, sitting on the firestep, slapping his knee, and throwing back a long drink.

"Sir, that's too bad. I apologize about that," Wilson laughed, and continued, "So anyway, then there's the Velociraptors. During the Cretaceous Period, fossils were found in Mongolia. About the size of a St. Bernard—about 100 pounds, a big mouth full of razor sharp teeth, some big old claws. So in essence, the Velociraptor is a giant killer turkey. Just think of this, just think if Mr. Franklin had gotten his choice, we would have a killer turkey as our national bird," said Wilson, as all faces were in full blank stare.

"Beggin' yer pardon, Gen'ral, Sir. Back to the trial we were talkin' about," said Shea.

"Shea," said Gen. O'Rourke, cutting him off, "Capt. Sullivan, will talk to you about that later."

"Yessir, Gen'ral," replied Shea.

Smedley approached, "Gen. O'Rourke, excuse the interruption. Cordelia just delivered a message from Col. Gilhooly."

"Go ahead, me boyo, read it to me," said the General.

"Dear General Darlin', my fat arse cousin," said Smedley, chuckling. "The artillery boyos want to know if any of their rounds fell short into the middle trench."

"By Saint Michael," said Sullivan, as he looked to the heavens. "How would one know this?"

"You don't," said O'Rourke.

"Begging your pardon, General? If it did happen, the only thing I can think of is…"

General O'Rourke gently raised his palm in front of Smedley's face to cut him off, "What I'm thinking is that the charge bags might have gotten damp or wet."

"Thata hole is tore up purt-near to smithereens," said Shea.

"Nobody's alive to verify that story, because they were all blown to smidiríní, me boyo," said O'Rourke, as they all hung their heads. "So, in that case gentlemen, Smedley take out your writing utensil, paper, and prepare to copy this message." He dictated, "To Col. Aloysius leprechaun leper, with the shillelagh stuck up your arse, Finn Gilhooly, Esquire. It is my conclusion that there was no, say again no, short rounds. My report will reflect thus and such, etc., etc. Tell the men that they are going home to Thanksgiving and Christmas clean. Smedley, me boyo, this part is personal," he said, pulling out his monocle and Rosary, and watching as Smedley wrote.

"Yes, Sir, I understand," said Smedley.

O'Rourke continued, "Darlin' Aloysius, I saw your fall, but I felt the earth jolt more. Stroke of genius, me boyo, opening a new trench line like that. When your fat lard arse hit the earth, the 15 Germans and I were in single hand combat inside the trench and we were knocked off our feet. But, as you can see, I'm writing you back, meaning I'm alive, hippo fat. So top that Cousin Blowhard, etc., etc.. Give me regards to Cousin Bessie. Did you get all that Smedley?"

"Yes, I did, Sir?" replied back Smedley.

"Good, good. Oh, that man is so braggadocios—never let you get a word in edgewise," said O'Rourke, as he put his monocle away and relit his pipe.

"You should've seen us when we were in the Sixth Calvary. We get attacked by hostiles. We would get in a skirmish line and 30 hostiles would attack us, and if we dropped seven hostiles, his claim was that he got all seven of them with two shots and wounded 15 others off ricochets," said O'Rourke, chuckling.

"Mr. Smedley."

"Yes, Sgt. Wilson."

"Where are the three chicken hawks?" said Wilson.

"They were released to go back to HQ just before we went into battle," said Smedley.

"So, they're all nice and safe like?" said Wilson.

"I can't believe I made it through this," said Smedley as he looked at Wilson.

"Well just be thankful. A lot of good men didn't," replied Wilson.

"And Ron,"

"Yes Sgt. Wilson?"

"The war is over. The name is Mike. I find this helpful after you have been through a bad experience, to talk with somebody like Lieut. Washington," said Wilson as the two men shook hands

"Beatrice, what did you bring me?"

"Gen. O'Rourke, Sir. You just got an incoming message from Higher Headquarters," said Smedley.

"Go ahead, me boyo. Read it," said O'Rourke.

"It's from Jack. It says, 'We need you and Aloysius for a special mission. You need to handpick a crew of up to 30 men. Use that special Acquisitions and Procurement skill that you're famous for, because you will need three armored cars with 37 mm cannons. Your mission is two weeks from now. You and your detachment will report to Arkhangelsk, Russia; your job will be to protect the American supplies, to aid the Czechoslovakian Legion, and to protect the Trans-Siberian Railroad. Good hunting. Good luck. Signed, Jack.'"

"*Caidreamh mé dúbailt uainiú*," said O'Rourke. "Sgt. Smedley, I just said *fuck me double timing.*" O'Rourke hit his pipe against his hand and packed it with fresh tobacco. "As they say in America, that's bullshit. But orders are orders. As good lads, we carry these out. Capt. Sullivan, Capt. Washington. Do you know anybody that could fit that order? Around 30 men and three armored cars with firepower on them? The only thing I'm lacking is someone to interpret Russian."

Coming from behind General O'Rourke, a familiar German voice said, "I couldn't help overhearing your conversation. I know Russian perfectly."

General O'Rourke turned around to find General Got Rot.

"General. How come you're not on your way back to the rear?" said O'Rourke.

"Not enough room on the truck. Or it was fate that they said to wait by the second trench and they would be back," said Got Rot.

"So, you know Bull-shit-vik, do ya?" said O'Rourke.

"I thought I'd offer my services. It beats sitting in a POW camp— or I mean home with my God awful Brunhilda witch, bitch, wife of mine. My first wife passed on, God rest her soul.. Plus, the children moved out long before we lost her. I remarried five years ago. Except for my newest little one, I'd rather freeze my ass off naked fighting bad Cossacks and the Bolsheviks, than spend another night in so-called paradise in that hideous creature's cave. I met her in 1911, married her in 1912, I was castrated in 1913. Thank God for the war, I got them back. Help me, General, if you believe in God. Help me, for the sake of humanity and my sanity," pleaded General Got Rot.

"I suppose I could use you as a private contractor. Get some better clothes on, because you look like a Dunghill Beetle," said O'Rourke.

The men shook hands, and Gen. Got Rot said, "Thank you, Sir."

"Sgt. Smedley."

"Yes, Sgt. Wilson," said Smedley.

"We're back at war," said Sgt. Wilson.

"Sgts. Lightfoot. May I see both of you over here? I would like to talk to you in private," said O'Rourke walking to the other side of the trench.

They both replied, "Yes, Sir."

"Tell me something, John. How did you get the name Ugh?" asked Gen. O'Rourke.

"When Crow and I first met, we were both young bucks, pushing each other. But with him being so thickheaded that sometimes he would go as the Crow flies at a machine gun nest, artillery piece, trenches or whatever. He always said something about he could dodge the bullets. So, I tried to teach him to get down behind a log and use the three Cs: cover, camouflage, and concealment."

"That's Ugh. That is disgusting. That's how I got my name Ugh. I looked right back at Sullivan and said, 'Okay, Crow,' and we've been together ever since—Ugh and Crow, Crow and Ugh," said Sgt. Lightfoot.

"John Lightfoot it took me about one minute to realize, that I fought a noble Comanche enemy War Chief in 1883 under Gen. Cook in the Sierra Madre's in Mexico. On that particular day, me and Aloysius got the jump on this War Chief one night. He looked a lot like you, his name was Death from Above. Would you happen to be a kin, sir?" asked O'Rourke.

"Yes, General, I know, I saw you in Mexico, because, I was there, too. I was about eight, at the time, I stayed back about a quarter-mile behind. Saw the whole thing," said Ugh.

O'Rourke said, "For that time, we had your dad. Aloysius kept nattering that we were being followed."

"It took me about day to finally figure out, who you were Pia Pisuupu." said Ugh, with a chuckle.

"That old bastard called me Big Wind." said O'Rourke. with a bodacious laugh. O'Rourke relit his pipe.

"He thought you're going to bore him to death, by your constant talking back and forth with your cousin." said Ugh.

"Here now, I talk no more than the average man, but on the other hand, Aloysius will talk the teeth out of a Blue Nile alligator" said O'Rourke.

"That constant jabbering is why my father tried to escape, to get back across the Rio Grande," said Ugh, as Thug just listened to stories of his grandfather.

"He did, did he," said O'Rourke, with a big smile on his face. "How is his left hand? Lardhead took three fingers off of the right hand of Death from Above with a 50-90 Sharps. Good shooting, especially since he was ready to split my skull with a tomahawk."

"He always said he liked having three eyes, and yes he did learn to split a few skulls with a tomahawk, using his left hand." said Ugh.

"Not with his tomahawk in me hand," said O'Rourke, showing the tomahawk. "And me eye?

"It's in a pouch around his neck; he pulls it out once in a while and puts it in the middle of his forehead," said Ugh. "He said being your prisoner for 30 miles was agonizing. He was going to ask you, General, for your pistol, so he could put a bullet in his head. Your constant talking, incessant stories—he said he never got a word in edgewise. But your cousin, wherever he is at, Death from Above was going to slow roast him and feed him to the coyotes. He said if he ever ambushed you two, he would cut both your tongues out for the sake of his ears. If it wasn't for taking half his fingers off, truth be known, you'd have been his 110th kill and scalp. He got that later after his hand healed."

"Next time you run into dear old dad, tell him no hard feelings," said O'Rourke, reaching for a bottle of Bush Mills.

"That is the same thing he told me," said Ugh.

"Now that everybody's accounted for, we're heading back to the rear, we're going to let somebody else cleanup this mess," said Sullivan.

In the countryside of France on November 11, 1918.

Would it be forever known as the war to end all wars?

TWENTY-SIX YEARS LATER...
1941 IN THE SULLIVAN BASEMENT

Leonard yelled down the stairs, "Dad, are you still down there?"

Sullivan closed the satchel and ran his hands over the still smooth leather.

"Yes son. We'll be up to listen to your blarney. Helen, by golly, it's been a while since I've seen that bag. It's like rubbing a magic lamp and getting a bad genie. That's why I haven't looked for it in a long time, purposely. I still have nightmares. I smell the horrible stench of death, hear the screams of my men being torn apart by mortars and hand to hand combat, and feel the pounding of war throughout my whole being."

"Thanks Dad. I never knew what you went through or how you felt. Thank you for fighting in the Great War, and thanks for sharing your story with me. I'm proud you are my daddy." Helen kissed her father on the head and said, "Let's go back upstairs, Major Sullivan."

"By Saint Michael," said Sullivan as he looked to the heavens. "This wee satchel represents the war to end all wars. So many memories, some good, mostly bad." Sullivan put the satchel under his arm and stood. He said, "Well lass, as my old comrade, Captain Shea would say, 'Let's go have some of them thar vittles.'"

Leonard Sullivan—Orlando Bloom.

Decatur Shea—Tom Hiddleston.

James O'Keefe—Bradley Cooper.

Mike Wilson—Chris Pratt.

Stephen Forthright—Chris Evans.

Thomas Lightfoot—Raoul Trujillo.

Jonathan Lightfoot—Rudy Youngblood.

Ronald Smedley—Dan Fogler.

Oliver Martin—George Clooney.

Clancy O'Rourke—Liam Neeson.

Aloysius Gilhooly—Sean Bean.

Wild Bill—Robert Downey Jr.

Mary Magdalene Sullivan—Meryl Streep

General Got Rot—Christopher Waltz.

The Prince—Daniel Bruhl.

Josephine Zoe—Monica Bellucci.

Woman in Aeroplane—Marion Cotillard.

Alicia Perkeys—Alicia Keys.

Smith Jones—Nathan Smith Jones.

Sam Araujo—Michael Peña.

Stan Sato—Ken Jeong.

Randall Newman—Taylor Kinney

A.C.1

Richard Williamson—Will Smith.

Thomas Moffat—Chadwick Boseman RIP.

Samuel Ford—Michael B. Jordan.

Clarence Case—Anthony Mackie.

Peter Pick—Winston Duke.

A.C.2

Andre Hawkins—Keegan-Michael Key.

Anthony Smalls—Jordan Peele.

David Downs—Samuel L. Jackson.

Octavius Gathers—John David Washington.

Bartholomew Page—Wayne Brady.

A.C.3

Augustus (Gus) Washington—Denzel Washington.

John Henry Jefferson—Kevin Grevioux.

George Storms—Jamie Foxx.

Ceasar Bolt—John Legend.

Napoleon Newsome—Lonnie Lynn.

Makeup Greg Nicotero

Mickey Mouse, wouldn't this make a marvelous movie?

American's entrepreneurs invest in America and Americans.

ACKNOWLEDGMENTS

I would like to thank Teanglann English-Irish Dictionary for all the help on the Irish language.

And I would like to thank Michael Powell and Prof. Martin Flores from the Comanche Nation. with help on the Comanche language.

I would like to thank Carol Stoltenberg and the German-American Society for their help on the German language.

To Lisa Pelto. All my thanks in helping me develop this project, who I've come to love and have a friendship with, and who has taught me a lot as a mentor.

www.ingramcontent.com/pod-product-compliance
Lightning Source LLC
Chambersburg PA
CBHW020540020726
47494CB00006B/1853